A Twist Of Fate

by

Beverly Clark

Genesis Press, Inc

Indigo Love Stories

presented by Genesis Press Publishing

Genesis Press, Inc.
315 Third Avenue North
Columbus, MS 39701

ATwist Of Fate

ISBN: 0-7394-3508-6

Manufactured in the United States of America

First Edition

Chapter One

New Orleans

Camille King sat in the reception room of the Hadley Fertility Clinic studying the four couples and the three other women besides her waiting to see their doctors. Finding nothing out of the ordinary to hold her interest, she shifted her attention to the room's decor.

The Hadley Clinic was a modern, luxuriously decorated facility. When you opened the shiny, oak wood doors, you took in at a glance the three sets of expensive burgundy, overstuffed linen couches and matching lounge chairs, then the gleaming brass and glass coffee and end tables. And as you stepped inside the reception room, the final stroke of elegance was the hunter green and cream striped silk wallpaper and the plush wall-to-wall hunter green carpet that sank beneath your feet.

Straight ahead sat a smartly dressed receptionist behind a rich mahogany wood desk, typing information into the latest state-of-the-art computer. Camille had to admit that Dr. Hadley had spared no expense in his bid to impress his predominantly wealthy and upscale clientele.

Camille smiled, rubbing the swell of her stomach. She didn't care about any of that. Having a healthy baby was her number one priority. Although in the second trimester of her pregnancy, she had yet to feel her baby move. Could that be the reason Dr. Hadley had personally phoned her that morning and insisted - no - adamantly exhorted her to come in to see him this afternoon? A frisson of fear quivered through her. Please, God, don't let anything be wrong with my baby.

Charles Hadley wasn't her regular doctor. Surely Janet Broussard, her obstetrician, would have called her if there were any problems. And she hadn't. So if nothing was wrong, then what could Dr. Hadley possibly want to talk to her about? She guessed she would just have to wait and see.

Camille picked up one of the maternity fashion magazines from a nearby end table and thumbed through it. She would need to go shopping very soon for something else to wear. Because of her expanding waistline she now had to choose looser fitting dresses. Camille smiled, glancing down at the comfortable lavender, India gauze dress she had on. Just the other day she'd rummaged in the back of her closet and found several big shirts and pants with larger waistbands.

At the sound of the clinic door opening, she looked to see who had entered the room. She nearly swallowed her tongue when a tall, dark haired man with a light, honey-gold tan walked in. She guessed his age to be somewhere around thirty-four or five. Their eyes met, and his cobalt blue ones locked with her startled brown ones, holding them momentarily captive before releasing them. Her gaze dropped instinctively to his sensual mouth. And for a few renegade seconds she imagined how those sexy lips would feel on hers.

Camille slowly moved her tongue across her lips at the thought. She gulped several times before finally managing to wrench her gaze away from that beautifully shaped mouth. But the pull of attraction lured her attention lower to the area just above his shirt collar where its stark white color dramatically complimented his magnificent tan. She closed her eyes and shook her head to clear it. A woman in her condition had no business salivating over a stranger, even one as devastatingly good looking as this one.

When Camille opened her eyes, the man was talking to the receptionist. She looked with appreciation at how his beige sports coat conformed to his broad shoulders and impressive biceps. As if mesmerized, she observed with interest the way his expertly tailored pecan-brown slacks accentuated his muscular thighs and calves to perfection.

With much difficulty Camille returned her attention to her magazine. But even as she did so, her mind asked the question; Why was he here? Then she answered her own question. The Hadley Clinic was also a sperm bank. He was probably one of their choice donors. Her face heated up at the strangely erotic image it invoked.

Unable to win the battle to keep her eyes off him, Camille peeked over the top of her magazine once again and watched as the man signed in, then a few seconds later, walked over to a chair across from hers. And after picking up a newspaper someone had left lying on it, he sat down and crossed his right ankle over his left knee.

As if under a spell Camille riveted her attention on the bulge between his lean muscular thighs. Her throat went dry, and her face flamed hot with shame. What was the matter with her? She couldn't believe she was ogling the man like this.

* * *

Nicholas Cardoneaux definitely felt disoriented from his instant awareness encounter with the stunningly, attractive toffee-skinned woman with the huge melting chocolate eyes and long, cinnamon brown hair. No woman at first sight had ever rocked him like this. And for one insane moment the urge to caress her beautiful brown skin to see if it really was as warm and smooth and silky-soft as it appeared grabbed hold of him. He also found himself longing to breathe in her womanly scent, knowing intuitively that she would smell as sweet as magnolias. The thought caused his male equipment to harden painfully. He couldn't believe this was happening to him. Here he was in a room full of people, and his libido was showing him no mercy.

Camille felt the urge to go to the restroom, an all too frequent occurrence lately. In her agitation she stood up abruptly and the purse that had been in her lap fell to the floor and most of its contents spilled out. The stranger immediately rose from his seat, walked over to her and stooped to pick up the purse.

"You don't have to - " Camille began.

"It's all right, I want to," Nicholas said with a smile. He started retrieving the contents, while at the same time catching a glimpse of delicate ankles and a pair of perfectly shaped sexy legs that would give Tina Turner's competition. Coming across a picture wallet, his eyes locked onto a photo of the woman and an older man with his arm draped across her shoulder. He wondered whether he was her father or her husband. If the latter, that definitely put her off limits where Nicholas was concerned. And though he knew it was crazy, the thought of that being the case sent a feeling of disappointment knifing through him.

Looking down on the head of the stranger as he picked up the contents of her purse, Camille's eyes settled on his thick, black curly hair and she felt an overpowering urge to twirl several of the glossy locks around her fingers. Feeling uneasy with the path her thoughts had taken, Camille unconsciously moved her hand across the front of her dress.

Nicholas saw the gesture, and her stomach. Then it dawned on him what the bulge meant; she was pregnant. Why was he surprised? This was after all a fertility clinic. As he stood up, he wondered why her husband wasn't with her. If this lovely woman belonged to him, he certainly would have come with her. He cleared his throat.

"My name is Nicholas Cardoneaux and yours?"

"Camille King," she answered with a smile, holding out her hand for her purse. "Thanks."

"My pleasure." Nicholas smiled back as he handed her the purse. And as he watched her hurry into the ladies room, the name Camille tumbled through his mind. After a few moments, he decided that it fit her perfectly.

She appeared to be as delicate as the rose like flower of a camellia plant. And like that resilient plant, he had a feeling she also possessed its strength and vitality as well.

His thoughts suddenly jack-knifed to Lauren, a woman with whom he'd shared the last ten years of his life. She was blonde with green eyes and pale English rose skin. Lauren was fragile in body and mind; the exact opposite of Camille King he would venture to guess. And up until a couple of months ago, she too had been pregnant.

Only he and God knew how much he'd wanted that baby. Nicholas gritted his teeth in an effort to tamp down the pain. He and Lauren had tried without success for the last eight years to have a child. As luck would have it, when Lauren had managed to get pregnant, she had repeatedly miscarried. Then, with this last pregnancy, she had finally been able to hold onto to the baby past the danger period. His hopes had begun to soar, only to plummet shortly thereafter when she miscarried yet again. He breathed in deeply, refusing to dwell on what might have been.

He strode back to the reception desk. "I had a one o'clock appointment with Dr. Hadley," he said to the receptionist, pushing up the sleeve of his jacket and checking his watch. "It's well past that now. I'm a busy man. I have better things to do than waste my time in this clinic."

"We're sorry for the delay, Mr. Cardoneaux." The receptionist beamed an apologetic smile on him. "It won't be long now."

"That depends on your definition of long," he grumbled under his breath as he walked back to his seat. He couldn't help speculating about what Hadley wanted to see him about. Considering how urgent he had made it sound, Nicholas was surprised to be left cooling his heels in the waiting room.

The nurse called a couple named Miller. Obviously in love, the pair was no doubt eager to start a family, and Nicholas envied them. He and Lauren had been very much like them only to have their hopes repeatedly crushed. Now, he wanted more than anything to put that painful experience behind him, and forget this place existed and get on with his life.

When Camille returned to the reception room, she avoided looking at Nicholas and headed back to her seat. A few minutes later the nurse called her name and signaled that she should follow her. When they came to a small office, the woman asked Camille to take a seat in front of the desk, then she picked up a file folder and opened it.

"You're twenty-nine and at the end of your fourth month, Mrs. King?"

When Camille answered yes, she wrote it down.

"You were inseminated January 4th and 5th. Right?"

"Yes. Why are you asking me these questions when you already know the answers?"

"We just wanted to make sure our information is correct, that's all." She cleared her throat. "Due to a low sperm count you and your husband came to us to try our new treatment in hopes that it would improve that condition, and then later had the improved sperm stored with us for future use. Correct?"

"Look, was there something wrong with the sperm? And now you're telling me there's a complication with the pregnancy?"

"Oh, no! It's nothing like that," the nurse quickly answered. "Please, don't get upset. As far as I know your pregnancy is progressing normally and right on schedule."

"Since Dr. Hadley isn't my obstetrician and nothing is wrong, I don't understand why he wants to see me."

The nurse gave her a nervous smile. "You'll have to get the answer from him."

Camille frowned, trying to fathom why the woman was being so evasive unless something really was wrong, and she didn't want to be the one to tell her that it was.

The phone buzzed and the nurse answered it.

"The doctor will see you now, Mrs. King," she said, closing the folder and rising from her chair. "If you would follow me," Camille didn't know whether to feel relieved or apprehensive now that she was finally going to see the doctor.

* * *

In the reception room Nicholas was nearing the end of his patience as yet another couple and two of the remaining women in the room were summoned. Finally the nurse called him. As he strode into Dr. Hadley's office, Nicholas was ready to give the man hell when he noticed Camille King sitting in one of the two chairs in front of the doctor's desk.

"Why did you want to see me, Hadley?" Nicholas asked, his eyes narrowing on the doctor.

"If you'll just take a seat, Mr. Cardoneaux. I'll explain."

"Why is he here?" Camille demanded.

"Please, stay calm, Mrs. King." Dr. Hadley walked around the desk and sat in his chair. He pushed his gold-rimmed glasses up on his nose and picked up the two folders lying on the desk, then clearing his throat, looked at Nicholas then Camille. "The days you were inseminated, Mrs. King, Mr. Cardoneaux's wife, Lauren also underwent the same procedure."

"So what does that have to do with me?"

"Please, be patient. I'll make the connection. It was after you both had gone that we discovered the mistake."

"The mistake?" Camille gave him a blank stare.

"What mistake?" Nicholas demanded. "And why are you just now getting around to telling us about it after all this time?" he ground out.

Dr. Hadley grimaced and beads of sweat popped out on his forehead. "You see, we hired a new technician a few days prior to the procedure and - "

"What are you saying?" Camille's eyes widened and she rose from her chair.

"After the sperm vials were delivered to their respective examining rooms and the insertion syringes filled, we proceeded with the insemination on the assumption that everything was in order. As a result of that mistaken assumption Lauren Cardoneaux was inseminated with your husband's sperm. And you with Nicholas Cardoneaux's."

Chapter Two

Shock flew through Camille's mind. The room started spinning and she swayed, then everything faded to black.

As she started to crumble to the floor, Nicholas in a lightening-quick motion, caught her, lifted her in his arms, and carried her over to the couch.

Dr. Hadley rushed around his desk. "I assure you, Mr. Cardoneaux, nothing remotely like this has ever happened in our clinic."

Nicholas glared at the doctor. "I don't want to hear your assurances or excuses. Don't just stand there, man, get her a glass of water!"

Hadley quickly moved to obey, dashing from the room, returning almost immediately with the water.

"Now you can get out, Nicholas commanded as he took the water from the doctor's unsteady hand.

"Mr. Cardoneaux, I'm after all a physician. I can

help - "

"You've done enough, don't you think? For your sake you'd better hope and pray that she's all right. My attorney will contact yours about the repercussions of this clinic's blunder."

Needing no further prompting, Dr. Hadley hurried out of the room.

Nicholas studied Camille's now wan, but still lovely face. He couldn't believe it! His child was alive and thriving inside this woman's womb. He sat the glass down and vigorously rubbed the inside of her wrist.

As she came around Camille felt as though she were drifting in a haze.

Nicholas said in a gentle, coaxing voice, "Camille, can you hear me?"

At the sound of Nicholas Cardoneaux's deep voice, the haze subsided and she opened her eyes and blinked several times. It took a few seconds for reality to set in. And when it did, she raised herself to a sitting position.

"Tell me that what Dr. Hadley said isn't true," Camille said, her eyes pleading with Nicholas to deny it.

"I'm sorry, I can't tell you that. Here, drink this," he said, bringing the glass of water to her lips.

Camille took several sips before pushing it away.

"But that means my baby is - "

"Mine not your husband's," he finished.

"Oh, my God! It can't be true. What am I going to do?" she cried as tears spilled down her face.

"Camille, please don't cry." Nicholas pulled her into his arms, her tear-filled voice ripping at his heart. Why had she said I instead of we? She had a husband didn't she? Dr. Hadley had referred to her as Mrs. King. That had to mean there was a Mr. King, didn't it? If that were so, why had she excluded him? He was as much a part of this as she. The staggering revelation that the baby his wife was carrying wasn't his was bound to make him mad as hell, but that couldn't be avoided. It was a fact he would have to accept.

"You don't have to worry about a thing," Nicholas soothed. "We'll work something out. I promise."

At his words Camille cried harder. At a loss as to how to comfort her, Nicholas held her closer, and as he comforted her, the reality of his situation began to unfold. The child he'd always wanted wasn't lost to him after all. Camille and her husband would probably be more than happy to give the baby to him after it was born considering the circumstances. And Nicholas intended to see that the Kings were generously compensated. He was elated!

"Mr. Cardoneaux, I - " Dr. Hadley said as he stuck

his head around the door of his office.

"We don't have anything further to discuss, Hadley."

"But we do," he said entering the room, "if you're thinking about suing or possibly seeking to close down the facility. We help so many couples who wouldn't otherwise be able to have children."

Ignoring the plea, Nicholas said. "I hope you fired the one responsible."

"Yes, we did of course."

"Mrs. King is obviously upset. You need to call her husband."

"That would be quite impossible since the man is dead."

Nicholas was stunned, but also relieved. Now he wouldn't have to deal with an irate husband. It should be a simple thing convincing Camille King to give him custody of the baby.

"Does she have any other family?"

"A mother and younger brother. I'll have my nurse call them," Hadley said, picking up the phone.

Nicholas could see that Camille was still under the after affects of shock and wasn't taking in what was being said.

Dr. Hadley's nurse entered the office. "I couldn't

reach either of her relatives, doctor."

"Then, I'll take her home," Nicholas asserted. His words seemed to bring Camille out of her stupor.

"No. You don't have to do that, Mr. Cardoneaux," Camille answered.

"How did you get to the clinic?" he asked her.

"I drove. And I can drive myself home, thank you very much." Camille swung her legs off the couch.

"I think you'd better sit for a while until you get your bearings."

Camille ignored his directive and stood up anyway.

Nicholas advanced toward her. "Look, you're in no condition to drive."

"I can take a taxi."

"You'll be more comfortable in my car. I can have someone drive your car to your house later today."

Camille started for the door, but after taking only a few steps, she swayed on her feet. Nicholas was there and scooped her up in his arms.

"You're one stubborn woman, Camille King."

"Put me down. I can walk."

"Obviously you can't," he said heading for the door.

The nurse opened it and preceded them out of

the doctor's office. As Nicholas carried Camille through the waiting room, he heard familiar voices.

"Isn't that Nicholas Cardoneaux, Richard?"

"Yes, it is. We haven't seen him since he and Lauren . . ."

"Great," Nicholas swore under his breath. Phyllis and Richard Collier. A couple, who like Nicholas and Lauren, had had fertility problems and had gone to the Hadley clinic. They also happened to be members of the same country club. Before exiting the clinic, he sliced them a quelling look.

Once outside in the warm, humid afternoon, Nicholas shifted his light burden to a more comfortable position and headed for his car. Seconds later he slid the key into the lock of a silver Lexus.

When Camille looked around them and saw that people were staring, she squirmed in her self-proclaimed protector's arms.

"Would you please put me down?"

"I will when you're securely settled inside my car," he answered. "Now, where do you live?"

Realizing the futility of arguing with him, Camille told him Orleans St. in the Quarter and glared at him. She'd never met a more arrogant, overbearing man in her life. She found it next to impossible to believe that he could actually be the father of her baby. For the past four months she had believed she was carrying her late husband's child. And what about Lauren Cardoneaux, this man's wife, who happened to be pregnant with Elroy's child? Tears welled in her eyes.

Nicholas saw them and the sadness and lingering shock on Camille's face, and his heart went out to her. What must it be like for a woman to find out she had conceived a strange man's child instead of her husband's?

After a few minutes Camille wiped the moisture from her eyes with the heels of her hands and asked. "Where are you taking me? This isn't the way to my house."

"You need time to compose yourself, so I'm taking you to Audubon Park. It's only a couple of blocks from here."

"What if I don't want to go?" she challenged.

Nicholas just smiled and kept on driving.

What an impossible man he was, Camille fumed. He was evidently a law unto himself. She thought about his words of comfort. What did he mean when he'd said they'd work something out? What was there to work out? This baby was hers. There could never be any compromise where her child was concerned. Although Nicholas Cardoneaux might be the biological father, it didn't mean she would let him have a say about it. She already loved her baby and would do whatever it took to protect and keep her. Camille moved her hand across her stomach.

"Are you in pain?" Nicholas asked, concern furrowing lines on his forehead. "If you are I'm taking you to emergency."

"I'm not in any pain. I feel fine. Or at least I would if you would take me home."

"Oh, I will - later."

Camille sighed in frustration. There was no changing his mind. She'd just have to bide her time. And after he took her home she wouldn't see him again. Surely he wouldn't want to lay claim to this child under the circumstances. Camille suddenly remembered where she'd heard his name; it was on the television. The Cardoneaux family owned a multimillion-dollar construction and architectural business, and were no doubt high up in the social register.

"What were you thinking?"

"How badly I want you to take me home."

"We've been all through that."

"And you're still going to do exactly as you please. To hell with what anybody else thinks or wants. Right?"

"You're a quick study," he said, flashing her a

charming yet annoying smile.

"Of all the . . ." Camille decided not to say anything more. It wouldn't do any good anyway.

After a few minutes, he said. "So it's to be the silent treatment, is it? Look, Camille I only have your well being at heart."

"My well being as a person or only as the vessel nurturing your seed? And by the way, I'm Mrs. King to you."

Nicholas grinned. "Considering our present predicament, it seems kind of odd to be so formal with each other. You can call me Nicholas." He guided the car off St. Charles Avenue and drove down Hilary and on to Leake Avenue. "I came this way because we would have had to walk quite a ways if I had continued down St. Charles, since cars are banned from entering the front section of the park."

"I know all that. I do happen to live in New Orleans."

"Sorry. Listen, Camille, I know you're no happier about this situation than I am, but we're going to have to deal with it and each other. You're carrying my baby."

"Correction. The baby I'm carrying is mine."

"Correction. The baby you're carrying is ours."

"What about your wife?"

Nicholas grimaced. "I am no longer married. Lauren and I were divorced after she lost our - the baby."

"Divorced? And she lost the baby!" The words 'lost the baby' echoed through Camille's mind. Nicholas's wife, ex-wife, had lost Elroy's child! Camille gulped. "How long ago?"

"Two months. You see, as a result of a car accident Lauren suffered a miscarriage and had to undergo an emergency hysterectomy."

"How awful! I'm so sorry."

"So am I, for her. Finding out she could never have any more children nearly destroyed her and contributed to the destruction of our marriage.

"I can see how it would have."

"Then you can understand where I'm coming from. I thought I'd lost my child, but to know that it's alive..."

Camille started to say, this baby is part black, not exactly the child you had envisioned. But she changed her mind because judging from his words, the sound in his voice and the look on his face, that didn't seem to matter to him. She had a feeling in the pit of her stomach that he was going to give her problems. And if he did, how was she supposed to deal with him?

Nicholas helped Camille out of the car and they

headed through the entrance to the Audubon Zoological Garden along River View Drive, which paralleled the Mississippi. He found a place where they could sit quietly and talk.

"Next time we come here we can catch the Mombasa Tram and—"

"There won't be a next time, Mr. Cardoneaux. There wouldn't be a first if not for your arrogance. The only thing I want you to do is take me home. Then you can forget about me and the baby and get on with your life and let me get on with mine."

Nicholas wanted to tell her that this was only the beginning between them, that he intended to get custody of his child, but he decided that now was not the time to bring it up. Once he has made her see that he could do more for the baby than she, then maybe he would begin to get somewhere with her. The way things stood, he was going to have a more difficult time convincing her of that than he had figured.

He spotted a bench beneath an old oak tree that was thickly draped with Spanish moss. He brushed the bench off and waited for Camille to sit down. When she did, he eased into the empty space beside her. An ICE CREAM ON TAP truck stopped several yards away, and a crowd quickly gathered around it. When a boy came away licking a double-dipped ice cream cone, Nicholas saw the look of longing in Camille's eyes.

"You want one?"

"I really shouldn't."

"Why not?"

"I don't want to gain too much weight."

"You want an ice cream and I'm getting you one. What's your favorite flavor?"

"Strawberry."

Nicholas smiled. "Mine too." He flagged down the truck before it moved on and brought back two double-dipped ice cream cones, one for himself and the other for Camille.

She took the offering and devoured it with relish.

Nicholas could have sworn that he heard a low moan of pleasure escape her lips. He took his napkin and reached over and dabbed at the drops of melted ice cream that had dribbled on her chin.

"Thanks. This is good."

"I can tell you rarely indulge yourself. You're going to have to do it more often. And I intend to personally see to it that you do."

"Look, Mr. Cardoneaux - "

"Call me, Nicholas."

"I don't need you in my life. Okay? I was doing

just fine without you."

"Dr. Hadley said you are a widow."

"That doesn't mean I'm desperate for money or starving for a man's attention."

"Don't be so defensive. I never thought for one minute that you were. How long has it been since your husband - you know."

"Elroy died a year ago."

"What made you decide to go ahead with the insemination?"

"A family was something we had both wanted. When we had gone to the doctor, we found out Elroy had a low sperm count. The doctor suggested that we go to the Hadley Clinic since they were having success with a new treatment to improve that condition. Although Elroy's sperm count improved, we didn't try for a baby right away. You see, Elroy was a jazz musician and after years of trying to establish himself, his career was finally starting to take off. And since he was older we decided to have his sperm stored for future use."

"I see," Nicholas said, digesting what she'd said while picking up on what she hadn't. It was really Camille who had wanted the baby. Elroy King's career had been his main focus. "Was he the man in the picture?"

She frowned. "What picture? Oh, that's right

you saw my photo wallet. Yes, that was Elroy. After he died it took me a

while to pull myself together. But I did and decided it was time to go ahead and have a baby. And now ..."

"And now to find out you're pregnant with another man's baby... And not just any man's baby, but a white man's baby."

"Look, I don't care about that. All I care about is my baby."

"Surely you don't want to raise a - "

Camille stood up. "I think you'd better take me home right now."

"We're going to have to discuss this sometime, Camille. It might as well be now. What I want you to know is that I'm not going to go away."

Camille was ready to argue the point when she felt a sudden fluttering movement inside her abdomen. She gasped dropping the rest of her ice cream cone and sat back down on the bench.

"What's wrong?" Nicholas's eyes widened in concern. "Is it the baby?"

"I-I think I just felt her move."

"You did?"

"Here," she indicated the area. When she saw the look of anxious anticipation in his eyes, compassion moved her to take his hand and press it to her stomach.

Nicholas felt a slight movement beneath his palm and a rush of emotion welled in his eyes.

"My child is really alive," he said, still awed by the revelation.

Camille didn't know what to say. She could understand what he was feeling, but she didn't want him getting any ideas.

"I want you to take me home."

Nicholas brushed the moisture from the corner of his eye and blinked several times. He sensed her withdrawal and knew that she didn't want him to have anything to do with her or the baby. Well, she wasn't the only one involved. It was his baby too. And he wanted it and he intended to have her. Her? Nicholas smiled. At least he and Camille agreed on the sex of their unborn child.

"Camille, there has to be a way to settle this."

"If you're considering trying to take this baby from me once it's born, don't even think about it. I'll fight you every step of the way."

Nicholas gritted his teeth. "I think you're right. I'd better take you home before we both say things we'll regret," he said, picking up her ice cream cone and dumping his and hers in a nearby trash can.

Camille saw the determined set of his jaw and knew it portended trouble. Why couldn't he just forget about her and the baby? It wasn't as if he couldn't find a woman of his own race to have babies with. She was sure any number of them would jump at the chance.

Suddenly those renegade feelings of desire she'd felt when she first laid eyes on Nicholas at the clinic came rushing back. For a few brief moments her heart raced. There was evidently a potent attraction working between them. One she had to ignore. But can you really ignore it? This man is fine to the bone, you must admit, a little voice echoed through her brain. Are you sure that nothing can come of that attraction, girl?

Of course she was. They came from two entirely different worlds not to mention different races. Suddenly the significance of who fathered her child hit her for the first time. Nicholas Cardoneaux was a descendant of one of New Orleans' most aristocratic families. Did she have the right to keep her baby from knowing him? Or Nicholas from knowing his child. Oh, God, what should she do?

Every now and then as he drove, Nicholas stole a glance at Camille. He could tell she was deep in thought. Probably, wondering how she could get him to back off. She just didn't understand that there was no way on earth he would ever do that. He wasn't sure how they were going to resolve this, but he knew that he would do whatever it took to get custody of his child.

Chapter Three

When Nicholas drove up in front of her mother's house, Camille saw her brother sitting in the porch swing. Since the confirmation of her pregnancy, her mother had insisted that Camille move in with her and her brother until after the baby was born. She hadn't liked the idea of Camille living all alone in the big house Elroy had left her. Camille dreaded telling her family the truth about the baby. Especially, her brother.

Her mother would be understanding because she was liberal minded. But Jamal was another story entirely. He barely managed to be civil to white people - white men in particular. He was one of those black Americans who blamed the white man for most of the ills befalling the black race. Camille didn't completely agree. In her opinion some people in this modern-day world, whether black or white, brought certain tragedies on themselves. And for the most part life was what you made of it. But she knew her brother held a different view on the subject. She also knew some of the reasons for his attitude. If only their father had lived to help guide him. Their mother had inculcated manners into her son, but despite that training he often abandoned it around white people, vocally venting his frustration and resentment.

Camille put her hand on the car door handle, but hesitated before opening it. Finally she let out a resigned sigh. She might as well get this over with.

Nicholas got out, quickly skirted the car and opened the door for her. As he did so he took in at a glance his surroundings. He'd never been to this section of the French Quarter. The lawn was well tended and the house freshly painted white with a blue trim. Twin Magnolia trees stood like sentinels on either side of the wrought-iron gate. What immediately caught his attention was the hostile look on the face of the young black man on the porch. Upon seeing Nicholas and Camille head up the walk, he rose from the swing, stepped off the porch and started toward them.

"Where's your car?" Jamal asked his sister, casting a wary look at Nicholas.

"This is Nicholas Cardoneaux. Mr. Cardoneaux, my brother Jamal Parker."

Nicholas smiled and extended his hand.

Jamal glared at him ignoring the gesture. He asked Camille, "Did your car break down?" He asked

Camille. You should have called me. I would have picked you up."

"I know you would have. Dr. Hadley's nurse did call, but you had evidently left to pick Mama up from work."

Nicholas could feel the hostile vibes emanating from Jamal Parker and sought to extinguish them. "It was all right. I was there and offered to take her home."

"That's right, Jamal. In answer to your question, no there's nothing wrong with my car. I just wasn't up to driving it home."

He frowned. "Why? Are you sick? Is something wrong with the baby?"

"No, I'm not sick. And the baby is fine."

"Then?"

"I'll explain later." Camille turned to Nicholas. "There's no need for you to stay."

Nicholas's jaw flexed taut with tension. "There's every need. And you know the reason why."

"What's he talking about, Camille?" Jamal demanded.

Seeing that the situation could get out of hand Camille said, "Maybe you had better go, Mr. Cardoneaux." She looked at Jamal and asked, "Is Mama in the house?"

"Yes, she is. We just got in twenty minutes

before you did." He turned to Nicholas. "Don't let us keep you. I'll take care of my sister from here on out."

Camille thought for a minute, then looked at Nicholas. "On second thought maybe you had better come in the house."

A curious frown formed on Jamal's face. "Why are you inviting him into our house? It was good of him to bring you home, but it's time for him to leave."

"Jamal! Would you stop with the heavy big brother act. I have something important to tell you and Mama. And Nicholas - Mr. Cardoneaux is part of it. Now can we go in the house? Please?"

Nicholas felt like strangling Jamal Parker. He could see that his attitude was upsetting Camille. And he wasn't going to stand for it even if he was her brother.

The front door opened and out walked a tall statuesque black woman, dressed in a kente cloth caftan. Nicholas assumed she was Camille's mother because they shared the same delicate, exotic facial structure and toffee-brown complexion. He didn't pick up on any hostile vibes coming from her. And for that he was grateful as well as relieved.

"Camille, who is our visitor?" the woman asked.

"His name is Nicholas Cardoneaux, Mama. Nicholas - I mean Mr. Cardoneaux, my mother Hazel

Parker. Mama, we - I need to - ah talk to you."

Nicholas picked up the conversation. "I drove your daughter home from the Hadley Clinic, Mrs. Parker."

Jamal's eyes narrowed. "For some mysterious reason she has yet to reveal, Camille was unable to drive her car home so Mr. Cardoneaux here, kindly volunteered his services."

"I think we'd all feel better if we went inside," Hazel suggested.

Jamal glowered at Nicholas, but without saying another word, preceded them into the house.

"You'll have to forgive my son, Mr. Cardoneaux. I somehow failed to instill proper manners and common courtesy into him. Please, come on in." Once they were in the living room, Hazel said to Nicholas, "Have a seat. Would you like some lemonade or a cold drink of water?"

"No, thank you, Mrs. Parker."

Camille walked over to her mother. "Mama, I have something to tell you, but I don't know quite how to begin."

Hazel smiled. "Just spit it out, sugar."

Nicholas liked this straight-forward woman. He could see where Camille got her gutsy spirit.

"Now that we're all in the house, I want to know what's going on, Camille," Jamal insisted.

Ignoring her son's outburst, Hazel smiled at her daughter. "You said you had something you wanted to tell me, sugar?"

Camille sat down on a chair across from the couch where Nicholas was sitting. Jamal remained standing. Hazel sat next to Nicholas.

"Mama," Camille began, "I learned that- that. I can't say it," she cried covering her face with her hands.

Hazel's brows arched with concern and she rose from the couch and knelt before her daughter. Taking her hands in her own she asked. "You're scaring me, sugar. What is it?"

Before Camille could answer Nicholas rose from the couch and answered. "Mrs. Parker, today we learned that the baby Camille is carrying is mine, not her late husband's."

"What?" Jamal spat.

Hazel shifted her gaze to Nicholas, then back to Camille. "I don't understand. How can this be?"

"Evidently the technician at the clinic made a mistake with the sperm vials. You see, my wife had gone to be inseminated the same day as Camille and there was a mix-up."

"Are you telling us your wife is carrying Elroy's baby?" Jamal said, although his voice sounded incredulous, it was liberally laced with sarcastic amusement.

Nicholas glared at him. "If you must know, my wife was in a car accident and lost the baby. Look, I can see you have issues, but my concern is for Camille and our child."

"Our, Is it?" Jamal let out a humorless laugh. "I don't see that you have a problem. After the baby is born, you're welcome to claim it."

"Mama, if you don't do something about him, you'll be minus a son because I'm going to kill him."

"I'm sorry, Camille," Jamal quickly apologized, "I didn't really mean it about the baby."

"I sure hope you didn't," she answered.

"How do you feel about all of this, sugar?" Hazel asked her daughter.

"I don't know how I feel, Mama. It was and still is a shock."

Jamal broached a question, deliberately allowing his distrust to seep into his words. "How do you know this isn't some kind of scam, sister girl?"

"Jamal, please."

Nicholas spoke up. "We'll have to talk about this another time, Camille. When we can do it alone." To Jamal he said. "I don't want her upset any more than necessary." He returned his gaze to Camille's face and smiled. "We'll talk later."

"I don't see the point, Mr. - Nicholas. There's nothing to talk about. This is my baby. And my family and I will handle it."

"I'll call you," Nicholas adamantly persisted. "Give me your phone number."

"You don't have to give it to him, Camille," Jamal inserted meaningfully.

Hazel shot her son a silencing look. "This is between Camille and Mr. Cardoneaux, Jamal."

"She's my sister. And it's up to me to protect her."

"You don't have anything to worry about," Nicholas said strongly. "I only want what's best for her and our child."

"So you say. We'll just have to wait and see how true your words prove to be."

Ignoring Jamal, Nicholas said to Camille. "I'm going to need your phone number. And also your key so I can get your car back to you."

Camille told Nicholas the phone number and then took the car key off her ring and handed it to him.

He turned to Hazel and smiled. "It was a pleasure meeting you, Mrs. Parker." Then he said to Jamal before leaving. "Whether you like it or not I intend to talk with Camille. I wouldn't advise your getting in my way." With that Nicholas walked out the door. The battle lines were clearly drawn between them.

"Who does he think he is?" Jamal started after him.

Hazel caught her son's shirt-sleeve. "You will leave him alone."

"For now, but if he hurts my sister, I'll make sure he lives to regret it," he said heading into the kitchen.

"Oh, Mama. What am I going to do?" Camille cried.

"The first thing you're going to do is go upstairs and rest. You look like you're about ready to drop."

"I am," she sighed and giving her mother her weary smile, Camille went straight upstairs to her bedroom, but she didn't lie down right away. Instead she walked into the adjoining room that her mother and brother had converted into a nursery.

She'd had Jamal paint the room a soft yellow and stencil a furry rabbit, teddy bear and lamb border on the walls. He had started carving a swinging cradle. She smiled proudly at his workmanship. Her brother was an exceptionally gifted carpenter. She only wished he were as gifted when it came to displaying tact and diplomacy. She knew the reasons for his attitude even though it didn't excuse his behavior.

Like the majority of young men, Jamal had wanted very badly to succeed, and had considered college the route to take to achieve that goal. Unfortunately college life hadn't been right for him and he had dropped out after his first year. He'd blamed his failure on his instructors and counselors, who all happened to be white, for suggesting that given his talent for carpentry, he should enroll in trade school. Jamal hadn't seen it as sound advice; he'd considered it a put down. It was then his resentment and bitterness against white people had begun to fester. It didn't help that over the last six months he had received quite a few crushing rejections from prominent construction companies in and around New Orleans. And as a result he was temporarily unemployed.

Camille rubbed her finger across the surface of the unfinished cradle and smiled. Although she understood her brother and his hangups and loved him anyway, it didn't mean she was going to let him or anyone else tell her what do. And that included Nicholas Cardoneaux, especially Nicholas Cardoneaux.

She walked back into her bedroom, kicked off her shoes and lay down on the bed. She was exhausted. The entire situation was all so unreal. One minute she was expecting Elroy's baby and the next...

This just couldn't be happening to her. What had she ever done to deserve it? She closed her eyes and the vision that danced before her mind's eye wasn't Elroy King's strong African-American features, but Nicholas Cardoneaux's handsome tanned face, black curly hair and mesmerizing blue eyes. And that body.

Whoa, girl.

She felt her baby move and splayed her hand over the area. Her baby was real and growing larger and stronger everyday. Camille had had her life all mapped out before this happened. She had made plans to return to teaching music at the junior high school in the fall. She had also intended to resume giving private piano lessons. But her real joy came from teaching the under-privileged kids at the Children's Center during the summer months, even though it wasn't exactly how her mother had wanted her to use her musical talent. Camille recalled a conversation years ago between her and her mother. It was shortly after her father died...

"Your father worked every spare moment and saved every dime he could get his hands on so you could study with Ellis Marsalis to be a jazz pianist. Not just any jazz pianist, but the best. And all you want to do is teach music. Sugar, you have a chance to be great."

"But I want to teach others to appreciate music

the same as I do, Mama."

"You can do that when you're done with your music career."

"I want teaching music to be my career, Mama. I love playing the piano, but -"

"Not everyone is born with your special talent. Xavier wanted you to become an icon in the jazz music world. You don't want to disappoint him, do you? Sugar, please just think about it. Your father was so proud of you."

Camille had felt pangs of guilt. And for the next ten years she had done as her mother wanted, but soon after marrying Elroy, she did what she truly loved; she taught.

Her husband had encouraged her to pursue her heart's desire. Now he was gone, along with her dreams of having their child. Instead the baby she was carrying was Nicholas Cardoneaux's. It all seemed so unfair. Tears welled in her eyes and trickled down her face.

She lifted her wedding picture from the night-stand.

"Oh, Elroy. What am I going to do? It wasn't supposed to be like this. You should be alive and here with me. This child should be yours and mine."

All she had left of her husband was the money

from his insurance, some pictures, momentos and the house he'd bought six months before he died.

Camille closed her eyes, willing sleep to come, hoping somehow that in sleep she could find peace. But deep in her soul she knew it was only wishful thinking and that no amount of sleep was going to solve her dilemma.

Chapter Four

Nicholas strode out to his car without sparing a backward glance at the Parker house. If he hadn't left when he did he was sure he and Jamal Parker would have come to blows. The man's attitude grated on his nerves. His insults he could handle, but the fact that he was Camille's brother didn't entitle him to have a say in what happened with regard to his child. He and Camille would make that decision.

Nicholas reached for his cell phone and arranged to have someone meet him at the clinic to get Camille's key, then deliver her car to her house. He also called his office and had his secretary cancel his remaining appointments. There was no way he could conduct business this afternoon.

After leaving the Quarter, he drove through West End Park to the Southern Yacht Club. He got out of his car, then walked past the club and headed down to the marina where his yacht was anchored.

"Mr. Cardoneaux," a man called out. No one told me you would be coming today."

"It was a spur of the moment decision, Claude. If the Creole Lady isn't ready to - "

"We always keep her at the ready, sir. Just give us a few minutes and we'll be under way. Where did you have in mind to go?"

"A place that's quiet. Whenever I have some heavy thinking to do, sailing on Lake Ponchatrain aboard the Creole Lady always seems to help me."

Claude smiled. "I understand. I know just the place."

Nicholas went below to his cabin and changed into the khaki slacks, cotton knit shirt and trekking boots he kept on board. He started to leave the cabin and join Claude at the helm, but instead sank down on the bed. The shock from the day's revelation had set in, and suddenly Nicholas was exhausted.

The last time he'd been aboard the Creole Lady was the day his divorce from Lauren became final. Before that he'd tried for weeks to talk her out of getting a divorce. When she remained adamant, he had sought psychological help for her. The doctors had agreed that the loss of the baby and her inability to have another had warped her thinking. They had worked with them both to no avail, and after only a few sessions Lauren was more determined than ever to end their marriage. Disregarding the doctors' advice, and Nicholas's entreaty to give it another chance, she'd flown to Jamaica and gotten the divorce. In a matter of days it was final, and Nicholas had taken the Creole Lady out past Barataria to an uncharted island for a time to lick his wounds. Now once again he needed the solace only sailing the Lady could give him.

* * *

When the breathtaking panorama of Joyce Wildlife Reserve came into view, Nicholas felt the tiredness and tension in his body start to melt. So eager to reach his destination, that before Claude could drop anchor, he jumped onto the pier, and was headed for his favorite spot.

Ten minutes later as he walked up to the gates of Swamp Walk, he waved to Joseph, a park ranger he'd known since childhood. Nicholas liked this place because it was obscure and he could count on being the only one on the grounds at this time of day. Swamp Walk was a 1,000-foot boardwalk that led deep into Manchac Swamp.

When Nicholas and his brother, Phillip, were little boys, their parents had taken them to Joyce Wildlife Reserve, where they would slip away into the swamp to hide out. Suddenly he smiled as he stood watching the egrets and herons swoop overhead. Here he felt at one with nature. It was even comforting to see the alligators. Especially the mother alligators as they fiercely guarded their nests. They reminded him of his own mother.

Suzette Cardoneaux was overprotective of her sons. As youngsters, he and Phillip had been allowed to play with only certain children, those from impeccable backgrounds. Yet somehow they'd managed to find their own friends, much to their mother's chagrin.

The air was humid, and the lush greenery grew in profusion everywhere you looked. Tupelo and Cypress trees and the ever present weeping willows were all around. And with each step into this tranquil paradise, he felt himself relax a little more until a peaceful calm had completely engulfed him. As he continued on his walk, Nicholas thought about Camille and their unique situation. He found a huge protruding root from a giant tupelo tree and sat down on it.

How was he supposed to handle this situation? From his brief exposure to Camille, he sensed that she wouldn't be easily convinced to give up the baby. But somehow he had to do just that. He wanted this child. He'd yearned to hold a baby of his own for far too long to lose out now.

Several hours passed before Nicholas was ready

to head back to the boat. He had thought that by the time Claude had guided the yacht into the marina thirty minutes later, he'd have decided what to do, but such wasn't the case. He reasoned that if he turned things over to his lawyers there would not only be a scandal, but a nasty court battle. He'd never subject Camille and his child to something like that. There had to be another way to resolve his dilemma and he would find it.

* * *

That evening Nicholas drove through the alley of oak trees leading up to the front door of the Cardoneaux mansion. The estate had been named Magnolia Grove in 1798 and had been called that down to this day. He was proud of his home. It was a perfect example of classic Greek revival architecture, with its eight white, doric columns and galleried first and second floor. Rhododendron and azalea bushes flanked the big house as well as the cottages on either side of the mansion. They had once been used in the 1800s as guest houses when balls were the fashion.

Magnolia Grove, originally a five thousand acre plantation, had been in the Cardoneaux family since the early 1700s. Following the 1930's depression, Nicholas' grandfather, Andre Cardoneaux, had share cropped several thousand acres, but had kept for his personal use the house and the fifty acres surrounding it.

Jacques Cardoneaux, Nicholas' father, had eventually sold the forty-five hundred acres and started Cardoneaux Construction. And when Nicholas had joined the family business, the architectural firm had been added. Under his direction the company had expanded and profits doubled in the following eight years.

As the eldest son, Nicholas was expected to produce the first Cardoneaux heir. Because Lauren had been unable to carry a child to term, over the years he had come to assume that his brother Phillip would be the one to provide one. Now since Camille King was expecting his child everything had changed. The joy he felt couldn't be measured. He didn't care whether it was a boy or girl; he wanted his baby living under his roof.

Nicholas saw his mother walk out on the porch and his joy swiftly faded. What would she think about this latest development? He'd find out because he intended to broach the subject at dinner. He was sure that Phillip would support whatever decision he made, but his mother was another story entirely. She was old southern aristocracy down to her French manicured toe-nails.

"Nicholas, you're late," she complained. "I called the office, but no one could tell me where you'd gone. You really shouldn't do that, dear. I was worried about you.

It's not like you to be so inconsiderate."

"I'm sorry, Mother. Something came up. Where is Phillip?"

"He called to say he'd be late - again. One of his patients had a heart attack and he's with him now. I wish he'd gone into practice with Maurice. He said your brother was the best doctor of internal medicine to come along in a great while. I'll never understand why he chose to work at the New Orleans Community Hospital, rather than with Maurice."

"He has nothing against Dr. Longet's practice, Mother. It's just that Phillip believes his services are best utilized where people are in real need."

"Don't lecture me, Nicholas. Wealthy people get sick the same as the poor ones."

"I really don't want to get into this with you, Mother. Phillip is the one you should talk to, not me."

"You know he won't listen. He's every bit as stubborn as you and your father."

Nicholas heard the catch in her voice whenever she mentioned his father. He had died in a yachting accident three years before, and his mother still grieved for him daily. Maybe the news of a grandchild would ease her pain and loneliness.

* * *

"A mix up? What kind of mix up?" Suzette asked, putting her fork down as she and Nicholas dined in the formal dining room an hour later.

"Mother, the child Lauren lost wasn't mine."

"What do you mean not yours!"

"A mistake was made."

"But you just said that I'm to be grandmother. Are you telling me that some strange woman is carrying it!"

"That's exactly what I'm telling you."

"I don't understand. Whose child had Lauren been carrying? How could something like that have happened? I warned you and Lauren about going to a place like that. Have you spoken to this woman?"

"Mother, I'll answer your questions if you give me a chance. Yes, I've spoken to her."

"And has she agreed to give you custody?"

"No. We haven't gotten that far."

"How much money does she want? It always comes down to that, you know. I take it she's not well off."

"I don't know the answer to that."

"She's probably not. We'll hire an investigator and - "

"No, we won't. I intend to handle this personally, Mother."

"Don't be ridiculous. What is the woman's name?"

"Camille King."

"Is she related to the St. Charles Parish Kings?"

"I doubt it."

"No matter, we'll find out all there is to know about her. Poor Lauren. Does she know?"

"No, Mother, and I don't want her to. She's suffered enough. And anyway she's not part of this."

"I guess you're right. Do you know who fathered her child?"

"Does it matter? Lauren lost the baby, Mother."

"He was probably a nobody."

Knowing his mother's position on ancestry, Nicholas knew he was in for it once she found out Camille and Elroy King were black. He didn't care what she thought, though. She could rant and rave and pitch a hissy fit if she wanted to; he intended to get custody of his child.

* * *

Camille hadn't gotten very much sleep the night before. This morning she woke up to a queasiness in the pit of her stomach and had to make a quick dash for the bathroom. She hadn't had morning sickness since the initial first two months of her pregnancy, and guessed it was the stress of yesterday's revelation that had caused it this time.

"Are you all right, sugar?" Hazel Parker asked her daughter.

"Just a bout with morning sickness."

"You were up late last night. I heard you walking around."

"It was hard for me to get to sleep. I couldn't seem to drive Nicholas Cardoneaux from my thoughts."

"Of course you couldn't. The man is the father of your baby."

"Biologically speaking."

"I believe he thinks of himself as more than that, sugar."

"He'd better change his thinking then. I don't intend to let him into my life or my baby's. He's a wealthy man. Surely he can make another baby with someone else."

Hazel frowned at her daughter's words. She'd seen the look in Nicholas Cardoneaux's eyes. He wasn't the kind of man to give up on anything he wanted. He was no doubt used to getting his own way. Where exactly did that leave her daughter? And her grandbaby?

"The two of you are going to have to talk, Camille."

"I don't see why. There's nothing for us to talk

about. Trust me, he's not going to call. He's probably forgotten about us already."

"I wouldn't count on it."

"He has no choice. This is my baby."

"And his."

"Why do you keep saying that?"

"Because it's the truth, whether you choose to accept it or not. He has rights, you know."

"Not to my baby he doesn't."

Jamal strode into the kitchen.

"When and if Cardoneaux calls, are you going to tell him where he can go? Or do you want me to do it?" he asked Camille.

"This is not your business, Jamal."

"You're my sister," he said, as if that was explanation enough.

"You're going to have to let her deal with this by herself, Jamal," Hazel chided.

"She's never dealt with a high-powered man like Nicholas Cardoneaux. These rich old southern aristocratic types think they own the world. Mark my words. If you get involved with him he's going to give you problems, sister girl." With that he exited the kitchen.

Camille sat down at the table. She had a sinking feeling her brother was right.

"Don't pay any attention to him, sugar."

"I think I should. What he said about Nicholas Cardoneaux is probably dead on. If Jamal is right, Nicholas will call and much more besides."

"Not necessarily. Maybe he won't call."

"You think not? Now I'm worried that he will. You heard him, Mama."

"Maybe he'll settle for just setting up a trust fund for the baby."

"He told me he's wanted a child for years. And Jamal seems sure he's going to want to do more than that. If I could just make him see that my child wouldn't fit into his world."

Hazel shook her head. Where was all this going to end? She knew one thing for sure. She wasn't going to stand by while Mr. Nicholas Cardoneaux or anyone else hurt her daughter and grandchild.

Chapter Five

It had been almost two weeks since the incident at the Hadley Clinic and the scene at Camille's house. During that time Dr. Hadley had called Camille pleading with her to sign a waiver stating that she wouldn't sue or seek to close down his clinic. She had assured him that she wouldn't, but couldn't speak for the father of her child.

That first week Camille had managed to be out of the house so that if Nicholas Cardoneaux had called she wasn't there to answer the phone. When she was at home and had seen his name on the Caller ID, she hadn't answered. And she hadn't returned any of the messages he'd left. By the beginning of the second week, and there had been no more messages or phone calls, Camille had begun to relax. Like she had told her mother, he had probably given up when he realized that her baby wouldn't fit into his world.

Camille had continued teaching piano and music at the Children's Community Center, and her life was gradually gettting back on track when she heard the music room door open and there, standing in the doorway was Nicholas Cardoneaux, looking for all the world like an angry Greek God.

"Wha- what are you doing here?" she asked.

"What do you think? Why haven't you returned any of my phone calls, Camille?"

"Look, Mr. Cardoneaux, I saw no reason why I should. How did you know where to find me? Never mind. You've obviously had me 'checked out' so to speak."

"There's nothing wrong with a father being solicitous of the woman who is carrying his child."

"You had no right to - "

"I had every right, Camille. Like I said before, I'm not going to go away. You might as well get used to seeing me because I'm not going to let you shut me out of my child's life."

"It's not even born yet." Camille rose too quickly from her chair and suddenly felt dizzy. Nicholas was there, supporting her, and helped her back into the chair.

After a few moments she recovered and looked at him. He gazed into her arresting face. God, she was beautiful. He shook his head to clear it. He had to remember his objective. He had to keep in mind that what he wanted was for Camille to give him custody of the baby

- not access to her body. He noticed that her skin seemed to have a special glow. Being pregnant with his baby had probably given it that.

His baby.

He still had a hard time believing this miracle.

"Camille, I told you we needed to talk. And we're going to even if I have to kidnap you to bring it about."

"Why can't you just leave me and my baby alone? She can never be a part of your world. Can't you see that?"

"No. I can't."

"You mean you don't want to."

"Whatever. That baby you're carrying is a Cardoneaux. My daughter deserves the best. And she deserves to be with people who will love her."

"Are you saying I won't?"

"No. I'm not saying that. You're putting words in my mouth."

"We're never going to agree on what's best. I'm this baby's mother and I think she belongs with me. No judge is going to award you custody."

"I wouldn't be too sure about that. I'm this baby's father. I don't want to get lawyers involved in something you and I can work out ourselves. But if you force me to - "

"You'll bring them into it, right? Please leave, or I'll have the security guard escort you out."

"Camille, I'll call you at home and this time you'd better pick up that phone or else I'm coming over to your house."

Before she could say anything, Nicholas was gone. She got up from her chair and walked over to the window and glanced out in time to see him get into his car and drive away. Camille turned away from the window and returned to her chair and pulled open her desk drawer and lifted out an old magazine she'd borrowed from the Center's library.

On the front page was a picture of the Cardoneaux family, and in the society section she came across an article about them. His mother was a queen bee if she'd ever seen one. Camille wondered how she would take having a racially mixed grandchild. How would she treat the baby? Frowning, she chose not to think about it. She shifted her gaze to Phillip Cardoneaux. He closely resembled Nicholas. She couldn't help wondering what his reaction would be to the situation. Had Nicholas even told his family about the baby?

After finishing for the day, she decided not to go directly to her mother's. She needed to go to a place where she could think undisturbed so she drove to her own house in Treme, a section of New Orleans where many prominent musicians made their home.

As she got out of the car, Camille smiled. Her husband had loved this house. The two of them had just started decorating it when he died suddenly from a stroke while performing at Preservation Hall. It was the chance that every serious Jazz musician would sell his soul for. That night there had been standing room only. Just being asked to perform at the Hall was an honor bestowed on very few jazz musicians. That night Elroy had been so excited...

"I've finally arrived, baby girl."

Camille just smiled. She wasn't fond of the endearment, since she was fifteen years younger than her husband. It made her feel more like his daughter than his wife. She had never told him that though.

"Aren't you happy for me, Millie?"

"Of course I am."

"You don't sound like it. When I make it to the big time we'll have that family you've always wanted. I promise.

"I thought you wanted that too."

"I do, but later. Right now I'm on top of the world, baby girl."

Camille remembered feeling like second best.

Her mother and her friend Deja had told her that a lot of women found themselves taking a backseat to a man's career. But that once the novelty wore off, she'd have her husband back.

As she walked through the living room to the music room, Camille stopped and stared at her husband's portrait on the wall. His eyes were closed and he was holding his saxophone, blowing on the mouthpiece between his lips. He'd died doing what he loved. She went upstairs and stopped in front of the bedroom she'd shared with Elroy. Her mother and brother had removed all his clothes and stored his personal possessions in the attic until she felt ready to go through them.

She moved on to her bedroom. After deciding to move out of the master bedroom, she had the largest guestroom redone for herself in ivory and peach. The connecting door opened into her dream nursery. Unlike the one at her mother's house, this one had every conceiveable item a baby was ever likely to need.

Now, knowing the child she carried wasn't her husband's made it all seem surreal somehow, forcing her to question her feelings about the house. She no longer felt the same about it. She'd had several offers for it since her husband's death and had considered selling it at one time, but after being inseminated and learning she was pregnant, she'd changed her mind.

And now?

"Oh, God, why did this have to happen to me?" She climbed into the bed and lay on her back staring out the window at the clear blue sky. Although it was a cloudless afternoon, her life was far from sunny. What should she do? What could she do? He seemed determined to install himself smack dab in the middle of her life and her baby's. Her attempts at keeping him at bay hadn't worked.

Camille sighed. Somehow she had to persuade him to forget about her and the baby.

You and what act of congress, girl? a voice inside her head taunted.

* * *

The woman could make him so damned mad. Nicholas fumed as he paced back and forth in his study at Magnolia Grove. Well he wasn't going to let Camille exclude him from his child's life. She had better get used to seeing him because he intended to be around for at least the next twenty years and beyond.

"What's bothering you, Nick?" Phillip asked, standing in front of the doorway to the study. "Is it safe to come in?"

Nicholas smiled. "Of course it is. I'm just letting

off steam, that's all."

"Mother told me about the mistake at the fertility clinic. I'm thinking there's more to the story than you've told her. Am I right?"

"You have no idea how right you are. Close the door and sit down while I enlighten you."

Once Phillip had made himself comfortable, Nicholas unburdened himself. By the time he'd finished, the smile had faded from his brother's face, a look of concern replacing it.

"You do have problems, big brother. Mother is not going to be pleased when she finds out."

"You think I don't know that. I have enough to deal with as it is. Camille King is one stubborn lady. She refuses to listen to reason."

"You mean your perception of it."

"My perception? What are you saying?"

"I know you, big brother. It's either your way or the highway."

"I'm not that inflexible."

"Oh, yes you are. Lauren is the only other person to upset your equilibrium like this. You thought you could change her mind about the divorce, but found out differently. I tried to warn you, but you wouldn't listen. Remember?"

How could he forget. Nicholas hated to admit it, but his brother was right. He couldn't help it that he was a dominating male. It was in his genes he guessed. What was he going to do about Camille? He certainly wouldn't be able to intimidate her. She was too feisty by half.

"I'm going to call Camille in a few minutes."

"What's you're game plan?"

"I don't really have one."

"Yet."

"Phillip, you make me seem like some kind of calculating ogre."

"I don't mean to. Look, I have late night duty at the hospital so I have to go. You'll figure out the best way to handle this. I have every confidence in you, big brother."

Nicholas wondered if he really could figure it out as he watched his brother leave. He walked over to the phone, picked up the receiver and punched in Camille's phone number.

"Hello."

"Camille?"

Silence.

"I called to invite you out to dinner so we can talk."

Still no response.

"I know you're there, Camille."

"I don't see- "

"I'll pick you up in half an hour. Be ready," he growled and hung up. Damn it, he had lost his temper - again. He'd have to learn to control himself around her.

"Nicholas."

"Mother!"

"That was the King woman, wasn't it? Judging from the sound of things she's being less than cooperative."

"It's my problem, Mother and I'll handle it."

"If you find you can't make any headway with her, let me try. I'll make sure she sees reason."

"No! Absolutely not."

"But, Nicholas - "

"I mean it, Mother. Don't interfere."

Chapter Six

"The nerve of the man," Camille muttered in annoyance as she changed her clothes. Just because he happened to be the father of her baby didn't give Nicholas Cardoneaux license to order her around. She'd listen to what he had to say and then...

And then what, girl?

She didn't know. If he persisted in disrupting her life what could she do to stop him?

You may have to allow him concessions.

Camille heard a knock on her bedroom door, then her brother asked if she was decent. When she replied yes, he opened the door and walked in.

"Mama told me that you're going out to dinner with Nicholas Cardoneaux. Is it true?"

"Jamal - "

"Is it true?"

"Yes."

"I thought we were in agreement that you were going to stay away from him?"

"We are, but I can't just pretend he doesn't exist."

"Why can't you? Maybe I should have a little talk with him."

"Even if you did, it wouldn't change anything. He's the father of my baby."

"Yes, according to him and that fertility doctor. It may not even be true? What proof does he have? Only the clinic's word. It seems strange to me that they would wait so long to reveal this so called mistake."

"Why would Dr. Hadley lie? Why would Nicholas- I mean Mr. Cardoneaux -want to claim my child if it wasn't his? It wouldn't make any sense."

"Maybe that clinic was conducting some kind of weird experiment. Who knows. I don't have all the answers, but I wouldn't trust anything Cardoneaux or that doctor says."

"Because they're white? That's not a good enough reason, Jamal. I think I should at least listen to what Nicholas has to say."

Jamal threw his hands in the air. "He's already got you calling him by his first name. You just don't understand men like him, Camille. They take what they want and walk away. If that baby is his and he wants it, he's going to do whatever it takes to get it."

"He doesn't seem like that kind of man."

"That's just it, you don't know what kind of man this Nicholas Cardoneaux is. Let me handle this for you."

"You make it sound like a business deal. No, Jamal."

"Mark my words, sister girl, you're going to be sorry you didn't let me deal with him." With that said he left the room.

Camille sank down on the chair before the vanity. Could her brother be right and she was making a mistake? Underestimating Nicholas? Or relying on Dr. Hadley's word that this baby actually was Nicholas's? What if the baby didn't look white? There were tests she could take to determine paternity, but they would have to wait until after the baby was born.

It looks like that's exactly what you're going to have to do.

* * *

Camille sneaked glances at Nicholas as he drove. He was wearing a cafe au lait summer suit, with cream-colored shirt and tie. The contrast between his suit and his honeyed tan made him look fantastically sexy. She shook her head. She had to stop doing this. The reason for this evening was to discuss the baby and what part if any Nicholas would play in its life. Camille's objective was to change his mind not let him change hers. She returned her attention to the scenery passing the side window.

Nicholas had seen the flash of desire in her eyes and realized that she was as attracted to him as he was to her. His eyes caught on her full bottom lip and then dropped to her breasts and on further to the swell of her stomach. God she was beautiful.

You've said that before, Cardoneaux. What does it have to do with your getting custody of your child?

Nothing. But she was the mother of his child and he admired her.

Admiring her is one thing, Cardoneaux, but...

But what?

But is it wise?

No, damn it, but he desired her, damn it. He desired her like crazy.

"Where are you taking me, Nicholas?" Camille asked as he headed in the direction of East New Orleans.

"Some place quiet where we can talk."

"Look, Nicholas, there is really nothing to talk about."

"I beg to differ with you, Camille. That's my child you're carrying. That very fact gives me certain parental rights."

"Why should you want to exercise those rights?

You could marry again and have other children."

"You mean white children. It's really a moot point. You are already carrying my child. She'll be my heir."

"Is that all that you want her for?"

Nicholas sighed, gritting his teeth in frustration. "I think we should wait until we get to the restaurant to discuss this."

They were silent during the remainder of the ride.

Camille's eyes widened in surprise when Nicholas pulled into the parking lot of La Provence, a French restaurant she and her husband had gone to on several occasions.

"Judging from your expression you've been here before."

"Elroy and I ate dinner here a few times."

"Would you prefer we went somewhere else?"

"No. This will be fine. Let's go in and get this over with."

"Camille, I - "

"Having this discussion was your idea not mine. If it were solely up to me - "

"I know what you'd do, but since it isn't we'll go inside." Nicholas helped Camille out of the car and cupping her elbow escorted her into the restaurant. The maitre d' appeared and showed them into a small private dining room.

"The wine steward will be with you momentarily. Would you like to order an appetizer, sir? Madam?"

"Yes, I would." He glanced at Camille. "What would you like?"

"I'm really not hungry."

Nicholas took her menu and ordered the quail gumbo.

Camille's mouth began to water. She remembered how delicious it was.

Nicholas smiled when he saw her expression. He was glad to know that she had a healthy appetite.

"How does marinated rack of lamb sound for the main course?"

"All right, I guess."

"Make that two," Nicholas instructed the waiter. The wine steward arrived. "We'll have two glasses of your special non-alcoholic rose. You see, she's pregnant," he said proudly.

The steward glanced at Camille and then at Nicholas. He raised his eyebrows, smiled and then congratulated them before walking away.

"Why did you tell him that?" Camille demanded.

"It's only the truth," Nicholas answered simply

with a smile. "Relax. I'm proud you're carrying my child."

"There's no need for you to broadcast the fact to the entire world."

"I'm not doing that."

"When the novelty wears off, you're going to regret going public. What will your family and friends think?"

"My family will go along with whatever decision I make. I am after all head of the family since my father's death a few years ago." He wasn't worried about his brother, but his mother was another story. "As for my friends, what they think doesn't really matter."

"Because it's either your way or the highway. Right."

Nicholas quirked his lips into a smile, remembering that his brother had said the same thing. Was he really that bad?

"What can I say to make you see reason?"

"If by reason you mean forget that you're carrying my child. I can't do it. And there is nothing you can say that'll make me feel differently."

Camille wondered what it would take to get through to him.

You might as well try another tactic. You'd have a better chance convincing a leech to voluntarily let go of its dinner. Nicholas could imagine what was going through Camille's mind as he watched the changing expressions on her face. She just didn't know that there was no argument, logical or otherwise, she could present that would make him forsake this child.

"Give it up, Camille. Our dinner has arrived. Please, just enjoy."

The lamb was wonderful. And the freshly baked bread made Camille groan in pleasure. She eyed the dessert cart with longing. On it was Tarte Aux Fraises, a cold fresh strawberry tart, Ladyfingers, Gateau A l'orange, orange sponge cake topped with an apricot glaze and slivers of almonds.

"Which one appeals to you?" Nicholas asked.

"The Gateau à l'orange."

Nicholas smiled. "It was a favorite of mine when I was a boy. Still is." He indicated Camille's dessert preference to the waiter and told him to make it two.

Maybe the way to her heart was through her stomach. Once her appetite was appeased and she was relaxed, then perhaps they could talk calmly and rationally about their situation.

Keep on dreaming, Cardoneaux.

Camille put her fork down and picked up her napkin and wiped her mouth. When she raised her eyes, she realized that Nicholas was watching her and smiling.

"Would you like more dessert?" he asked.

"No. I've had enough, thank you. We might as well get on with it."

"There's no need to make this a battle, Camille."

"Because you intend to win the war. Right?"

This wasn't going at all the way he'd hoped, Nicholas thought. He didn't want to give her an ultimatum. That would only make her more defensive and dig her heels in deeper. He realized now that full custody was out of the question. "Is it because I'm white that my being the baby's father bothers you so much?"

Camille was silent for a minute. "No, it's not that. I don't know you. I had my life all mapped out."

"Then I came along and derailed your plans. There's no reason why we can't share this child. She needs two parents."

"What kind of arrangement did you have in mind?"

"I don't know. It's why we need to discuss where we go from here."

"It would be easy if you'd - "

"Forget it, Camille. Don't you understand? I can't forget about this child."

"Why can't you?"

Nicholas' expression softened. "I've wanted a child of my own, it seems, forever."

"Even if the mother is black?"

"She could be red, yellow or purple; it wouldn't make any difference."

"Your family might not agree with that." Camille saw Nicholas's self-assured look waver for a second. She was right. Was it his brother or his mother or both who might take exception to the idea? "You're not as confident as you pretend. Are you?"

"It doesn't matter whether they approve or not."

"Are you sure about that? Family is important."

"Not more important than my own child, Camille."

Why was he being so stubborn about this? They were worlds apart. It would be impossible to share this baby. She was sure his family's opinion was more important to him than he was willing to admit.

"Look, Camille, I know where you're going with this. I'll just have to prove how wrong you are."

"Why bother? It won't make any difference. Don't you see that. We're not getting anywhere, Nicholas. Please, take me home."

He could see that it wouldn't do any good to continue the discussion this evening, but they would definitely continue it another time. He didn't know what he had hoped to accomplish? But this little go-round had made Camille more resistant than ever. He was sure her brother would be only too happy to add to her obstinacy. What next? He wondered.

Nicholas didn't try to talk to Camille as he drove her home. He would only have succeeded in antagonizing her. A pregnant woman didn't need that kind of stress. The last thing he wanted to do was endanger her or his unborn child.

Camille saw the solemn expression on Nicholas' face and wondered what his next move would be. She had to protect herself and her baby no matter what. She wouldn't allow anyone to hurt her whether directly or indirectly. She was curious about Nicholas's family, though. Something about them made him unwilling to share that information with her. What kind of people were they?

Nicholas drove up in front of the Parker house and switched off the engine, then turned to face Camille.

"This is not the end by any means. So don't think you can avoid me."

"Or you'll do what?" she challenged.

"Don't push me too far, Camille."

"Meaning?"

"I refuse to argue with you. I'll be in touch."

"I just might leave town for good."

"You won't do that. I've learned quite a bit about you, Mrs. King."

"Like?"

"Your family is here for one thing. I think you'd better go inside. Your brother is scowling at us through the window. If looks could kill, I'd be a dead man."

Camille glanced in that direction and sure enough she saw that Jamal was watching them. She got out of the car. "Jamal has only my happiness in mind."

"He's being overprotective. I'd never harm you or the baby."

"He doesn't believe that."

"But you do, don't you?"

"I really don't know you, Mr. Cardoneaux."

"Oh so it's back to formality, is it? There is one way to remedy that. Get to know the real me, Camille. You might be surprised. I promise you I'm as normal as the next man."

"That's just it, this situation is as far from normal as you can get."

"I know that. But you're having my baby. Our baby, Camille. She will be a part of both of us. I'd better go or run the risk of setting off World War III. Think about what I've said. Please. Our child deserves the best we can give her."

Camille watched Nicholas drive away before slowly heading up the walk. Jamal met her halfway.

"How did it go?"

"It went just fine."

"Is that all you're going tell me?"

"Jamal, please. I want to go to bed. I've had a long day."

"And they're going to get even longer before this is over."

"Jamal, leave it. Okay?"

"I can't do that."

"I know you love me, Jamal, but you're going to have to let me deal with this myself. Good night," she said and went into the house. As she passed by her mother's room on the way to her own Camille saw that the light was still on, but she decided to wait until tomorrow to talk to her.

She walked into the nursery and picked up a teddy bear from the crib and hugged it to her chest. How was this nightmare going to end?

* * *

Nicholas didn't go straight home to Magnolia Grove. Instead he drove around for a while. When he was sure his mother had gone to bed, he headed home. He wasn't up to an interrogation session with her.

You're going to have to face her sooner or later, you know. She's not likely to give you any peace until she knows the complete unvarnished truth about the baby's mother.

This was his problem. He was the only one who could solve it. What he didn't need was interference. Things were difficult enough as it was. As he lay in his bed after showering, his thoughts drifted down a different path. He was remembering the softness of Camille's skin, those melting chocolate eyes of hers. He hardened at the thought of - no he wasn't going to give in to desire. Concern for his child had to take precedence over lust.

Is it really lust you feel for Camille, Cardoneaux?

He had to admit it was more than simple lust. Why couldn't he have both Camille and his baby?"

You know why.

Camille is beautiful, intelligent and the mother of his child. Why couldn't he have both? He would have to think about the possibility.

Yes, he liked the idea. He more than liked it.

Chapter Seven

"How did your evening go?" Hazel asked her daughter the next morning as she entered the kitchen. "You didn't come to my room when you got back. I was expecting you."

"I wasn't up to discussing my problems, Mama. As far as the evening went, we didn't resolve anything. One thing it did was let me know how serious Nicholas is. His determination frightens me."

"Did he threaten to take the baby away?" Jamal asked from the doorway. "If he did -"

"You'll do what, Jamal!" Hazel inquired. "You're such a hothead."

"Mama, I can't stand by and do nothing."

"You could let your sister handle it."

"Since Elroy died she's only had me to look out for her. And I intend to keep on doing it."

"Mama, Jamal, please stop it. I can't take much

more of this. Maybe I should move back to my own house."

"No, don't do that, sugar. We didn't mean to upset you." Hazel glared at Jamal. "At least one of us didn't."

"What are you going to do, sister girl?"

"I don't know, Jamal, but I'm going to find a way without your help."

"Good luck because you're going to need it," he said on the way out the back door.

"You going to the Center today?" Hazel asked.

"No. Me and Deja are going shopping." Camille smiled and moved her hand across her stomach. "My little girl is beginning to really make her presence more profoundly obvious."

"You so sure it's a girl?"

"I haven't had an ultrasound yet, but yes I'm sure. Nicholas thinks so too."

Hazel monitored her daughter's expression closely. From what she could see Camille wasn't immune to Nicholas Cardoneaux. Not by a long shot. She wondered if there was a chance that—no surely not. It wouldn't be an easy path to trod should anything happen between them.

* * *

"I've been asking around about Camille King," Suzette Cardoneaux told her son as they sat eating their lunch at the mansion. "And no one that I know has even heard of her."

"Mother. I thought we agreed that I would handle this."

"I know, but, Nicholas -"

"Back off, Mother. I mean it."

"There's something you're not telling me, isn't there?"

"Mother," he warned.

"Oh, all right, but I still think you should -"

"I know what you think."

"And it doesn't matter to you." she persisted.

"Mother, please, not today. I've got a lot on my mind. The last thing I need is your interference in my personal life."

"Interference! That baby happens to be my only grandchild. Maybe if I had interfered in your personal life earlier you and Lauren might still be married."

"I doubt that very seriously." Nicholas wiped his mouth with a napkin and then rose from his chair. "I have to go in to the office."

"You went back there last night, didn't you? You were so tired this morning you couldn't even get up.

You're behind in your work because you've been so busy trying to placate this woman."

He glared at her.

Suzette put up her hand. "All right. I won't nag."

"Thank you."

As Nicholas drove to work he thought about Camille and what he should do. He didn't want to pressure her, but he was anxious to resolve this. More than anxious actually. He'd told her he would prove that she and her brother were wrong about him. But how should he go about doing it? He conceded that he would have to give her space.

When he stopped at a light, Nicholas realized where he was. Across the street was the exclusive baby store called Baby Blvd. He parked in front of it and got out. He stood watching as a couple walked out of the store with smiles on their faces and holding hands. The woman looked to be about eight months pregnant.

Nicholas felt a stab of pain pierce his heart when he thought about the miscarriages his wife had suffered. They'd lost four babies. With each loss it destroyed a piece of his soul. When Lauren had passed the danger period, and it looked like she would carry the last baby to term, they had bought furniture for the nursery. The room had been painted a soft white and the furniture was gilt trimmed white French Provincial.

Nicholas thought about the child he and Camille were having. Since they both felt sure it was going to be a girl, he had decided to have the nursery painted pink and furnished in oak wood. He could hardly wait to have his daughter under his roof even if it was only part of the time. Deciding against going in, he got back in the car and drove away. One goal was clearly etched in his heart and mind; and that was getting closer to Camille so that he could at least talk her into considering shared or joint custody.

* * *

"You're so picky, Camille," Deja complained as she and Camille left yet another maternity fashion store with very little to show for several hours of shopping.

Camille laughed at her friend's woebegone expression. "I have to find just the right outfits to wear. Hardly anything I've seen so far really appeals to me. Considering the rate I've been blossoming lately, I'm going to look like a whale by the end of this pregnancy."

Just as they crossed the street to the parking lot where she'd left her car, Camille saw Nicholas get out of his silver Lexus parked down the block and stand in front of Baby Blvd, one of New Orleans's most exclusive baby stores.

"What's wrong, Camille?" Deja asked looking at

her friend, concern lining her words.

"Nothing. I'm just tired. I think we should get something to eat and then head for home."

"We haven't been out that long or bought that many things." Deja stopped talking and followed Camille's line of vision. "Who are you staring at?"

"Nobody."

"Is that Nicholas Cardoneaux?"

"What makes you think that?"

"He looks exactly the way you described him?" Deja smiled and ran her tongue over her lower lip. "I know one thing, He sure is one fine hunk of a man with that coal black curly hair."

"How he looks doesn't matter."

"Believe me, it matters. You wouldn't say that if he looked like Frankenstein."

"Deja, Please. This is not funny. The man wants to take my baby away from me."

"You sure about that? Maybe he just wants visitation rights. Can't you guys compromise or something?"

"Visitation rights aren't all he wants. There can be no compromise between us. This is my baby, you hear me."

"Okay, okay. No need for you to get hostile."

"I'm sorry, Deja, but I'm not ready to talk about

Nicholas Cardoneaux with you or anybody else right now. Come on, let's go get something to eat."

* * *

"You didn't buy much, sugar," Hazel said when Camille and Deja walked through the front gate. She watched her daughter closely, trying to gauge her mood. Something was definitely bothering her.

"I tried to get her to buy more stuff, Miss Hazel," Deja volunteered.

Hazel frowned looking at Camille. "Are you sure you're feeling all right?"

"I'm fine, Mama."

"You didn't do too much walking, did you?"

"Mama, would you please stop fussing over me. I'm pregnant not an invalid."

Hazel glanced at Deja who hunched her shoulders and said. "She's been like this ever since we—"

"Deja!" Camille warned her friend.

Hazel eased an arm around her daughter's shoulder. "Since what? Tell me what's put you in this mood, sugar."

"I saw Nicholas Cardoneaux looking in the window of that exclusive baby furniture store on Poydra."

"I see. And that upset you?"

"What it means is he's planning to buy baby furniture. Or has already bought it. And we both know why. He intends to take steps to get custody of my baby and take her to live in his mansion."

"Maybe not," Hazel said thoughtfully. "He could be just—"

"Save your breath, Miss Hazel," Deja broke in. "I've tried to get her to see his side, but—"

"Deja!" Camille silenced her with a look, then returned her attention to her mother. "Mama, I'm not going to let him take my baby."

"Calm down. No one is going to take your baby. As I was about to say. He might just be preparing for when the child comes to visit."

"My baby is not going anywhere without me. Certainly not to the Cardoneaux mansion." Camille recalled Nicholas's words about possible legal action. He was obsessed with her child. Could he convince a judge to possibly give him full custody? Or joint custody?

Just as Camille and Deja stepped up onto the porch a Flowers Etc. van drove up. The delivery boy took a huge bouquet of flowers out of the side of the van and strode through the open gate.

"I'm looking for a Mrs. Camille King."

"I'm Camille King."

He smiled. "These flowers are for you, ma'am."

"Who—" She didn't have to ask, she knew who'd sent them. She took the flowers from the delivery boy and silently read the card. 'Camille, you are the loveliest mother-to-be in New Orleans.' signed Nicholas. Camille delved inside her purse for a tip.

"That's won't be necessary, ma'am. It's already been taken care of." He nodded and then said. "You have a wonderful day."

"They're from Nicholas Cardoneaux, aren't they?" Deja inquired excitedly, clapping her hands and grinning.

"I'd say Nicholas Cardoneaux is trying to rack up brownie points, sister girl," Jamal said as the delivery boy passed him and made his way to the van.

"You shouldn't be aggravating Camille, Jamal," Deja cautioned him.

"What you need to do is mind your own business."

"The flowers are beautiful, aren't they, sugar?" Hazel said in a bid to defuse a possible confrontation between brother, sister and friend.

"You're right, they are." Camille smiled stroking one of the delicate flowers and sniffing a silky petal.

"He's just buttering you up," Jamal interjected. "Can't you see that."

"And you accuse me of not minding my own business," Deja slipped the words in with the ease of a swift knife thrust between the ribs.

"Jamal, Deja, please don't."

"I'll take these flowers in the house and put them in water." Hazel smiled, easing them from Camille's fingers. To Jamal she said. "I don't want you upsetting her. Then looked at Deja. "Or you either."

Once their mother had gone into the house, Jamal continued. "Camille, you can't trust Nicholas Cardoneaux. He doesn't really care about you. The only reason he's being nice is because he wants custody of the baby."

Camille didn't respond to his words, she just walked wearily over to the porch swing and sat down.

Putting her hands on her hips Deja said to Jamal, "You heard Miss Hazel. If you don't back off you're going to have her to answer to. You know from experience that being on her bad side is not a place you want to find yourself," she finished, then flopped down on the empty space beside her friend.

Jamal scowled at her and then shaking his head went into the house, banging the screen door shut behind him.

"That man's got some serious attitude problems," Deja said sagely.

"I thought you and he were...close."

"We are or we were, but right now he's got entirely too many hang-ups for me."

Camille smiled. "You told me you liked challenges."

"Challenges, yes, but I'm not into scaling granite walls. You heard him." Concern crinkled Deja's brows. "What are you going to do, girlfriend? I'd say judging from the flowers, Mr. Nicholas Cardoneaux is courting you."

"Because he sent flowers! Don't be silly. It doesn't mean anything."

"You don't know that."

"I know what he's trying to do and it's not going to work. It won't convince me to give him custody of this baby. I don't care if he sends me a whole field of flowers."

Deja shook her head and didn't say any more.

* * *

Nicholas couldn't keep his mind on his work thinking about Camille. He glanced at his watch. She should have gotten the flowers by now. He wondered what she thought of them.

His phone buzzed. He smiled, thinking it could be Camille and grabbed the receiver. "Yes, Marsha."

"It's Dr. Charles Hadley on line 2."

Nicholas pushed the button. "I thought I made it clear that my attorney would - "

"You did. But Mr. Cardoneaux - "

"You have no idea what kind of problems your mistake has caused. You've complicated not only my life, but also the life of my child's mother. And all you're worried about is your damn clinic."

"What happened wasn't intentional. Mrs. Suzette Cardoneaux - "

Nicholas eyes narrowed. "What about my mother?"

"She called the clinic trying to coerce information about Camille King from my nurse."

"What? When?" Nicholas demanded.

"Earlier this afternoon."

Right after his little talk with her, Nicholas thought. He cleared his throat. "You spoke to her personally?" he asked.

"Yes."

"What did you tell her?"

Affront in his voice, the doctor answered. "We didn't tell her anything if that's what you're insinuating. To do so would be completely unethical. Despite what you think about us we - "

"What exactly did she say?"

"She threatened to - "

"You can disregard it. I'll take care of my mother. This has nothing to do with your clinic's culpability in causing the situation in the first place, Hadley. My attorney will be in touch with yours."

"Mr. Charbonneau, you've got to be reasonable about - "

Nicholas hung up the phone. He'd warned his mother about interfering. Evidently, she hadn't taken him seriously. Well, he intended to make himself clear once and for all.

* * *

"Mother!" Nicholas roared as he stormed into the living room at Magnolia Grove.

"Nick, what's wrong?" Phillip asked, looking up from a medical journal he'd been reading.

"Where is she?"

"Upstairs." Phillip sighed. "Okay, what has she done now?"

"She's been interfering in my life, that's what. I told her I would handle the situation with Camille. But what does she do? The minute my back is turned she calls the Hadley Clinic and grills Dr. Hadley and his staff about Camille."

Suzette Cardoneaux swept into the living room with a smile on her face. "Nicholas, Phillip. You're both home."

"Didn't you believe me when I told you not to interfere?"

Her smiled faded. "I only - "

"If you do one more thing, Mother, I'll -"

"You dare to threaten me, your own mother. You owe me some respect, Nicholas Andre Cardoneaux."

"Respect? Respect means considering another's rights, which you have chosen to blatantly ignore."

"Oh, don't be so melodramatic, Nicholas. If you would only - "

"What? Let you run my life the way you see fit. I don't think so. You're interference stops right here, right now or - "

"Nick." Phillip put down his book and advanced toward his brother. "Maybe you should - "

"Stay out of it, Phillip," Nicholas said in an angry clipped voice. "This is between me and our dear mother."

"Nicholas, you can't just let that woman have my grandchild. That baby is a Cardoneaux and belongs here with us. You can't tell me you don't think the same thing. Can you?"

"That's not the point."

"It's exactly the point."

"I might think the baby belongs with me, but I have to consider her mother's feelings. Camille and I are probably going to have to come to some kind of compromise. So for the last time back off, or I'm going to move out of this house. Do I make myself clear?"

"Nicholas, you can't mean that."

"Don't put me to the test, Mother. If you don't believe me just do or say one more thing. Am I finally getting through to you?"

"Yes," Suzette said stiffly and with head held high walked out of the room and up the staircase.

"You were kind of rough on her, don't you think?" Phillip asked.

"No, I don't. Mother has to learn that I'm serious about her interference.

"There shouldn't be any doubt in her mind after this. If there ever was. You know how she is."

"Yes, I do." He grimaced. "That's what bothers me. Once she learns that my child's mother isn't white, all hell is going to break loose."

there, Camille!" he warned.

She wanted to rail at him and tell him to leave her alone and a few other things, but decided it would only make matters worse if she did. She was at a loss as to how to deal with this man.

"Are you there, Camille?"

"Yes, I'm still here. I'll be ready," she said and hung up.

Unsure himself of what they'd accomplish this evening, he slowly cradled the receiver. Maybe nothing, like last time. He started pacing the length and breadth of his bedroom, one hand anchored at his waist, absently rubbing his chin between his thumb and forefinger with his other hand. But then again if Camille let herself come to know him, she'd realize his interest in the baby wasn't a whim or some possessive kick he was on, that his feelings for the baby were every bit as strong and as genuine as hers were, and that they could find a way to work something out. Right now they were at odds with each other.

Nicholas stopped his pacing and walked over to the connecting door leading into the nursery, ambled over to the rocking chair by the window, and sat down to watch the sunset. He couldn't believe the turn his life had taken. After longing for a child all these years he'd finally gotten his wish, but not at all as he might have expected.

The mother of his child was of another race and wanted nothing to do with him. Or so she said. He knew she was attracted to him. He'd seen it in her eyes when they first met. Why was she fighting him so hard? He was just as attracted to her but wasn't resisting the feeling. Even though he could understand her reluctance on one level, he couldn't help wondering how much of it had to do with race. She'd denied that it had anything to do with it, but there was her brother Jamal who had issues and was openly hostile toward him. He was grateful that her mother hadn't put up any color barriers. Could he build on that tiny seed of hope? He could tell that Camille and her mother were close. If he could get Hazel Parker to - to what?

He'd asked Camille to give herself time to get to know him. But that cut both ways. He needed the same time and opportunity to really get to know the real Camille.

Nicholas raked his fingers through his hair. The fact that he didn't know how to handle this situation really bothered him. He'd only had trouble maneuvering things or people in the direction he'd wanted them to go with two people; Lauren, about the divorce and now with this stubborn black woman named Camille King who was carrying his child. He had to somehow make her see how important this child was to him and get past the walls she'd built against him for whatever her reasons. He got up and walked back to his room to shower and change.

Chapter Eight

When he drove up in front of the Parker house, Nicholas saw Jamal sitting on the porch swing. Didn't the man ever go anywhere? Why did he always have to be home when he came to see Camille? Was it too much to hope that they wouldn't have yet another confrontation? Confrontation or not, he intended to see Camille. As he got out of the car she stepped out on the porch. Nicholas's gaze swept her body. Seeing the soft swell of her stomach, knowing that he was the cause, made his insides jerk and his heartbeat accelerate. Camille had on a blue sundress that outlined the womanly fullness of her breasts and tempting curve of her hips. He ached to slip the thin straps off her shoulders and kiss her delicate skin. Then lower the bodice past her hips and caress the juncture between her...

He shook his head to clear it. He had to stop giving in to these arousing thoughts and feelings. The child should be uppermost in his mind.

Who are you trying to fool, Cardoneaux, a little voice taunted.

"Are you ready?" he asked Camille.

"Camille," Jamal rose abruptly from the swing.

"I'm going with him, Jamal."

"But- all right." He glared at Nicholas. "If you hurt her in any way, Cardoneaux - "

"I won't. You're going to come to realize that one day."

Nicholas cupped Camille's elbow and guided her down the walk to his car parked just outside of the gate and helped her inside. "Where are we going this time, Nicholas?"

"You make it sound like I'm escorting you to the gas chamber. Camille, I'm not some kind of unfeeling monster. Please, give me a chance to prove my sincerity where you and the child are concerned, and dispel any negative ideas you have about me."

Camille was beginning to believe in that sincerity, but it didn't mean she would give him her child. Maybe Deja was right and she should allow him access to the baby once it was born. She wondered if he would be satisfied with simple visitation rights. Somehow she didn't think so. He was a dominating male and wanted everything his own way. What belonged to him, he kept and protected. The thought of how it could be if he decided to be difficult made her shudder. She knew he'd be a formidable force to reckon with.

Nicholas noticed the waves of changing expressions on Camille's face and wondered what was going through her mind.

"Camille?"

"You asked me to give you a chance and I'm considering it. That's all I can promise."

"It's enough - for now."

For now! Camille wondered if she was making a big mistake. But what choice did she have. He could take her to court if she denied him the right to see his child. She wasn't sure now if she wanted to keep him from doing that. Oh, God, why did life have to be so complicated.

"Don't look so down. We can work through this, Camille."

She didn't see how. They lived in worlds that were poles apart. How would getting to know him bridge the giant gap yawning between them?

You could start with this baby, the voice of reason counseled.

"I hope you're right, Nicholas."

Nicholas smiled one of his killer smiles that made her heart beat a little faster and the other parts of her body ache. She was a young, healthy woman. These involuntary desires brought home how much she missed having a man in her life. Although that might be true, there was no way she'd allow anything to happen between her and Nicholas. It would only complicate the situation even more if that were possible.

What about for your child's sake?

God this was an intolerable situation with no resolution in sight.

Nicholas heard the uncertainty in Camille's voice and saw it in her face. It seemed to echo his own. There had to be a way to work this out. He would prefer to raise his daughter himself, but if he had to share her with Camille he would. His earlier thoughts of sharing a life with her and the baby came back to him. The idea was beginning to have a certain appeal and a feeling of rightness about it.

"What would you like to do on a night like this?" Nicholas asked.

Camille knew that he was trying to find a common ground between them. She felt that if they were around other people there would be less chance of the evening escalating into a battle.

"Have you ever walked along Moonwalk promenade?"

"Many times. But I haven't been there since my brother and I were kids. Whenever we visited our great-aunt Marie-Lorraine, we'd go to a spot just before you came to Washington Artillery Park and stretch out on the benches and watch the traffic as it moved along the Mississippi."

"Jamal and I used to do that too."

"You seem surprised that I should have gone there. Why is that?"

"Considering your background, I thought..."

"That remark smacks of snobbery around the edges."

"I didn't mean to offend - "

"I think you did. I can't help that I was born into money, Camille."

"I'm sorry. Do you forgive me?" She smiled.

When she smiled at him like that, Nicholas could forgive her just about anything. The movement of her soft full lips took his breath away. He groaned, wriggling uncomfortably to quell the throbbing between his legs. If just watching her smile did this to him how would...

Don't go there, Cardoneaux.

Tell that to his unruly libido.

Nicholas parked the car and he and Camille strolled along Moonwalk. He'd forgotten the exhilaration of watching the river and the lights and hearing the foghorns blow. He could only guess at the reason for their coming here. It was probably the thought of them being alone together that made her uneasy. If it was, she wasn't the only one. Being near her certainly unsettled him.

"How would you like to go to the Cafe du Monde?"

"Yes, that sounds good. The Elkins Jazz Quartet is playing there tonight," Camille remarked. She had always enjoyed the casual ambiance of the sidewalk cafe.

"I've heard them play. They're very good."

"Yes, they are."

The scent of Nicholas's citrusy cologne, and the combination of warm humid night air and silvery moonlight was having a titilating effect on Camille's senses. Awareness of him heightened at his touch on her elbow as he escorted her to the restaurant.

Nicholas could feel her eyes on him as he looked for a table reasonably close to the bandstand, considering the considerable crowd. He could tell that the place had lightened her mood. If he could think of other places to take her and things to do with her and took the time to patiently work his way into her life and affection, then maybe...

She'd give in? Keep on dreaming. What about

her brother and your mother?

He would deal with them when he had to.

Nicholas studied Camille's face as she listened to the music completely absorbed by it.

The bandleader came over to their table.

"Excuse me. You're Camille King, aren't you? I heard you play at a concert five years ago. I have one of your albums. You were fantastic. How about joining us on the next song."

"I don't know - "

The man smiled. "We'd be honored, Ms. King."

"Go ahead, Camille," Nicholas encouraged.

"All right," she said to the man, "if you really want me to." Camille rose from her chair and followed the man to the bandstand and sat down at the piano.

Her touch was magical. Nicholas had no idea she was so talented. He knew she taught music, but... Camille seemed to slide into the music with the ease of a warm knife into cold butter. When her eyes closed on a particularly poignant part, he wanted to touch her, to feel what she was feeling. Like a diamond, there were so many facets to this beautiful woman. And he found himself wanting to explore every one of them.

When the music stopped there was a hush followed by enthusiastic applause from the listeners.

Camille bowed, then returned to her table.

"You were fantastic. I hope our child inherits her mother's musical genius."

"Thank you, Nicholas."

"Have you ever considered returning to your career as a jazz Pianist?"

"No."

"Why not?"

"I love playing, but I want to share my love of music by teaching others to appreciate it. My mother was disappointed when I chose not to continue performing, but I had to be true to myself. Can you understand that?"

"With a talent like yours, I can see why she would feel that way. You play magnificently. But I can also understand where you're coming from. You have to do what you feel is best."

"I never thought you'd understand."

"Believe me, I do. My mother wanted me to pursue a career as an artist."

"You paint!"

"Would you like to see some of my work."

"Yes, I would." She frowned in confusion. "But I read that you were the CEO of your company as well as an architect."

"That's true. I was also drawn to painting, but I

wanted to be an architect and help create and build beautiful homes even more."

As they drank orange juice and ate beignets, pillow-shaped doughnuts draped with powered sugar, Camille realized that they thought alike about quite a few things. They both pursued their own dreams in their own way despite opposition.

"When do you want to see them?"

"Them?"

"My painting's."

"You're serious, aren't you?"

Nicholas smiled. "When would be a good time for you?"

"Tomorrow is Sunday. Would the afternoon be all right?"

"Perfect." He glanced at his watch and picked up a napkin and wiped his mouth. "It's getting late, I'd better get you home. We wouldn't want Jamal calling the New Orleans Police Department. Or better yet coming after me himself." He laughed.

Chapter Nine

Sunday dawned bright, warm and sunny. It had rained during the early morning hours, leaving the abundant greenery and flowers with a fresh dewy appearance. Camille was expectant, anxious for the time to go by so Nicholas could take her to his house to view some of his paintings. She'd seen pictures of the Cardoneaux mansion in the magazine she'd borrowed from the Center library.

What was this excitement strumming through her at the prospect? She found it nearly impossible to sit through the Sunday services. Her mother noticed and on the way home questioned her about it.

"Nicholas is coming by this afternoon, Mama."

"What does he want this time?" Jamal asked. "As if we all didn't know."

"Don't start with me this morning, Jamal."

"I'm not. I'm only speaking the truth. You keep letting him come here and take you there, he's going to think he has a claim on you."

"Jamal."

"Wake up, Camille."

"Jamal, that's enough," Hazel reproved him.

"Not hardly, I won't let up until she discovers for herself what this guy is like, and what he's really up to. And believe me, he is up to something, Camille."

"I know you think he doesn't really care about me, Jamal, but you could be wrong."

"I doubt it. I don't want to see you get hurt."

"I won't be. I'm taking it one day at a time. If I see that Nicholas isn't sincere - "

"He's not going to show his true colors until it's too late. All he wants is the baby."

"Jamal, you don't know that," Hazel interjected. "He seems like -"

"He's gotten to you too," he said incredulously. "Both of you are going to be sorry you didn't listen to me."

A long silence pervaded the car during the remainder of the ride home. After Camille and Hazel got out of the car, Jamal drove off.

"What's the matter with him, Mama?" Camille asked as they headed up the walk.

"He has a hard time trusting white people because of what happened at the university. And then later when he tried to get a job."

"I understand about the university. But a lot of what happened later was mostly his own fault."

"You and I know that, but try telling him."

"I have, but he won't listen to me. Even so it's not fair of him to be so rude to Nicholas. He's not responsible for what happened to him."

"Evidently, your brother thinks that he is because he's the head of a multimillion-dollar company, that has in the past in his opinion, not been as fair toward hiring blacks as it could have been."

"That might be true, but his attitude toward Nicholas seems to reach far beyond that. He's made it personal. It's as if Jamal blames Nicholas for every evil committed against him. And that's definitely not fair."

"I know it isn't, but life is rarely fair, sugar. Once Jamal realizes that Nicholas is no threat to you then maybe he'll see him in a different light. We can only hope that he comes to realization before the baby is born."

* * *

Nicholas pulled up in front of Camille's house several hours later and saw her standing on the porch. And seeing no sign of her brother, he breathed a sigh of relief. His heartbeat speeded up when he got a good look at Camille. Today she was wearing a loose-fitting white, short-sleeve dress that set off her toffee-brown complexion to perfection. The gold chain around her neck glittered against that beautiful skin. Her long hair was in a single braid, draped over one shoulder. He could see her Native American and Creole ancestry in the fine high cheek boned structure of her face. If their daughter resembled her mother she would be a beauty.

He got out of the car and strode up the walk. "You're looking especially lovely today, Camille. Not that you don't everyday."

"Thanks for the compliment."

"Is your mother home. I'd like to say hello to her."

"I'm afraid not. She went to visit a friend about half an hour ago."

"I have to warn you that I'm no Monet or Thomas Kinkade."

"That doesn't matter. Let's go! I'm anxious to see for myself how good you are."

"I just don't want you to be disappointed."

"Oh, I'm sure I won't be."

Nicholas drove up to the corner of Orleans and Royal Street and made a right turn, continuing straight until he came to Conti, then swung the car into the parking lot across from the Puissaint Contemporary Art

Gallery.

Camille had expected Nicholas to take her to his house and was disappointed.

"I had no idea your work was being displayed at a gallery. I took for granted we'd be going to your house."

Nicholas picked up on the disappointment in her voice. He hoped that she didn't think because he hadn't taken her to his house that he was ashamed to. He had quite a few of his paintings in his studio at home, but he thought it would be better for now if he took her to the gallery. He'd been avoiding telling his mother about Camille because he didn't relish the reaction she was sure to have.

Coward.

He just wanted peace.

At what price?

"You must be very good," Camille said jolting Nicholas out of his disturbing thoughts.

"A friend of mine owns this gallery. He took pity on me three years ago and has displayed my work ever since. I still paint occasionally when I can find the time. I'm thinking about delegating more responsibility to our company vice-president and my personal assistant so I can devote more time to painting and other things."

Like bonding with an infant daughter after he'd

gained custody, Camille thought, suspicion rearing its head.

Nicholas saw the look on her face when he had added other things. He realized that he'd made one step forward and fallen two back. He'd have to watch what he said and did.

Camille had seen this particular gallery in passing many times, but had never gone inside. She'd always admired these classic two-story buildings with their intricately designed, black wrought iron railed upper floors.

Nicholas could tell as he escorted her inside that Camille was impressed. He was glad he'd had the foresight to call his friend earlier that morning to make sure that the paintings were displayed to best advantage. He had to admit that he was as anxious for her to view his work as she appeared to want to see it.

A man of medium height walked up to greet them, smiled and then said, "Nicholas, why haven't you ever brought this lovely creature to my gallery before."

"You're full of flattery, Henri. May I introduce Camille King. Camille, my friend, Henri Puissaint."

"Pleased to meet you." Henri Puissaint was a charming man in a slightly rough-edged way. He was obviously part black; his skin was several shades lighter than hers and he had worldly-wise gray eyes. It surprised her that he and Nicholas would be friends. Jamal would definitely find it hard to believe. She herself, evidently had more to learn about Nicholas.

"You may call me Henri." His brows crinkled in momentary puzzlement. "I have heard your name before, but can't seem to place it."

"I performed for a few years in concerts as a jazz pianist."

"Oh, yes. I remember hearing one of your albums a few years back. I often wondered what happened to the artist. You had an unbelievably magical touch."

"Thank you for saying that, Henri."

"I was only speaking the truth, cherie. I will show you to the blue room where Nicholas's paintings are displayed. Please follow me."

When they entered the room the warm ambience seemed to reach out and welcome them. Blue and gold velvet drapes adorned the windows and gold wall-to-wall carpet covered the floor. A soft gasp escaped Camille's lips when she came to a portrait of a plantation. It seemed to stand out from the background almost like a three dimensional puzzle. She was no art critic, but in her opinion Nicholas was a master with a paintbrush. The accuracy and brilliant execution of his strokes was astonishingly close to perfection. She could see why his mother had encouraged him to be a world-renowned artist.

"This is a likeness of Magnolia Grove, my family's ancestral home," Nicholas explained.

Camille remembered seeing the house on the cover of a magazine. He had certainly done it justice.

"The likeness is uncanny," Henri remarked. "Over here is one he did of a steamboat and the next one is a view of the Mississippi river from the banks just a ways beyond the New Orleans wharf. It is unbelievably life-like, don't you agree?"

"Absolutely." Camille recognized the spot. "The painting is wonderful, Nicholas."

"Do you really like it?"

"Oh, yes. You've captured the feel of freedom and the river's wild beauty once you've departed New Orleans."

"You seem to understand exactly what I was trying for."

"I feel that same sense of freedom when I play the piano."

"Would you like to have the painting?"

"Are you serious?"

"Very serious." Nicholas revered her with different eyes. Camille was a warm sensitive woman. He thanked God that he'd been able to touch on yet another subject they both could share. There had to be others. And he would discover them if she would only give him the chance.

"I'll have my assistant wrap it up for you." Henri smiled.

"How long have you two known each other?" Camille asked Henri when he returned moments later.

"Since we were boys. Nick used to sneak away from Magnolia Grove and come to the Quarter and play with me. One time his mother followed him. Talk about somebody losing it, I didn't think I'd ever see my friend again. But clever old Nick must be some kin to Houdini because he managed to slip away, and often times brought his brother with him so we could all hang out together."

"I can't picture Nicholas ever doing something like that."

"You mean because he's filthy rich. I don't think that ever mattered to him."

"I wish you two would stop talking about me as if I wasn't here."

"Did I lie?" Henri arched a teasing brow.

"No." Nicholas laughed. "You're still as impossible as ever, Henri."

"Now, you wouldn't want me to change, would you?"

Camille felt the heart-deep camaraderie between Henri and Nicholas. This was yet another side of his personality unfolding before her.

"I will be closing the gallery in about half an hour. I would like it if you and Nicholas joined me and my beautiful wife Jolie for dinner."

Camille looked at Nicholas, and then Henri. "I'd love to, but are you sure your wife won't mind on such short notice?"

"Even with our two children away visiting their grandparents, I'm sure she has probably prepared enough food to feed an army."

"He might look like he doesn't eat much, but believe me, Henri is a one-man army when it comes to packing away good food," Nicholas said wryly.

"I don't ever remember hearing you turn down a second helping of Jolie's dinners, Nick," Henri kidded.

"And you won't either. We'll look around until you've closed the gallery, then follow you upstairs."

Camille knew of several people in the Quarter who lived above their shops. Most upstairs rooms were built using open-air architecture in which one room opened into another with a balcony view from the continuous gallery and loggia enclosed French doors or windows. And to reach Henri's living quarters, they had to climb a staircase that spiraled upward to a landing that had a large lace-covered oval window.

Just then a lovely caramel-skinned woman met them at the top of the stairs.

"Camille, my wife, Jolie," Henri introduced. "Nick you already know."

Jolie offered her hand. "I'm pleased to meet you, Camille. Knowing my husband, you're staying for dinner. Right?"

"I hope it's not an imposition."

"Oh, no. As he and Nick have probably already told you, I usually cook enough food to feed an army. The army mostly being my husband."

Henri clamped a hand to his chest as if wounded. "You cut me to the quick, my heart."

Camille laughed, enjoying the spicy, but loving repartee between Henri and his wife. It reminded her of the way her father and mother had gotten along. She thought about the eight years she and Elroy had been married. They had had a kind of repartee between them, but only on a superficial level. Since Elroy was quite a bit older than Camille, it was more of a mentor and protégé kind of relationship between them.

Nicholas saw the reflective expression on Camille's face when she looked at Henri and Jolie. He couldn't help wondering if it made her think of her marriage to her late husband. The sharp thrust of jealousy stabbed him at the thought of her in another man's arms. Even though that other man had been her husband.

"My Jolie is a chef at Antoine's, Camille," Henri proudly revealed. "Tonight we are having her famous pompano en papillote."

Camille's mouth watered. She thoroughly enjoyed the lump crabmeat and shrimp that topped the dish, and she closed her eyes when she tasted the jambalaya. The only other person who could do it justice was her grandmother.

"I love it when people enjoy my cooking."

"I'm sure the owners of Antoine's consider you a state treasure, Jolie," Camille commented between bites of shrimp.

"I don't know about the state, but you are certainly my treasure," Henri said to his wife with a suggestive smile and a sexy wink.

Camille laughed and so did Nicholas. Their eyes met and held for a moment before Camille looked away.

"Now for dessert," Jolie said rising from her chair and heading into the kitchen. Seconds later she brought back a peanut butter and praline pie topped with whipped cream.

"I'm surprised Henri doesn't look like a butterball, if he eats like this everyday," Camille remarked as she slipped another forkful of the delicious dessert into her mouth.

"He's lucky to be one of those people who can eat anything in any amount and still not gain an ounce." Nicholas laughed.

"Are you jealous, my friend?"

"Don't pay any attention to these two, Camille." Jolie smiled.

Nicholas watched Camille and the natural instant friendship that sprang between her and Jolie. If he could just keep Camille in this mellow, relaxed mood during the rest of her pregnancy then...

Then what, Cardoneaux?

While Henri and Nicholas sat on the balcony laughing and joking with each other, Jolie and Camille sat at the table in the kitchen sharing a cup of tea.

"How long have you known Nick, Camille?" Jolie asked.

"Not long."

"Am I prying?"

"No. We have a rather unique relationship. You see, Nicholas is the father of my baby."

"Really!" Jolie's brows arched in surprise. "How and when did that come about? I didn't know he was seeing anyone."

Camille explained the situation to Jolie.

"To say your situation is unique is putting it mildly."

"Nicholas wants this child, but I can't give her to him. I love her already. He's mentioned shared or joint custody, but I don't know about that. So what do we do, Jolie?"

"The two of you will just have to find a way to work it out. That's all I can tell you. How do you feel about Nick?"

"We're only involved because of the baby. There are no romantic feelings between us." When Camille saw the at-least-not-yet look in Jolie's eyes, she reached for a change of subject. "What do you know about his relationship with his family and ex-wife?"

"Not a lot. His brother, Phillip, is cool. I met his mother only once and Lauren twice. And believe me it was enough for me. Henri and I weren't exactly their cup of tea. Excuse the pun," she said raising her teacup to her lips and taking a sip. "I know Lauren desperately wanted to give Nicholas a child. And when she found out it was no longer possible, she went off the deep end and got a divorce. It hit Nick hard when she lost that last baby and had to undergo a hysterectomy. He was willing to adopt, but Lauren wasn't. It had to be a child of his blood or none at all."

Nicholas stuck his head in the kitchen doorway. "I hate to cut the evening short, but it's getting late and I should be taking Camille home.

Although she was a little annoyed by his high-handed assumption that she was ready to leave, Camille smiled at Henri and Jolie. "I enjoyed myself. We'll have to do it again."

* * *

During the drive back to her house, Nicholas noticed that Camille had been very quiet. He parked the car and turned to her.

"What's wrong?" he asked.

"I suppose you're used to making decisions for other people. But I for one don't enjoy having them made for me."

"Is that what you think I did?"

"I don't think, I know. You're so used to doing it you probably don't even realize it."

"Camille."

She opened the car door and headed up the walk. Nicholas got out of the car and caught up with her.

"Look, I didn't mean to offend you."

"I'm sure you didn't. I don't see how we're ever going to work anything out. Is the reason you didn't take me to your house because you haven't told your family about me and the baby?"

"I have told my mother about the baby, but not about you. My brother knows everything. The reason I haven't told my mother is not because I'm ashamed that you're carrying my baby."

"I think it is."

"I couldn't just spring it on her. I am going to tell her. You have to give me chance."

"I don't think waiting will help. All you want is the baby and I can't and won't give her to you, Nicholas. It's that simple and that complicated. Good night."

"Camille, wait! I've realized that. And as I said before we can share - " She ignored his entreaty and Nicholas watched her go into the house and he groaned in frustration when she slammed the door. This entire situation was making him crazy. Whatever he did or didn't do wasn't ever the right thing. What should his next step be?

Chapter Ten

"You've been brooding since Sunday, Nicholas," his mother commented at breakfast a few days later.

"What did you say, Mother?" he said absently.

"You've been thinking about that woman again. Haven't you?"

"Woman? What woman?"

"Don't be obtuse. You know very well who I'm talking about. The woman who - "

"Mother dear, don't start."

"Start what? The King woman is carrying my grandchild and you expect me to keep quiet!"

Nicholas rose from the table. "I don't intend to have this conversation with you, Mother."

"You can't run away from this, Nicholas."

"I'm not. I'm handling it my way. If you don't approve - well..."

Phillip walked in. "Sorry I'm late." He looked from his mother to his brother. "Oops. You and mother aren't- "

"No, we're not because I'm leaving for the office."

"He's running away from his responsibilities is what he's doing."

Nicholas's eyes narrowed and he glared at his mother. "And just how am I doing that?"

"By not taking steps to insure that the child, who is a rightful Cardoneaux, comes here to live with us where he or she belongs." She shifted her gaze to her younger son. "The only thing your brother seems interested in is seeing the child's mother. What he should be doing is convincing her to relinquish custody to him."

Phillip frowned. "Taking a child away from its mother is a bit harsh. Even for you."

Nicholas flinched because that was exactly what he had once contemplated doing. But since coming to know Camille there was no way he could ever do that now. He just had to hope that she would consider shared custody.

"This shows all the signs of escalating into a slinging match. And I haven't got time for it." Nicholas glanced at his watch. "I knew I shouldn't have stayed another minute longer." Nicholas shot a look of sheer annoyance at his mother before heading for the front door.

Nicholas fumed as he drove through the gates a few minutes later. But his mood began to lighten at the thought of seeing Camille. It had been three days since he'd dropped her off at her house. He had called daily asking after her health, and she'd given him monosyllabic answers to his inquiries, refusing to tell him when he might be able to see her again when he asked. He had to find a way to reach her, really reach her before the baby was born. The thought of going to court in order to see his own child turned his stomach.

It occurred to him that he might start with one of the things he and Camille had in common. He loved working with children and evidently so did she since she taught them music at the Children's Center. Why couldn't he be an art instructor there? He'd have to contact the head of the Center of course. Nicholas smiled, wondering how Camille would feel having him around on a regular basis?

What was so ironic was that the Center was one of his mother's pet charities. Nicholas was surprised that she and Camille hadn't met. But then when he thought about it, he knew why they hadn't. His mother's secretary usually took care of all the things her employer considered too mundane.

Nicholas grimaced. There was no getting around the fact that he would have to introduce Camille to his mother and soon. It wouldn't do for her to find out from anyone other than him. One thing was sure. Whenever he did tell her, it wasn't going to be any picnic.

* * *

Camille sat gazing out the window of her classroom. She'd been avoiding seeing Nicholas for the past few days because it had really bothered her that he hadn't taken her to his house on Sunday. She hadn't mentioned how she felt to her family. Jamal's opinion would be no big surprise. Her mother would be understanding and sympathetic. But these feelings were something she would have to come to grips with on her own.

She knew it wasn't fair or reasonable not to consider Nicholas's side. It couldn't be easy telling his family - well he had told his brother - but not his mother who might have big-time objections to her intrusion into their lives, and eventually her baby's entry into the family because of who her mother was.

This was a situation near too impossible to call because she knew how serious Nicholas was about this baby. But had he really thought about how it would impact his life. Or hers for that matter.

"Camille."

Jolted out of her reverie, she focused her attention on the man standing in the doorway. "Mr. Shelton.

Come in." Although he was the administrator of the Children's Center, he rarely came to her classroom unless he wanted her opinion on something.

He smiled as he walked in. "If you're not too busy I want to run an idea by you. It concerns someone I'm considering hiring at the Center."

"Oh. Please, sit down." Camille was curious.

"Lynn Harmon, our art teacher will be leaving us to take a position in San Francisco at The Art Institute. And we'll be needing a replacement. I've spoken to some-one who is qualified and most eager to take over her class. He has a degree in art and art appreciation and is a painter himself. I believe you know him. His name is Nicholas Cardoneaux."

Camille swallowed the lump that had suddenly risen in her throat at the idea. She didn't know how to feel about it. Had he used his influence to free the position so he could take it over? Seeing to it that Lynn had an offer she couldn't refuse. Her brother had tried to warn her about the power and influence wealthy men often wielded if and when they chose.

"So, what do you think?"

"Well, I - "

Mr. Shelton's brows rose and he shot her a ques-tioning stare. "You have seen his work, haven't you?"

"Well, yes I have. And he's very good, but that doesn't mean he'd be a good teacher."

"True." Mr. Shelton rubbed his chin between his thumb and forefinger.

Camille watched him thoughtfully. There was more to it, she could feel it.

Mr. Shelton cleared his throat. "And there's something else. Mr. Cardoneaux's mother is on the board of directors. And she is by far one of our most generous supporters. And I wouldn't want to offend her. You understand."

"Yes, I'm beginning to." Camille wondered if Nicholas's mother would continue to be so generous, once she found out who Camille was.

"You said you'd seen Mr. Cardoneaux's work and he was good. His teaching here would be ideal if he has a rapport with children."

"Mr. Cardoneaux is the head of a multi-million-dollar business, Mr. Shelton."

"I'm aware of that."

"Surely a busy man like that wouldn't have time to devote to teaching."

"I see your point. But he has assured me that he would adjust his schedule, freeing himself to teach art two days a week. He also said you would appreciate his willingness to be flexible."

"Oh, I do. It seems to me you've already made up your mind to hire the man and don't really need my input."

"You don't have any real objections, do you, Camille?"

"No. Mr. Cardoneaux is very talented. He could possibly be an asset to the Center."

Mr. Shelton smiled a happy, relieved smile. "I'm glad to hear you say that. I'll contact him this afternoon about joining us."

As she watched the man leave, Camille thought about the effects of this action. Was Nicholas really interested in the kids and the Center? Or was this merely a means to an end, by getting closer to her and eventually her baby. What would his next step be?

* * *

Nicholas stood watching Camille as she instructed a blind girl, who looked to be about ten years old, on how to play her scales. He winced every time the child hit a wrong note, but Camille was patient and had her repeat the exercise until she could do it without a mistake, then congratulated her, making it seem like it was a virtuoso performance. The child smiled and reached for her cane. Camille definitely had a way with children. He could see that she was going to be a great mother. He waited for the child to leave the room and then remarked. "You were wonderful with that little girl."

Camille looked up at the sound of Nicholas's voice. "Thank you." He certainly hadn't wasted any time getting there. Dispensing with preliminaries she asked. "What I'd like to know is, was getting the position here some kind of grand-stand gesture to impress me? Or are you genuinely serious about teaching?"

"I may be head of a company, Camille, but it doesn't mean I can't apportion time for something I consider important. I've worked with kids for the last ten years. I've been a Big Brother and a counselor at Lake Ponchartrain's Children's Summer Camp for the past six years."

Camille had to admit that his credentials were impressive. And having seen some of his work, she knew he could be good for the kids.

"So what's the verdict?" Nicholas said, interrupting her thoughts.

"You won't have a problem with me, Nicholas. I've decided to give you the benefit of the doubt."

"I guess I should be grateful for small favors."

"Nicholas."

"It's all right, Camille. One day I'm going to

make a true believer out of you where I'm concerned."

"Now you're moving into the personal. And we shouldn't be discussing this here."

"You're right." He smiled. "I start working here next week."

Her expression seemed to say so soon. What could it mean? Nicholas wondered. Would being near him disturb her more than she was willing to admit to herself? Could he actually be making headway with her? Was patience the key to securing inroads to this proud stubborn woman?

Seeing the speculative look, Camille started gathering her things.

"I didn't see your car when I pulled into the parking lot."

"It's in the shop. I caught the streetcar."

"Then I'll drive you home."

"That's not necessary."

"Camille."

She sighed wearily. "All right, if you insist."

"I do," he grinned. "It's not like I'm not asking you to walk the last legs of a journey to the electric chair, now is it?"

"No, it's not." She laughed. "I'm sorry."

"I want to know why you were so abrupt with me

on the telephone the last few times I've called to ask how you were?"

"I wasn't."

"Yes - you were. And when I asked when I could see you again you put me off, refusing to give me an answer."

"Answer me this, Nicholas, would you have taken me to your house to see your painting? When you offered to show me some of your work I had assumed it would be at your house. And when it wasn't, I got the distinct impression - oh never mind."

"Camille, I'm not ashamed or embarrassed to be seen with you or to take you to my house."

"It seemed like it to me."

"You're the mother of my unborn child, for God's sake."

"Then why haven't you told your mother about me? You said you'd told her about the baby, but not that the baby's mother is black I'll bet."

"Well no, but - "

"But what, Nicholas. Are you afraid she'd treat me the way she treated Jolie. Jolie told me how your mother reacted to her and Henri's being invited to your house for dinner. She hates black people doesn't she? That's it. That's why you didn't take me to your house.

And it's why you haven't told her I'm black. You know she'll be less than pleased to know that. If it's how she truly feels, time is not going to change her mind, Nicholas. Why don't you just back off and forget about me and this baby and get yourself an acceptable wife and have pure white children."

Nicholas's eyes glowed. "Stop it right now, Camille. It isn't about that. Neither you nor my mother are going to dictate what is or is not acceptable regarding my own child. Do you understand? Now, if you're ready I'll take you home."

There was nothing more to say. Camille picked up her purse and Nicholas took her workbag and she preceded him out the door. On the way to her house she replayed the scene in her mind. She believed him. Nothing short of a hurricane would divert him from his purpose; that of being a father to this child. She'd finally come to completely accept that now. But where did they go from here?

"I'm going to tell my mother about you, Camille."

"When, Nicholas?"

"I don't know. It has to be handled carefully."

"No matter how careful you are, it won't change the outcome. That's something you're going to have to accept."

Nicholas knew she was right. He was being a coward by not spreading everything out on the table. He had to admit that a part of him did care what his mother's reaction would be. But a much more important part didn't. This was his child and nothing or no one was going to keep him from giving her all the love he could give her.

As they drove up in front of the Parker house, Nicholas saw Jamal step down from the porch. He helped Camille out of the car, took her work bag and cupping her elbow escorted her up the walk. Jamal strode right past them and out the gate without saying a word to his sister. When Nicholas felt Camille stiffen, he wanted to go after Jamal, drag him back and make him apologize for hurting her like that, but decided that it would only make matter worse.

"I'm sorry about that, Nicholas."

"Don't be. It's not your fault. He feels the way he feels. And like you, he needs convincing."

"Nicholas."

"It's all right I'm up to the challenge."

Camille didn't know what to say. She'd never met a more single-minded man than Nicholas Cardoneaux.

"Do you get seasick sailing on a boat?"

"No."

"Would you like to go sailing with me on

Saturday?"

"I don't know."

"Say yes. I promise you'll enjoy yourself. It'll do you good to get away. I know this hasn't been any easier for you than it has been for me, Camille."

"You're right, it hasn't," she admitted.

"Then you'll come?"

"What time do you want me to be ready?"

"6:00 a.m. It isn't too early for you, is it?"

"No, I'm an early riser."

"Look, I know you're tired so I'm not going to hold you. I'll see you on Saturday."

Camille stood watching as he strode down the walk to his car. When she saw him drive away, she sat down on the porch swing and let her mind drift.

"Camille. Girl, didn't you hear me calling you?" her friend Deja asked as she stepped up on the porch. "I saw Nicholas drive away. Have you two come to any kind of agreement?"

"No - not exactly."

Deja grinned. "Not exactly?" She put her hands on her hips. "And why not?"

"Now don't go there, okay?"

"He's fine to the bone, girl. What's your problem?"

"You don't understand."

"Oh, I think I do. You have feelings for the man, don't you? I mean deep feelings if that dreamy look in your eyes when I walked up was anything to go by. Admit it, girl."

"Even if I do, and I'm not saying that, it doesn't make any difference."

"I'd say it can make a big difference, if you want it to."

"Deja."

"I'm serious." She put up her hand. "All right, I'll shut my mouth. Where is that brother of yours?"

"Why do you want to know? I thought you two weren't talking anymore."

"Well, we aren't. But - "

"But you still care about him, don't you? Now who's not facing her feelings?" Camille laughed. "We're a pair aren't we?"

"Yes, we are."

"I -I don't know where he went or when he'll be back."

Deja quirked her lips. "What's he done now?"

"When I came home with Nicholas a while ago, Jamal wouldn't even speak to me. In fact he walked right past me as if I wasn't there."

"Wait until I see that man. I'm going to give him a piece of my mind."

"No. Don't do that. There's enough tension between us already."

"You shouldn't let him get away with that. It's not right."

"I know, but I'm at a loss as to what to do about it."

"You can deal with it later. I haven't heard you play that beautiful piano in the living room in a while. How about giving your best friend a private concert?"

Camille knew what her friend was doing and she indulged her.

Chapter Eleven

Saturday morning found Camille sitting on her front porch swing waiting for Nicholas to arrive. She'd put on her first pair of maternity jeans that morning. Smiling, she stroked her fingers across the swell of her stomach. Now nearing the end of her fifth month, her body was really starting to blossom.

Her smile faded. Was she doing the right thing getting involved with Nicholas? She was still trying to decide when she saw him drive up. Her heart lurched against her ribcage as he uncoiled his tall, handsome frame from the car. She had to admit that the sight of him brightened her day.

It does more than that if you're truly honest with yourself, girl.

She wanted to deny it, but she couldn't.

"Are you ready?" Nicholas asked, an easy smile playing at the corner of his mouth.

That smile did crazy things to Camille's insides.

The man looked like a model on the cover of G Q magazine. He was wearing beige corded Levi's and a blue short-sleeve shirt. And had a long-sleeved white sweater tied around his neck. The wind had blown several stray raven-black curls across his forehead. Sexy didn't begin to describe him.

"Yes, I'm ready," she said softly.

Nicholas thought Camille never looked more beautiful. Beneath her canvas hat, her brown eyes sparkled and her skin glowed with health and vitality. The pink shirt she was wearing brought out the copper tinge in her brown complexion, making her cheeks appear to have a rosy blush.

His gaze dropped to her stomach. Inside her their child thrived. He raised his eyes upward and when they reached her face, her soft full lips instantly mesmerized him. He felt an odd flip-flopping sensation in his chest, and he barely managed to contain the sudden urge to take her in his arms and kiss her breathless.

"Where are we going sailing?" Camille asked, her question scattering his train of thought.

"On Lake Ponchartrain," he answered, taking her canvas bag.

Camille smiled. "It brings back fond memories of when Jamal and I were little and our uncle used to take us out on the lake in his tugboat."

Nicholas began to relax. "Cruising on the Creole Lady isn't nearly as interesting as that. I'm afraid you might be disappointed."

"I doubt that."

Camille's eyes widened when they reached West End Park and minutes later Nicholas drove through the gates of the exclusive Southern Yacht Club. Only the wealthy old southern aristocratic families belonged to it. And of course the Cardoneaux's would be charter members. She suddenly felt out of her depth.

As he helped Camille out of the car, Nicholas noticed the uneasy look on her face. As he walked around to unlock the trunk and lifted out the picnic basket, he wondered if this outing was a good idea. Only time would tell.

Nicholas held out his arm to her and she wrapped her arm around it and they headed down to the marina.

"Here we are. This is the Creole Lady."

A man walked up to meet them and Nicholas introduced them. "Camille, this is Claude, the best skipper in New Orleans."

She extended her hand and smiled. "I'm pleased to meet you, Claude."

"I'm pleased to meet you, ma'am." He took the

basket and Nicholas helped Camille climb aboard the yacht. "We'll be shoving off in fifteen minutes, sir," Claude said, disappearing below with the basket.

Camille watched as the boat slowly eased away from the pier out onto the open water. And minutes later when they approached the Lake Ponchartain Causeway, she thought about her father and the times she and her family had driven across it to the Mandeville resort where he had worked. She recalled to mind the once-a-year picnic the resort gave for the hotel staff and their families. It was one of her most cherished memories.

Breathing in the invigorating salt-sea air and reveling in the feel of the soft cool breeze brushing against her face, she suddenly felt very content.

Nicholas took Camille on a tour of the boat and showed her some of the cruiser's rope work and the different knots they used in their day-to-day operation. He even let her try her hand at tying a Fisherman's Bend knot on a mooring warp ring. Then he guided her to a pair of seats in the cockpit area, a few feet from where Claude stood navigating.

Apparently having noticed her fascination, Claude began telling Camille what he was doing, and about the functions of the different sails and the rigging.

"Do you want to steer for a while?" he asked.

Camille looked to Nicholas. "Oh, may I?"

He smiled then nodded his head at Claude who instructed her how to hold course. It was exhilarating to feel the boat move under her direction. Sensing her excitement, Nicholas signaled Claude that he would take over for a while, then turned to Camille.

"Now, aren't you glad you came."

"Oh, yes."

"Today is all about relaxing and being comfortable in each other's company, Camille. No serious thinking today. Deal?"

She smiled. "Deal."

At noon Nicholas spread out their lunch under a shaded awning set up on deck.

Camille's face lit up. "Why these are some of my favorite foods. How did you know?"

Nicholas grinned. "I must confess, I asked your mother."

There were several insulated containers. One flat one held specially seasoned, lemon-peppered Red snapper. There was spinach salad in another container. Crab cakes and red beans and rice in yet others.

"This is a feast," Camille extolled. "Where did you get all this?"

"Your mother told me you were partial to the food

at Palm Court Cafe, so I had them prepare the basket."

"Everything looks fantastic. I have to admit that I'm starved."

"We can't have that, can we?" He held up a forkful of red beans and rice and brought it to her lips.

"Umm, this is so good," she said, tasting before taking the fork from him and helping herself.

Nicholas loved watching her eat. He could tell that she was really enjoying her food.

She caught his eye and patted her stomach. "It's the baby." She laughed, between bites of crab cake. "She's really hungry."

Nicholas grinned. "And from what I can see, so is her mother."

"You wouldn't be trying to call me greedy on the sly, would you?"

"Who moi?"

"I have an excuse. I do happen to be eating for two."

"And I couldn't be happier about it," he said, awe softening his words. "You seem so certain about the sex of our child. Do you know for sure whether we're having a boy or girl?"

Camille swallowed another bite of crab cake. "No. I won't know until I have an ultrasound, which will be done on my next appointment.

"I'd like to come with you."

Camille put her fork down, suddenly serious. "I don't know if that's a good idea."

"Could it be you who is ashamed to be seen with me?"

"Touché. We both evidently have things we need to work on."

"You're right. For the sake of our child we'd better do something about it pretty soon."

"Are you sure you really want to get that involved? If you do you can mark paid to your well-ordered life. I guess you know that."

"Please, stop trying to dissuade me from being a part of my child's life. I understand that adjustments and compromises will have to be made. And I'm more than willing to do that."

Camille wondered if he really knew what he was promising. There were so many obstacles to overcome. The major one of telling his mother, he hadn't even hurdled yet. Would she have just as prejudiced a view of their relationship as Jamal? The situation and the problems seemed insurmountable.

As though guessing her thoughts, Nicholas said. "If we do it together we can make it work. Come on, Lady.

Nothing serious today, remember?"

"Aye aye sir." She saluted and then smiled. "Nothing serious today."

* * *

They arrived back at the marina, just in time to watch the great orange ball of sun dip into the water, making the New Orleans skyline gleam in the late afternoon light.

"I've never seen New Orleans like this." Camille remarked. "She's magnificent."

"I know." He watched her, pleased that she was pleased. "Where would you like to eat dinner?"

"Maybe you should take me home."

"Are you tired?"

"A little."

"And you're not hungry?"

She was about to say she wasn't when her stomach growled loud enough for him to hear. She bowed her head. "I'm ashamed to say I am."

Nicholas laughed. "Don't be. You are after all eating for two as the old saying goes. What do you have a taste for?"

"I know we had the red snapper, but - "

"But what?"

"Well, I've been craving fish and seafood a lot

lately. Jamal says I'm either going to grow a shell or sprout fins."

Nicholas grinned. "I know the perfect place."

"Where?"

"Let it be a surprise," he answered, enjoying the curious, slightly annoyed look on her face.

* * *

When Nicholas parked across the road from the restaurant, Camille's brows arched when she read the sign. "Brunings?" She had never eaten here before, but had heard of it. The place was set on pilings over the water.

"It's the grand-daddy of all New Orleans seafood houses," Nicholas said. "Did you know that it's the city's third oldest restaurant after Antoine's and Tujague's. Theodore Bruning opened his doors in 1859. According to what I've learned, there used to be separate doors for the ladies."

"Really!"

Nicholas laughed. "Yes, really. I also read that they used to have spittoons and slot machines back in the 1930s and 40s."

"Spittoons! Yuk."

"You don't mind if I chew a little tobacco. Do you?"

"Nicholas!"

"Just kidding."

"I sure hope so. That's nasty."

They laughed, found a table and started thumbing through their menus.

"The fried seafood platter with stuffed whole flounder sounds good," Camille said mentally licking her lips.

"It's the star attraction. Order the spicy boiled new potatoes instead of fries. If you do, they'll throw in an order of onion rings. Believe me, they're to die for."

An hour later Camille pushed her plate away. "If I eat another bite I'll burst."

"Me, too," he said patting his tight flat stomach. "You want to take a walk down Lakeshore Drive?"

"Sounds heavenly."

Nicholas drove them to Lakeshore Drive Park, and soon they were strolling along the shoreline.

"I've always thought the shoreline and seawall were fascinating." Camille told Nicholas.

"So have I. The city had daring engineers create them, where before there was nothing but marsh. They transformed the seawall into a protective barrier for the city during hurricanes. Some call this stepped seawall the longest grandstand in the world."

Camille could sense the admiration and respect he held for the engineers who had created this feat.

"It does remind you of a grandstand, like the one at Marine World. You expect to see a whale leap up from the water. So beautiful - "

"I agree."

Their eyes met and held, then they were silent for a moment.

Camille felt desire instantly pulse to life within her. She knew it was more than mere attraction. She had tried to relegate what she felt to lust, but knew it was more than that. A bond existed between them that had little to do with sex or the fact that they had created a child together. She didn't know what to call it.

Be honest, girl.

I am.

No, you're not.

No, she wasn't. She wouldn't exactly call it love, but knew it was an emotion stronger than mere fondness or lust.

She definitely wasn't ready to go there.

"You're kind of quiet. Are you sure you're feeling all right?" Nicholas asked.

"I'm fine."

"You won't get an argument from me about that."

he grinned.

Although it was dark, she could see the flash of white teeth and the blue-black sheen of his hair in moonlight, and it made her stomach flutter as though a whole battalion of butterflies had taken up residence there.

When he stopped walking and drew her close, and lifted her chin, placing a tender kiss on her lips, desire blazed through her causing her nipples to tighten in arousal.

"Nicholas," she gasped.

"Oh, Camille," he said, enfolding her in his embrace, kissing her again, only deepening it this time. When he heard her moan, and he delved his tongue between her lips, his heart rate increased and his manhood swelled and hardened. As he drew her closer, he closed his eyes.

Camille felt the evidence of his passion as he rocked his lower body against the cradle of her pelvis. And instead of drawing away, she reveled in the feel of his desire for her. She knew she should stop this before it got out of hand, but when he continued to move against her, she lost whatever resistance she possessed.

"Nicholas."

He drew her off the path and under a tree and kissed her again.

Camille dropped her bag and slipped her arms around his neck.

He groaned and slid his fingers into her hair. The sweet taste of her mouth was driving him crazy. He knew it would be like this between them. His hands eased down her back and he moved them around to her breasts and caressed her nipples through her thin shirt. When he felt the tips harden into pebble-like peaks, he nearly choked on his desire. And as if with a mind of their own his hands eased around to the small of her back to her buttocks and squeezed gently.

"We have to stop this, Nicholas," Camille rasped out.

"Camille, I can't. I want you. I want you so damn much." He groaned continuing to caress her body.

"No, we can't," she said pushing against his chest.

The sound of a foghorn brought him back to reality. They were in a public place behaving as though they were alone in the privacy of a bedroom. He didn't know what had come over him.

"You're right we can't. I'm sorry if I've - "

"I think it's time you took me home."

"Camille, I - "

"Please, just take me home."

Nicholas let out a frustrated breath and willed his aroused flesh to calm down.

"Look, Camille..."

She turned away to straighten her shirt. "It's all right, Nicholas."

"No, it's not. I shouldn't have done that." What had he been thinking? He'd wanted to prove himself and what had he done? He'd practically taken her clothes off and ravished her in public. What must she think of him and his lack of self-control.

Camille didn't dare say anything to Nicholas. Her body still tingled, still wantonly craving what his had offered. What was the matter with her? She was acting like a sex-starved widow. Where was her pride? Her sense of right and wrong?

Do you consider what you felt for this man to be wrong? She didn't know anything anymore. She wasn't supposed to feel anything close to this for him. Only problems would arise if they became involved past their sense of responsibility to their child. She knew that. Then why was she asking—no—begging for heartache?

They were silent during the drive to the Parker house.

Camille glanced at Nicholas's taut profile, trying to guess what he was thinking. Was it possible that he was thinking about her in the same way she was thinking about him? Would it be so wrong to let herself care for him? According to her brother, Nicholas had his own agenda, and she'd be a fool to think she seriously figured in his plans. That after he got what he wanted from her, he wouldn't have anymore use for her. Surely not. But was she absolutely sure of that?

Nicholas pulled up in front of the house and cut the engine.

"If I've offended you, I'm sorry. It was never my intention."

"You didn't offend me, Nicholas. It was my fault as much as yours. Things just got out of hand that's all."

"Don't misunderstand me, I don't regret kissing you. Not for one moment. What happened was a culmination of the feelings building inside me since we met."

"Nicholas, don't."

"Don't what? Have feelings for you? It's already too late for that. They're there and I can't stop them. And frankly I wouldn't, if I could. You're a beautiful woman, Camille and I desire you like mad."

"You don't know what your saying. It's only because I'm carrying your baby. Once she's born you'll forget all about those feelings."

"I don't think so." He cupped her face and kissed

her tenderly on the lips. "In fact I know not. You look tired. I think you'd better go inside."

"Nicholas, I - "

"Don't say anything. What's between us is stronger than you're willing to admit. I understand, and I can live with that - for now, because I believe those feelings will deepen."

Camille didn't say anything more. Her emotions were impossibly tangled, and she didn't know what to say. She moved to open the door. Nicholas walked around and helped her out.

"I want you to come to my house tomorrow evening. I'm going to introduce you to my mother."

"Maybe you should tell her about me first."

"I've decided that it won't make any difference whether I do or not because she's going to have to accept that you're the mother of her grandchild."

"In essence you're handing her a fait accompli. Accepting that I'm black may be more than she is willing to accept."

"You may be right. But she'll have to accept it eventually. And that I care for you. End of story."

Hardly the end, Camille thought. More like the beginning.

"Well, will you come?"

"I don't know."

"Now who's is being a coward."

Why had she agreed to let him into her life?

Agreed? He never gave you a choice, girl. It was that or go to court. Going along with him at the time was the only thing you could do and you know it. Since things have changed, it's up to both of you whether your relationship goes any further.

"I'm not a coward, I just - all right, I'll come."

"Good." Nicholas put his arm around her shoulder and urged her up the walk to the porch.

"I don't want you reading more into my decision to do this than is there, Nicholas. I can't in good conscience keep our child from knowing her father and his family. They're as much a part of her as mine are."

He nodded. Look, I'll be here at six o'clock to pick you up."

"I'll be ready."

He turned her face toward him and kissed her forehead and then smiled at her before turning to walk back to his car.

"You still don't believe, do you, Camille?" Jamal said opening the screen door and stepping out on the porch. "What's it going to take?"

"Were you purposely waiting up for me to come

home? If the reason is what I think it is, I don't appreciate you spying on me, Jamal."

"I wasn't spying. It's not like you were trying to keep anything secret. You let the man kiss you in front of the whole neighborhood."

"Jamal, please. What I do and where, is my business."

"I'm only trying to keep you from making a huge mistake."

"Look, I'm tired and I'm going up to bed. You coming in?"

"No, I think I'll pay a visit to - "

"Don't you dare go anywhere near Nicholas."

"You're kind of protective, aren't you?"

"Jamal."

"I wasn't going to go there. Does that make you happy? I was going to drop by Deja's."

As she watched her brother stride through the gate and head down the street, she smiled. She hoped that he and Deja got back together, but knowing her brother he'd probably do something to screw things up as usual. Well he would have to deal with his own problems. Right now she had more than enough on her own plate.

Chapter Twelve

Nicholas went sailing early Sunday morning hoping to absorb all the tranquility he could store up because he knew he was going to need every bit of it to deal with his mother that evening. It wasn't so much that he cared what she thought about the race of his child's mother, but he wanted peace between them all.

Keep on dreaming. You'd have a better chance of living on the sun without burning up.

Nicholas showered and dressed and was on the way out the door to pick up Camille when his brother stopped him.

"Mother told me you were bringing a guest for dinner before she left for the club this morning. I don't have to ask who that guest is. Do I?"

"I'm bringing Camille."

"Do you think that's wise?"

"Why do you say that? Is mother in one of her moods?"

"No. But she was acting strange when she came

back from the club. Maybe you should clue her in before you bring Camille here. She's in her bedroom resting."

"I don't want to give her time to erect barriers."

"She's going to do that anyway, Nick. You know her feelings on certain subjects."

"You don't have to tell me that our mother is a first-class snob."

"It goes beyond that. She's obsessed with racial differences."

"Maybe manners and decorum will dictate her behavior."

"You hope. I wouldn't count on it."

Nicholas did have doubts, but he wasn't going to let his mother get away with insulting or embarrassing Camille.

Like you can stop her, a familiar niggling little voice mocked.

* * *

"You're really going to his house, aren't you?" Jamal asked Camille as he stood in the doorway of her bedroom, watching her as she sat in front of her vanity applying her makeup.

"I guess mama told you. The answer is yes, I am."

"So he's finally taking you to meet his family. It's

about time don't you think?"

"Jamal, don't, okay? I'm nervous enough as it is."

"I guess you have reason to be. If you want me to I can come with you?"

"Thanks, but no."

"You're not ashamed of me, are you? I know I didn't finish college like you did, but - "

"No, I'm not and you know it." She turned to face him. "Your not finishing college has nothing to do with it. It doesn't make you any less of person. There's nothing wrong with being a carpenter. The cradle you made for the baby is magnificent. Not just anyone can do that kind of work." Camille stood up. "How do I look?"

"Nice." Jamal smiled.

"Why thank you."

Hazel entered to room. "Sugar, Nicholas is downstairs waiting for you."

* * *

While he waited for Camille to come down, Nicholas took in the ambiance of the Parker living room. The other times he'd been there, he hadn't had a chance to because Jamal hadn't allowed him one. Nicholas noticed that the furniture was old traditional Creole French Provincial, the mahogany woodwork polished to a glass-like sheen.

A grand piano dominated. On top of it sat gilded-wood framed pictures of Camille and her family. He had thought that she was a carbon copy of her mother, but when he saw a picture of Camille standing beside a man who could only be her father, Nicholas saw that wasn't precisely the case: she had inherited the man's smile.

A brass accordion-like album stand was also spread out on the piano. It contained sepia-toned pictures of Camille's parents in their younger days. There were also snapshots of Camille and Jamal as children. And although he towered over her, Nicholas guessed that Camille was several years older than her brother. Even way back then Jamal had been protective of his sister. In one picture he held her hand and scowled into the camera as if daring anyone to object or wrench his hand away.

Nicholas admired Jamal's loyalty to and protectiveness of his sister if for no other than that he himself felt the same about his own brother.

A picture of Camille and her late husband caught his attention. Elroy King stood holding a saxophone and Camille sat before the piano. Both were smiling into each other's eyes. A twinge of jealousy twisted through Nicholas. But a second later a smile spread across his face because the baby Camille carried didn't belong to

Elroy King. Only with Nicholas had Camille shared that precious miracle.

"I'm ready, Nicholas. Shall we go?" Camille said, upon entering the living room.

Words lodged in Nicholas's throat at the sight of her. She was exquisite. She was wearing her hair up with a cascade of layered curls hanging down her back. Her cream-colored, sleeveless dress complimented her toffee-brown skin. Instead of camouflaging her stomach the soft lines of the cotton-knit dress charmingly showed off her condition. The hem of her dress stopped just above her knees exposing long gorgeously shaped golden brown legs.

"You look beautiful, Camille." Nicholas was finally able to utter as he walked toward her. He held out his hand and she placed hers in it.

"Before you take my sister anywhere, I want your word that you won't let your family hurt her."

"Jamal, please," Camille protested.

Nicholas held up his hand. "It's all right, Camille." He looked her brother in the eye and said. "You've got my word on it. Despite what you think of me, I care about your sister and would never hurt her or let anyone else hurt her." His expression made it clear that that also included Jamal.

"We'll see how much your word is worth when she comes home. Then we'll know who you really care about; my sister or your precious family."

"That's enough, Jamal," Hazel reprimanded.

"I think we had better leave now, Nicholas," Camille said glaring at her brother before urging Nicholas toward the door.

"Your brother really hates me because I'm white and because I have money. I don't know how to defend that," Nicholas said as they headed down the walk.

"Don't worry about it." It was ironic. Camille thought. It was usually the other way around.

"I don't know what to say to you, Nicholas."

"As I said before, your brother feels the way he feels and it's up to me to convince him otherwise. How to accomplish that miraculous feat just escapes me at the moment." He helped her into the car, and then slid behind the wheel. Turning to her, he smiled and said. "But I'll think of something." He started the car and they were on their way.

* * *

Camille's heart lurched up into her throat a half an hour later when Nicholas drove up to a towering, wrought-iron gate with the Cardoneaux name emblazoned on a bronze plaque inserted in a stone pillar to the right of it. In the near distance stood the Cardoneaux mansion. Her mouth dropped open at the sight of it. The pictures she'd seen in magazines at the Center library came nowhere close to doing it justice. Only Nicholas's painting did that. The house was simply magnificent. The house - no - mansion looked like something out of one of those pre-civil war period piece movies with its eight classic giant, white Doric columns spaced across the front and the galleries that wrapped around both the raised first floor, down to the elegant loggias strategically spaced on the above floor.

This was actually where Nicholas lived!

Nicholas saw the look of awe and sudden unease.

"It's just a house."

"It's more than that and you know it. I'm not sure I should go inside."

"You should and you are coming in with me. Unless of course you're ashamed to be seen with me," he teased, reminding her of what she'd said to him on more than one occasion.

"All right, but - "

He smiled and squeezed her hand. "It's going to be all right, Camille."

She felt less than optimistic that it would be. As they reached the porch, the double doors opened and out walked a man who could only be Nicholas's brother. The resemblance between the brothers was striking.

He smiled and embraced Camille saying. "I'm Phillip Cardoneaux. I'm pleased to meet you, Camille."

"I'm pleased to meet you, too, Phillip." Camille returned his smile.

Phillip let her go and took a step backward and glanced at her stomach. "You're expecting my niece or nephew. And I couldn't be happier about it. My brother has wanted a child for so long. He'd all but given up on it ever happening."

Camille could tell that she was going to like this man. He exuded genuine warmth, gentleness and naturalness around her. The article she'd read about the family said he was a doctor much loved by his patients. She could see why. She was surprised to learn that a man from his social standing practiced at a city hospital.

Nicholas sighed with relief at the success of the meeting. Now if only the meeting with his mother went equally as well. If not - no matter. He wasn't going to let her get away with anything.

"Welcome to our home," Phillip said moving aside for Camille and Nicholas to precede him into the house.

The living room was every bit as magnificent as the entry hall leading into it. Black and white checkerboard tile covered the floor. It was like stepping back into history.

Nicholas led Camille into the room and over to a beige, tan and black striped satin couch. A maid entered the room.

"Would you care for something to drink?" Nicholas asked Camille. "Tea, milk or juice?"

"A glass of water will be fine." Her throat had suddenly gone dry.

"Edna will get it for you." Phillip nodded his head at the maid, then turned his attention back to Camille. "I hope you've been feeling all right."

"Oh, I have."

"Who is your obstetrician?" Phillip inquired.

"Janet Broussard."

"I know of her. A very good choice, she has an excellent reputation."

"I'm happy with her."

"Phillip," Nicholas warned.

He smiled. "Please, forgive me. It's the doctor in me, I guess."

Nicholas cleared his throat. "Where is mother?"

"In her room freshening up. She'll be down in a few minutes."

Camille looked at Nicholas and then Phillip shaking her head, neither man proving to be what she had expected. She couldn't help wondering what their mother would be like. She didn't have long to wait to find out.

Suzette Cardoneaux appeared in the doorway.

"Am I late?"

"No, you're just in time." Nicholas smiled. "Mother, I'd like you to meet - "

Before Nicholas could finish his introduction, Suzette said. "I know who she is. I ran into Richard and Phyllis Collier this morning at the club and they filled me in. They mentioned seeing you both at the Hadley Clinic and enlightened me on a few details you neglected to mention." She glared accusingly at Nicholas and looked down her nose at Camille.

"Mother, you're being rude to our guest!" Phillip interjected.

"I think I have every right to be when I find that my son has purposely kept such vital information from me."

"Mother," Nicholas's voice took on an edge.

"Vital, how and in what way, Mrs. Cardoneaux?" Camille demanded to know.

Suzette didn't answer her, but instead looked to her son. "Nicholas, I need to speak to you in private."

"No, Mother. Whatever you have to say to me,

you can say it in front of Camille."

"All right, if you insist. Here it is. How do you know that you're really the father of her child?" she questioned baldly. "For one thing, you have no proof. For another, you have only the word of Dr. Hadley and his staff, both having clearly proven their obvious incompetence. They could be using you to cover over their mistake? This child could be anyone's."

"I don't believe you just said that, Mother," Nicholas roared.

"Believe it."

"How could you call your own grand-child a mistake," Nicholas continued. "The child Camille is carrying is mine."

"It's obviously what you choose to believe, because you want a child so badly. It's what Hadley and his clinic are counting on." She glared at Camille. "And she most definitely wants you to believe it." Her eyes narrowed. "This woman knows you have money and is probably out for all she can get."

Camille's last thread of control snapped and she shot to her feet. "For the record I don't want any of your money or anything else from you, Mrs. Cardoneaux. I'm this baby's mother and that's never going to change. I'm going to love her no matter who her father is. It's only because I'm black that you're so willing to believe that my baby isn't Nicholas's, isn't it? I have news for you, Mrs. Cardoneaux, I'm proud of who and what I am."

"Nicholas, really," Suzette sputtered indignantly. "Why did you bring this - this woman to our home? It's obvious that she doesn't belong here."

Camille shifted her gaze to Nicholas. "I see now why you didn't bring me here before." Jolie had been right on about his mother and her attitude, she thought bitterly.

Phillip moved to Camille's side. "I apologize for my mother's behavior."

"It's not your fault. Your mother is a free thinking adult, responsible for her own words and actions." Camille shifted her attention to Nicholas. "Please, take me home. If you won't I'll call my brother to come get me."

"I'll take you home." Nicholas glared at his mother. "I'll talk with you later," he said and followed Camille out the door.

"Camille, wait!" He said catching up with her.

"For what? So your mother can insult me, my baby and my ancestors?"

Camille, I'm sorry that she said those things to you."

"Being sorry doesn't help, Nicholas. Will it change the way she feels about me? What you said about

Jamal also applies to your mother; she feels the way she feels. She's never going to accept me or this baby. I had hoped - never mind. I don't want to talk about this anymore."

"Because she said what she did doesn't change anything, Camille. I know that I'm the father. That's all that really matters, isn't it?"

"You're fooling yourself if you believe that. There's more to it than that. Nicholas, don't say anything else, all right? I've heard all I care to."

There was so much more that he wanted to say, but knew she wasn't ready to listen. After this evening's fiasco, he wondered if she ever would be.

Chapter Thirteen

Jamal was sitting on the porch swing when Nicholas drove up. Just what she needed, Camille groaned. She knew once he found out what had happened all hell would break loose.

Camille turned to Nicholas. "Please, don't get out. Just go home."

Nicholas wasn't looking forward to yet another confrontation with Jamal, but he would be damned if he would back down from what he had to do. "I'm walking you to your door."

Seeing the determination on his face, Camille knew she would be wasting her time were she to even try to convince him to do otherwise.

Nicholas opened her door. Camille hesitated, but decided to get it over with.

Jamal, as if sensing trouble, met them halfway down the walk.

"Well, Cardoneaux."

"Jamal." Camille moved away from Nicholas toward her brother.

Ignoring his sister, Jamal glared at Nicholas. "Something happened didn't it?"

"Nicholas, please, just go," Camille tried again.

"No."

Jamal moved a step closer to Nicholas. "You don't have to tell me anything. I can guess from the look on both your faces it was something heavy. Your family rejected and insulted my sister, didn't they?"

Nicholas began. "I'm ashamed of the way my mother treated your sister. And I apologize for that. She may be my mother but she doesn't speak for me. No matter what anybody says I know the baby is mine and I also happen to care for Camille. Her being black doesn't enter into it. You can choose to believe it or not, Jamal. I don't give a damn. But I want you to know that I'm not going to walk away from my responsibilities to Camille or our child."

"What about your mother, man?"

"I'll handle her. What she thinks isn't law. Camille and the baby are my number one priority. I would have liked for my mother to have graciously accepted the fact that Camille is carrying her grandchild despite her personal feelings, but since she hasn't, that's her problem.

Her approval isn't essential. Not you, not my mother, or anyone or anything else is going to keep me away from Camille."

As Nicholas words sank in, the tension fizzled out of Jamal.

Camille put her hand on her brother's arm and smiled. "I'm all right. Really."

He didn't look as though he was completely convinced of that, but he backed off.

Nicholas focused his attention on Camille. "I'll call you after I've talked to my mother."

"Please. Don't bother."

"I'll bother because as I've said before, I'm not going to go away. I intend to be there for you in whatever capacity you need me. I'll see you at the Center tomorrow. We'll go to lunch and discuss what happened and your feelings about it."

"I don't see how discussing it is going to change anything, Nicholas."

"I do. Tomorrow, Camille." That said Nicholas strode down the walk to his car.

Camille turned to her brother. "I'm not ready to hear I told you so from you, Jamal."

"Oh, sister girl." He drew her into his arms. "I wasn't going to say that."

Tears spilled down Camille's cheeks. "I had hoped and prayed that because the baby was her grand-child, his mother would accept me."

"I know, you did. What I'd like to do is strangle his bitch of a mother with my bare hands for hurting you."

"It wouldn't change her thinking. The woman was so hateful, Jamal."

"I can imagine and I'm sorry you had to go through that. Now do you see what I've been trying to tell you? You have to put Nicholas Cardoneaux out of your life and keep him from complicating the baby's after it's born."

"That's easier said then done. She's his baby too. He is already possessive and she isn't even born yet."

"Given time he'll get over it and move on with his life."

"I don't see him doing that."

"Maybe his mother will convince him."

"I doubt it. He's his own man."

"Then he'll have to make a choice. Mark my words! Blood is thicker than water."

"This baby also carries his blood. How is he expected to choose between his child and his mother?"

"I don't know, but that's exactly what he's going to have to do. I don't believe you'll have to worry, though.

He'll eventually cave in. Once the novelty wears off, he'll lose interest in you and the baby and move on."

Camille had a feeling that the opposite would prove to be true. Jamal didn't know Nicholas as she was coming to know him. What she didn't know was how Nicholas was going to deal with this without someone getting hurt.

* * *

"Where is she, Phillip?" Nicholas demanded, storming into the living room at the Magnolia Grove.

"I think you should wait until you simmer down before you talk to her, Nick."

"On this subject I'll never simmer down."

"There's no need for you to shout, Nicholas," Suzette said descending the stairs."

"Oh, I think there is, Mother." He looked at his brother. "Phillip, please leave us alone."

"I don't think - "

Suzette smiled at her younger son. "It's all right, dear. I promise you there will be no blood shed."

Though reluctant to do so, Phillip left them alone.

"How you could say what you did to the mother of my child... Whatever progress I've made is shot to hell because of you and your stupid obsessive prejudice about race, color and social position."

"They're not stupid," she answered. "Nicholas, even if it proves to be your child, you're not obligated to claim it. After all Camille King's insemination was done without your knowledge or permission. All you have to do is disclaim paternity and walk away."

"Since you claim to know me so well, you should know I'd never abandon my own child for any reason. Certainly, not because of the color of her mother's skin. Or somebody's blunder. How could you treat Camille the way you did?"

"Because I don't believe the baby she's carrying is yours."

"Just the other day you were so eager for me to get custody and bring the baby here to live."

"That was before."

"Nothing's changed. I'm still going to be a father to that same child."

"You don't really know that for sure. My advice is to pay the woman off, back away and get on with your life, and find a suitable woman to marry and have a family with."

"You have tunnel vision where race is concerned and I can't for the life of me understand it. When Phillip and I were growing up you were like that. You never let us play with black children."

"For how much good it did. You sneaked around and played with them every chance you got anyway."

"Father never felt that way. Why do you, Mother? Just answer me that." When she didn't answer, he went on. "As far as I'm concerned, people are people no matter their race or the color of their skin."

"She and that baby would never fit into our way of life, Nicholas.

"That baby!" His eyes narrowed in fury.

Ignoring his response she continued. "The woman would end up being an embarrassment to our - "

"Don't say another word, Mother." His eyes shot fire. "I told you what would happen if you interfered in my life. Right now you've done more than interfered, you've complicated it beyond my wildest nightmare. I can only hope you haven't caused irreversible damage. I'm giving you until the baby is born to amend the damage you've caused. If you can't or won't apologize to Camille, you leave me no choice but to move out."

"You can't mean that, Nicholas!"

"I mean every word. After the baby is born she would be coming here to visit and with the way things stand she would sense the tension. Children are sensitive to that kind of thing. I refuse to live under the same roof with a woman who thinks and acts the way you have toward my child's mother."

"You can't just leave! I'm your mother, your own flesh and blood. I gave birth to you."

"The baby Camille is carrying has my blood. And after she's born she'll be my family too. Whether Camille is black, white or yellow she the mother of my child. Either you accept her or make no mistake I will leave this house. The choice is yours."

"Where will you live?" she sputtered.

"There are plenty of houses in and around New Orleans. In fact our company is due to complete one in the next few weeks."

"But this is your home, Nicholas."

"Mother, either you accept Camille and my child- your grand-child, or..." Nicholas let his voice trail away.

"You'd turn your back on your own mother for that- that -"

"Don't say it, Mother. For God's sake don't," he growled.

Suzette glared at Nicholas and holding her head high ascended the stairs without uttering another word.

Nicholas walked over to the bar and poured him-self a brandy.

"I heard you two shouting." Phillip said entering the room. "I might as well have stayed. You're really serious about moving out, aren't you?"

"Oh, yes. If she can't accept my child and the fact that Camille is her mother, then yes, I will."

"I never imagined that a child that isn't even born yet could tear our family apart."

"She isn't the one causing it. It's our dear mother's doing. It doesn't have to be that way, Phillip. Mother knows what she has to do. If she's not willing to do it, so be it. You think it doesn't hurt me to say those things to her?"

"There has to be another way, Nick."

"If there is I don't know what it is. Maybe mother will come around."

"You don't really believe that, do you?"

"What I don't understand is why she feels the way she does about race and color? Was it her upbringing? Could something have happened to make her feel this way?"

"I don't know. It might have. She's never told us about her childhood or anything about her side of the family."

"I've always thought that was strange, haven't you?"

"Yes. As far as I know the only relatives she has that are still alive are on her father's side. Aunt Laura and

Uncle Paul - and they are traveling somewhere in Europe."

"Believe me, Phillip, I want to understand her. I don't want to leave here, but I won't allow her to hurt Camille or the baby with her attitude. As it is, Camille doesn't want to talk to me. She was just beginning to soften and now..." he sighed. "I'm going up to bed."

Nicholas climbed the stairs and upon reaching the top, started down the hall. When he came to his mother's door, he reached for the knob, but suspended the action. He didn't want there to be hostility between them, but she'd brought it on her self with her rigid stand. This was the twenty-first century. He would have expected her to react differently. There was more to her attitude, much more. Whatever it was, it was connected to something she had refused to enlighten him or his brother on over the years. One day he would find out the truth.

Nicholas dropped his hand to his side and headed on down the hall to the west wing and his apartment. If his mother thought he would give in or change his mind about this she was sadly mistaken.

* * *

Camille stood in her nightgown looking out her bedroom window. It was well after midnight, but she'd been unable to fall asleep. Her mind kept replaying the scene with Nicholas's mother over and over.

A knock on her door scattered her musings, then her mother walked in.

"I heard you walking around. Jamal told me what happened. She put her arms around her daughter. "I'm so sorry, sugar."

"It was awful, Mama. Prejudice isn't new to me, but."

"I know. You would we've come a long way, but when something like this happens you begin to wonder if we've come as far as we'd like to believe."

"I didn't ask for any of this, Mama. I didn't ask for Nicholas to be the father of my baby. You'd think I planned it to hear his mother talk."

"She said that to you?" Hazel's voice rose along with her temper.

"Now don't you go getting upset, Mama."

"No one insults my baby like that and gets away with it. I'm thinking that maybe I should pay this Suzette Cardoneaux a little visit."

"No! Mama, this is my problem."

"I'd say she's the one with the problem and needs help sorting it out."

"Maybe this will help Nicholas see how impossible it is - "

Hazel shook her head. "No, sugar. I've seen that possessive look in his eyes."

"What should I do? He starts working at the Center tomorrow. I'll have to see him on a regular basis every week. I'm not sure I can handle it after last night."

"The two of you are going to have to talk. I don't see any way around it."

"What's there to talk about? His mother hates me and doesn't believe my baby is her son's."

Hazel shook her head. "I can't understand it. I've known a lot of white folks who were biased in their thinking about race, but when it comes to their grandchildren most are willing to put that aside. Blood is blood, sugar. Maybe after his mother has had time to think about it she'll - "

"You didn't see the look in her eyes. It wasn't hate exactly. More like she was afraid to accept the possibility that my baby is her grandchild."

"Afraid?" Hazel frowned. "That doesn't make sense. It's not something to be afraid of I wouldn't think. Either you accept it or you don't. There has to be another reason why she is so against the idea."

Could her mother be right? Camille wondered. But if that wasn't true what other reason could she possibly have for rejecting her own flesh and blood?

"Sugar, don't try to figure it all out tonight. You'd better get some sleep."

"I will, Mama."

After her mother left the room, Camille continued to look out the window, not really seeing anything. Her mind was locked into the situation she and Nicholas found themselves in. What did the future have in store for them? What would tomorrow bring? A change for the better or unbearable heartache.

Chapter Fourteen

Nicholas looked up from his morning paper when his mother entered the breakfast room. He started to say something, but the implacable expression on her face stopped him cold.

"I know you were upset last night and didn't mean half the things you said to me," Suzette began.

Nicholas's eyes narrowed. "About Camille and my moving out, I was and still am dead serious about that. Make no mistake, Mother, this baby is mine. Race isn't going to change that fact.

"If it's yours, it won't."

"What I can't understand is why you're so eager to believe it isn't mine."

She shot him a patient indulgent look. "Before you go getting more involved and laying claim to being the father, you should wait until after the child is born and have a DNA test done."

Nicholas threw his newspaper down on the table.

"There's no getting through to you, is there?" He gritted his teeth. "I don't need a test to confirm what I already know. I'm going to the Center."

Nicholas despaired of his mother ever accepting things when he saw the obstinate look slip into place like a mask.

"You'd better think long and hard about what I've said, Mother."

"You've made your views crystal clear, Nicholas."

He stood, staring at her for a moment, and then shaking his head walked out of the room.

* * *

The students in her last class had just left the classroom when Camille heard a knock on the door. She knew before it opened who was on the other side.

"I've come to take you to lunch," Nicholas said as he entered the room.

"All right." Camille didn't bother arguing, just lifted her purse out of the bottom desk drawer and let Nicholas escort her to his car.

Once they reached the parking lot, she said. "Nicholas, maybe it would be better if you didn't -if we didn't -"

"It wouldn't be better for either one of us, Camille."

She could see that she wasn't getting anywhere going this route and asked. "What happened when you talked to your mother?"

"I gave her an ultimatum."

Camille's eyes widened in surprise. "An ultimatum?"

"If she doesn't learn to accept you and our child, I'm moving out."

"Nicholas, you didn't?"

"Yes, I did."

"But if she feels - or she can't -"

"It's her problem, not ours. Maybe it was time I moved out anyway. It was unrealistic to think, in this day and age, that grown children and their families could live harmoniously under the same roof as their parents."

"You thought so before this."

"You're right, I did."

Camille put her hand on his arm. "You don't have to give up your home and your relationship with your mother, Nicholas. Just let us go."

"I can't, Camille. So don't ask me to. My mother has until the baby is born to realize how important it is that she accepts the way things are. I don't expect her to change the thinking of a lifetime over night. That would be wishing for the moon. I know that she's yearned for a grandchild for as long as I have a child. I'm hoping that desire will sway her."

Camille wondered what it would take for Suzette Cardoneaux to put aside her prejudices and welcome her racially mixed grandchild into the family? Maybe after actually seeing the baby - but did she dare hope that that would make any difference? She knew she wouldn't stand by and let anyone, grandmother or not, hurt her child. But despite what the woman had said, Camille was, for the sake of her child, willing to meet her halfway, but she would have to be the one to take the first step.

Nicholas chose Mona Lisa's for lunch.

As they waited for their food, Camille felt the weight of last night's fiasco pressing down on her like a ton of bricks. She couldn't say she was looking forward to the impending discussion.

"Don't look at me like that, Camille. God knows you have every reason to be upset. And I don't blame you after what my mother said to you."

"She truly believes the baby isn't yours. She brought up some questions I hadn't considered. That Dr. Hadley might be wrong and the technician hadn't really made the mistake he thought he'd made."

"Do you really believe that?"

"I don't know what to believe, Nicholas."

He took her hand in his. "Believe this! I care about you and our baby, Camille. I more than care." He leaned across the table and gave her a quick kiss on the lips."

"Nicholas, you're only saying that because - "

He kissed her again, stopping the flow of her words. "I'm not just saying this from the heat of the moment."

The waiter came back with their meal and Nicholas let her hand go.

Minutes later Camille licked her fingers as she ate. "Umm, I love their pizza. I can't wait to dig into this buttery fettuccini."

Nicholas smiled as he watched her eat. When she was halfway finished with her fettuccini he said. "Whether my mother changes or not, doesn't matter. I intend to live my life the way I want with whomever I want."

"But your mother - "

"Knows my feelings. Now that you know where I'm coming from, we can proceed."

"Proceed where? And how?"

"That's easy. We deepen our friendship, starting today."

"Deepen it?" She frowned in puzzlement. "But

how will that help?"

Nicholas scooted his chair around the table closer to Camille and put his arm around her shoulder and kissed her deeply.

"It'll help us grow closer."

Camille felt her heartbeat accelerate at his nearness. The subtle manly scent of his cologne aroused her and the electric response that charged to life between them when he had kissed her was overpowering.

"Nicholas, people are staring at us."

"Let them stare. You're not immune to me, are you?"

Camille lowered her eyes. "You know I'm not. I thought we were going to talk."

"I can't explain away my mother's attitude because I don't understand it myself. But I do understand where your brother is coming from. I have a feeling that something in his past evoked his hostile feelings. Evidently a white person or persons hurt him or someone close to him and he sees us all as being cut from the same cloth so to speak. That our thinking and ways of dealing with certain issues haven't changed."

Camille arched her brows in wonderment at Nicholas's perceptiveness. He had guessed right about Jamal's attitude and the reasons for it.

"I haven't had my head buried in the sand all my life, Camille. I'm aware of the prejudice and bigotry in this country, namely in the south. Don't look so surprised, you don't have to be black to relate to that. And I certainly don't condone it. Henri has been and still is a close friend of mine since we were boys. I never once considered him to be anything else. Neither skin color nor race ever entered into it as far as I was concerned. I'm not my mother."

She relaxed at his words and sought a change of subject. "There's one last piece of pizza left."

Nicholas shoved the tin her way. "Be my guest." When she had finished, he leaned over and wiped away a few drops of the sauce and cheese that had streaked down her chin. He swallowed hard as he observed her. God she was so beautiful. Desire heated his blood and he felt himself harden when his eyes came to rest on her full breasts that had become fuller since the first time he'd seen her. Fuller because his child was growing inside her, causing her body to blossom.

Camille felt Nicholas's eyes on her, caressing her with his heated appraisal. Her breasts tingled and her nipples tightened. When she felt her femininity moisten in arousal and her body grow increasingly warmer, she quickly reached for her glass of iced tea.

Girl, that won't cool you down. You're as hot for this man now as you were the day you first laid eyes on him.

I'm not. I'm a pregnant woman.

You may be pregnant, but you're still a young healthy woman and he is fine to the bone.

Nicholas saw the sudden rosy flush on Camille's skin. His heart raced. He could tell by the far away look on her face that her mind had strayed to a much more passionate subject than food.

He glanced at his watch. "It's time we headed back to the Center."

Back to reality, she thought as they left the restaurant. Driving along it occurred to Camille that Nicholas always took her to places in or near her neighborhood except the time they went to the Southern Yacht Club marina to go sailing and she mentioned it.

Nicholas frowned. "And?"

"Nothing."

"If you're thinking that I'm ashamed to take you around my friends, Camille, you're wrong, I'm not. You've already met Henri and Jolie. It's been for your comfort I've chosen places closer to where you live. If you like we can go to the country club or one of the plantation inns or restaurants in Kenner."

"Where, if not for me, you would normally go. Right?"

"Camille. That's not fair. People are normally creatures of habit. I'm no exception. We often get stuck in set routines. If you want to we can go to some of the places I frequented before we met. It doesn't matter to me where we go as long as we're together."

"Nicholas, this isn't going to work."

"Why won't it?"

"You know why."

"You mean because of my mother. I told you -"

"I know what you told me, that you won't let what she thinks influence you, but -"

"You don't believe me."

"I'm sure your mother frequents some of the same places as you do."

"Your point being?"

Camille let out a weary breath. "About your white friends? What will they think? The ones we saw at the clinic were certainly shocked to see us together."

"They weren't exactly close friends. And even if they had been I don't let any of my friends dictate whom I see and spend my time with."

Camille didn't reply. What could she say. Deep down she had doubts that his words could not assuage.

When they arrived back at the Center, she put her hand on the car door handle.

"Camille, one thing we need to clear up."

"And that is?"

"We shouldn't let other people influence how we feel about each other. What I'm trying to say is that we should live our lives the way we want to."

"To the exclusion of everything and everyone else. No man is an island, Nicholas. We need our family and friends."

"I'm not denying that, but we can't let what they think and feel and want rule our lives no matter who they are."

That struck a familiar cord with Camille. It brought to mind the relationship between her and her late husband. It had always been what Elroy thought, what Elroy believed they should do. It had taken her a long time to come to grips with that realization; the only reason he agreed to her retiring from the concert jazz stage to pursue a teaching career was that he was afraid her career would overshadow or upstage his.

It was the reason they had waited to try for a baby after his sperm treatment had been deemed successful. Because it was what he had wanted, they'd had his sperm stored for a later date. But that later date never came because he had kept delaying it, offering one excuse after another. It was only after Elroy's death that she'd gotten her wish and had conceived her precious baby. Then to find out that her husband wasn't even the father... At first it was a shock, but later she had begun to feel relieved.

Camille probed Nicholas's compelling blue eyes and knew instinctively that it would never have been that way between them. They would share their child and he would not dictate how she should feel or behave. He was tolerant of her brother and fair with his mother despite their obvious attitudes concerning the baby.

"When is your next doctor appointment?" Nicholas asked as they entered her classroom.

"Monday."

"I want to come with you. The last time we talked you did say that you were going to have an ultra sound, didn't you?"

"Yes."

"Look, if it's going to make you feel uncomfortable - "

"I'm not sure how I'll feel. Being pregnant is so new to me and I still feel awed by the process." She lovingly ran her fingers across her stomach.

"I am too. Look, since you enjoy seafood so

much, the Louisiana Crawfish Festival is coming up this weekend. Want to go?"

Camille mentally licked her lips at the thought of tasting light buttery, superbly-seasoned crawfish. She and her family had gone to the festival every year before her father died.

"I'd love to."

"Good. I'll pick you up in the morning at eight."

"I'll be ready. If you keep taking me out to eat all the time, I'll be fat as a butterball by the time I deliver this baby."

Nicholas noticed that in the last couple of weeks her stomach seemed to have grown quite large for the number of months pregnant she was, but he hadn't mentioned it.

"I'd better be getting to my classroom. I'm sure my assistant is wondering what happened to me."

Camille watched as Nicholas left the room. She couldn't help fantasizing about him. He was any girl's idea of a hunk. How was she expected to resist him? How she had this long, she didn't know. Nicholas seemed so eager to please her. Not that he didn't have his own agenda. Despite that, he was considerate and patient until pushed too far.

What about his mother? Camille couldn't help

obsessing about how this all would end. She didn't want to be responsible for alienating Nicholas from his mother, making him leave his home. He'd said that what his mother thought and felt wouldn't influence him. Could she really believe him? She would glean the answer soon enough, she guessed.

Chapter Fifteen

The state's favorite crustacean was honored during the weekend of the Louisiana Crawfish festival held in Breaux Bridge every year in the heart of Cajun country, the self-proclaimed "Crawfish Capital of The World." This particular festival was one Nicholas had thoroughly enjoyed since childhood. It was complete with food vendors, street performers and arts and crafts booths. He'd displayed several of his sketches there when he was just twelve. And to his amazement and joy, he'd sold quite a few of them.

"Are you enjoying yourself, Camille?"

"Oh, yes. This festival and the Greek one are among my favorites."

"We seem to enjoy doing a lot of the same things. The Greek Festival is a favorite of mine also. If you want to," Nicholas smiled totally entranced by the sparkle in her eyes, "We can go to the one held on the last weekend of the month."

"It's a date." A date. It dawned on Camille that he was courting her and had been almost from the time he discovered that she was carrying his child. Deja had been right. But should she let it go on? Or put a stop to it?

Like you can stop it, girl. The man is genuinely attracted to you. And your being pregnant with his child doesn't have anything to do with that.

For some reason she wasn't prepared to examine, she wanted so badly to believe that.

Any woman wants to believe that she's wanted for herself.

But this was a unique situation. Could Nicholas really separate his feelings for the baby from his feelings for her?

Time will give you the answer if you're willing to wait for it.

Nicholas helped Camille into a paper bib apron and to crack open the shells on her crawfish.

"You're treating me like a small greedy child," she complained.

"Right now, it's exactly what you look like," and she did too. She was wearing her long, brown hair in a braid that hung down her back. Her pink T-shirt, denim overalls and K-Swiss tennis shoes made her look about sixteen.

"I love hot water cornbread." She arched her brows looking to him for an affirming answer.

"Me, too," Nicholas answered. "Henri's mother used to serve it for dinner sometimes when Phillip and I ate with them."

After finishing their food, they strolled from one booth to another. Nicholas bought Camille several paintings and a sculpture of a mother and child from one of the Cajun artisans. He felt the sting of tears on his eyelids because it was like glimpsing a day in the near future when Camille would one day hold their child in her arms. His dream was so close to reaching fruition. He prayed to God that nothing would happen to destroy it.

"Are you all right, Nicholas?" Camille asked.

"I'm fine. It's nearly sundown. You want to go for a walk in the park before we leave?"

"I should after eating so much. I just couldn't help making a pig out of myself; the food was so delicious."

"Neither could I." Nicholas grinned, putting his arm around her shoulder and drawing her closer as they strolled through the park.

The sound of scurrying woodland creatures added to the earthiness of the scene. The overhead grounds lights came on as they made their way back to the festival. More people had arrived and had started dancing. A group called the Dixie Ramblers were performing.

Later Nicholas took Camille to Enola Prudhomme's Cajun Cafe in Carencro a few miles north of Breaux Bridge. Enola was the sister of the famous chef Paul Prudhomme.

"Umm, these sweet potato muffins are fabulous," Camille said taking another bite of the warm delicious little cake.

"I had an idea you would think so. You want to take a couple of them and a loaf of Enola's out-of-this-world banana bread home to your mother?"

"Oh definitely." Camille realized that although Nicholas was strong, he had a sensitive thoughtful side and that pleased her. "My mother's going to love it and so will Jamal. He's not all bad, Nicholas. He can be very loving and gentle."

"When I decide not to come near you, you mean."

"I've thoroughly enjoyed myself today," she said choosing not to comment any further on that subject.

Sensing her withdrawal, Nicholas followed her lead and said. "I wish we could experience this closeness all the time."

"Me, too," Camille answered softly.

* * *

Camille sat on the porch swing after watching Nicholas drive away. It was so peaceful out here, she thought. She could take time to think things out and look at her situation from a more objective standpoint. She could no longer deny to herself that she was falling in love with Nicholas. But she was afraid that she would end up getting hurt after the birth of her baby because these feelings Nicholas said he felt for her wouldn't last. She had to admit that his actions showed her proof of his sincerity. And after all actions did speak louder than words didn't they? But were they for her because of the baby? Could he possibly separate his feeling for the baby, from those he felt for her Camille?

"You're thinking about, him, aren't you?" Jamal asked as he walked up.

Camille hadn't noticed that he'd come home from his date with Deja.

"Do you think about, Deja?"

"That's different. She's my lady."

"Oh, is she? Since when?"

Jamal smiled sheepishly. "Since earlier this evening when we made up and she decided to give me another chance."

"I hope you don't blow it this time."

"Me too. Getting back to you and Cardoneaux. Are you really that serious about the guy?"

"And if I am?"

"If he's what you want there's nothing I can do to change your thinking about that. But Camille, you know how his mother feels about you. Do you really think she'll ever accept you into her family? How are you and he going to get around that? These questions are ones you need to ask yourself, sister girl," he said and strode into the house.

Jamal was right. Things were moving fast and she and Nicholas needed to consider what would happen if their relationship went beyond close all the way to love and ended in marriage.

Nicholas would be going to the doctor's with her Monday afternoon. As each day went by, the baby has brought them closer together. She had four months to go in her pregnancy. Four months in which her feelings for Nicholas would continue to grow. She could end up getting very badly hurt. She needed to think long and hard about everything.

Especially your heart.

Especially about that.

* * *

Nicholas left Cardoneaux Construction to meet Camille at the Center Monday afternoon. Today was the day she had her ultra-sound. He knew that the technician could tell the sex of their child. Did he really want to know? He believed and so did Camille that the child she carried was a girl. He found it next to impossible to contain his excitement. This was his child. His. The most beautiful word in the universe to him.

Just as he guided his car into the Center parking lot, Camille came outside. He could tell by her expression that she was just as anxious as he.

"Are you sure you're all right with this?" he asked her.

"Yes, I'm sure, Nicholas. Are you ready to go?"

"I'm more than ready actually," he said, helping her into his car.

Fifteen minutes later he pulled his car into the Delacroix Medical Center parking building. Inside the lobby they stepped into the elevator and Camille punched in the number to Dr. Janet Broussard's floor.

The office was warm and welcoming with its bright sunny yellow and green color scheme, he thought as they entered the reception room. The paintings on the wall were of tranquil scenes with happy babies, smiling mothers, toys and yards with flowers, jungle gyms and sand boxes.

"Have a seat. The doctor will be with you in a few minutes, Mrs. King," the receptionist told Camille.

Camille noticed the way the woman was eying Nicholas. If they were a fork and knife she would have devoured him piece by piece, Camille thought, annoyed by the woman's blatant interest in him. But could she really blame her? A woman would have to be blind or dead not to notice and appreciate a man as fine as Nicholas Cardoneaux.

And he's the father of your child. And attracted to you.

A few minutes later the nurse called Camille's name. She rose from her chair, as did Nicholas from his. He cupped her elbow and followed as the nurse led them to the doctor's office.

Janet Broussard's eyes widened in surprise when she saw them.

Camille cleared her throat. "Janet, this is Nicholas Cardoneaux, the father of my baby. He wanted to be with me when I had the ultra sound."

Janet smiled. "I'm always pleased to see the fathers' take a personal interest in the well being of the mothers and their unborn child. Pamela, my ultra-sound technician, is ready for you," she said showing them into a room several doors down the hall from her office.

Pamela smiled, as she welcomed them into the room. She instructed Camille to remove her dress and slip into the examining gown and then helped her get up on the table.

Nicholas watched with rapt interest as Camille lay back on the examining table. He was amazed by the swell of her stomach which looked even larger, bared, with her body in the reclining position. The technician squeezed a clear gel over her stomach and moved a small plastic wand over it. Images came into focus on the monitor screen.

"What do we have here?" Pamela queried.

"Is something wrong?" Camille said, rising up slightly in alarm.

"Oh, no." Pamela smiled reassuringly. "It looks like we have two babies instead of one."

"Two babies?" Camille gasped.

"Would you like to know their sex?"

Camille looked to Nicholas. He nodded yes.

"Yes, we would," she answered.

"The baby on the right is a boy." Pamela pointed to an area near the juncture of his thighs. "You can see the genitals. The other baby is a girl.

"Oh my God!" Camille exclaimed. "Two babies!

A boy and a girl." Tears spilled down her cheeks.

"We have a son and a daughter," Nicholas whispered reverently.

"Yes, you do." Janet said with a smile. "I thought I detected two heartbeats the last time you were here, Camille, but you had just found out about the mix up, so I decided to wait until you were farther along. I didn't want to say anything until we were sure. I take it you're happy about this latest development?"

"Oh, yes. I can hardly believe it."

"I'll have to prescribe a different regimen of vitamins for you. One geared more toward producing two healthy babies. How is your appetite?"

"Very good." Nicholas laughed. "She eats like a horse."

"Nicholas!"

"I mean like a woman eating for three," he laughingly amended.

"I'm glad to hear it," Janet chuckled. "Come back to my office after you've finished dressing."

Nicholas didn't know how to feel. He'd prayed for just one healthy baby. Now to learn that he would have a son, as well as a daughter was overwhelming. The expression on Camille's face was precious to watch. To him she never looked more beautiful.

* * *

After leaving the doctor's office, they stopped at the pharmacy to pick up Camille's new prescription.

"If you ask where I want to eat, Nicholas, I'll - "

He hunched his shoulders and grinned. "You have to admit that you have an extremely healthy appetite, Camille. Now we know why. Where would you like to have lunch?"

"You decide. I'm so happy I can hardly stand it. Two babies! We are so lucky, Nicholas."

"Yes, we are. Not just one baby, but two!" he grinned proudly, pulling his shirt away from his chest.

"You need to remember that you didn't do it by yourself. I had a little something to do with it."

"I love seeing you like this. What about names?"

Camille had decided on Solange Denae for her daughter.

"What is your father's name?"

"Jacques. And yours?"

"Xavier."

"Jacques Xavier Cardoneaux. I like the sound of that."

Cardoneaux. Camille hadn't thought about the last name.

"I like Xavier Jacques Cardoneaux," she said the combination experimentally.

He saw the wistful look in her eyes and the sadness because her father would never see his namesake. Nicholas sympathized; he missed his own father just as much. Camille was right family was important. It was a history of who and where we all came from.

* * *

The Palace Cafe was only a few blocks away so Nicholas decided to take Camille there. He knew she'd appreciate the atmosphere. It was a Parisan-style bistro. There were tables by huge plate-glass windows at sidewalk level. A sweeping staircase led to the second floor dining room if you wanted a quieter place to relax and enjoy your meal.

Camille was in a happy mood and chose to eat by the windows so she could watch the people go by. She picked up her menu and ordered the traditional pan-roasted oysters and crusty bread to soak up the rich and creamy juices.

Nicholas ordered pan-fried steak with a pile of skinny french fries.

"You'd better stop spoiling me," Camille said. "A poor girl like me might get hooked." She laughed.

"I enjoy watching a poor girl like you eat and

enjoy herself. You deserve to be pampered."

"You're right about that." she tossed back saucily.

"So try the signature, white-chocolate bread pudding with chocolate shavings on top. It's to die for."

"Bring it on."

They were as happy together, as they had ever been before.

* * *

Nicholas dropped Camille off at the Center so she could pick up her car and drive herself home.

When she got there, she parked the car and went straight to her room to take a nap. She found that she got sleepy at three thirty everyday. She had gotten into the habit of napping on the couch in the staff lounge at the Center on the days she worked. It was a luxury to crash on her own bed this afternoon.

She was having twins. She felt the excitement bubble inside her at the thought as she closed her eyes.

The smell of red beans and rice woke Camille and she followed the delicious scent to the kitchen where her mother stood in front of the stove stirring the pot.

"I knew the smell would bring you in here, sugar," Hazel said with a fond smile.

"Nobody cooks red beans and rice the way you

do, Mama. Zatarains eat your heart out."

Hazel laughed. "How did your doctor's appointment go?"

"Mama, I'm having twins!"

"Sugar, that's wonderful!" Hazel stopped what she was doing and hugged her daughter. "They run in my side of the family."

"What runs in the family?" Jamal asked, stepping just inside the kitchen doorway.

"Twins," Camille answered. "I'm having twins."

"All right! Boys or Girls?"

"One of each," she said proudly.

"I'll bet Cardoneaux was shocked. To have one racially mixed baby was one thing, but two. I wish I could have been a fly on the wall."

"Nicholas couldn't be happier, Jamal."

"Did he tell you that or did you just assume - "

"He's always wanted a child, and now to be blessed with two..."

"You sure he isn't just trying to impress you by pretending to be happy about this latest development. He may be happy, but his mother is going to pitch a hissy fit. I can almost see her face when she finds out."

"Jamal," Hazel chastened. "Mind your own business. You don't know how they feel."

"Mama's right, you don't." Camille walked over to the cabinet and took down the plates.

"This just complicates everything, Camille. Can't you see that?"

"Jamal, please. I don't want to discuss it, okay."

* * *

Nicholas sat behind his desk at Cardoneaux Construction with his feet propped up on it. He wasn't having just one child; he was having two. It was just so incredible!

The thought of his mother's reaction wiped the smile from his lips. How would this newest development go over? Probably no worse than when she thought there was only one child.

He heard the phone buzz and punched in his com-line. "Yes, Jennifer? Put him on. Phillip."

"How about having dinner with your doctor brother, only brother? Mother is dining with friends tonight. Since I have night duty at the hospital, it'll have to be a quick one. Frankie's sound good?"

"Perfect."

"You seem to be in a good mood."

"Oh, I am. I went with Camille to the doctor. We found out she's carrying twins; a boy and a girl."

"I'm happy for you, Nick. I know what this means

to you."

"Go ahead and say it."

"What?"

"Our mother, Phillp. You're wondering just like I am how she's going to take it."

"What can she say?"

"I'll meet you at Frankie's in half an hour."

* * *

When Nicholas got home late that evening, he found his mother reading on the couch in the living room.

"Mother, I have something to tell you."

Suzette looked up from her book. "You've changed your mind and - "

"No, I haven't," he said annoyed by her assumption that he would change his mind considering all he'd told her. "I found out today that Camille is carrying twins." He watched his mother closely, as he waited for her reply.

"It's just another thing that will entangle you even tighter in her web."

"Mother!"

"Don't you see - "

"I should have known better than to think..."

"Yes, you should have." Suzette returned her attention to her book, tuning her son out.

Nicholas gritted his teeth. He might as well start

packing. He refused to let his mother bring him down today. He was far too happy about this unexpected miracle.

Chapter Sixteen

Camille waited for her last music student of the day to finish practicing his scales.

"You did very well today, Rasheed. Tomorrow we'll move on to simple songs. And before you know it you'll be performing your first recital."

"All right!" the excited eight year old exclaimed happily as he rose from the piano bench and then scrambled out of the classroom.

Camille was busy writing comments on Rasheed's progress sheet when she heard a knock on her classroom door. She looked up in time to see Suzette Cardoneaux enter the room and she stiffened.

"I was just talking to Mr. Shelton and he regaled me with how lucky the Center is to have you working here."

"I enjoy teaching here. Why have you come, Mrs. Cardoneaux? I'm sure it wasn't to extol my virtues."

"I came to offer you a teaching position in New York, that'll be more rewarding than the one you have here."

"Why would I be interested in leaving New Orleans? My family, my friends, not to mention my child's father, all live here. You could care less about that, though. Right? What you're hoping to do is get me out of your son's life."

"What Nicholas doesn't need is you hanging around his neck like an albatross. The only thing you'll succeed in doing is bringing him down, Mrs. King."

"How would I be doing that? I'm giving him what he has wanted for years and couldn't have, Mrs. Cardoneaux. Not one, but two children."

"He's told me you're carrying twins."

"And instead of being happy for him, it's made you more determined than ever to get me out of the picture. I don't understand you." Camille threw her hands in the air. "You know how much these babies mean to him. How can you - "

"Those babies aren't his. If he disclaims paternity now, it'll be less painful for him in the long run."

"Or you." Camille's eyes narrowed. "You're so sure they aren't."

"Are you really that sure they are, Mrs. King?

There are tests you can have done before the birth."

"Yes, I know that, but there is a high risk of miscarriage. Maybe, that's what you want to happen. At any rate I'm not willing to take the chance just to appease you, Mrs. Cardoneaux."

"Think about my offer. It will always be good."

"I just bet it will."

"Leave New Orleans before it's too late. Nicholas doesn't love you. Doesn't that matter to you? The babies are the only thing he's interested in. Can't you see that? When he finds out they're not his, he'll forget you ever existed."

"You're wrong."

"Am I?"

"He cares for me."

"It's what you want to believe. We'll soon find out after your children are born. You'll be the one brought down low and humiliated." With that Suzette swept out of the room.

Camille stood balling and unballing her fists as she watched Suzette Cardoneaux leave. The audacity of the woman. How dared she try to bribe her to leave town. Jamal's words came back to haunt Camille. How was she going to deal with Nicholas's mother? He'd be furious if he ever found out what she had done. More importantly he'd be hurt. She could never tell him about that. She didn't want to be responsible for adding any more dynamite to an already explosive situation.

Camille was sitting in her chair, staring out the window when Nicholas entered the classroom.

Nicholas sensed that something was wrong. It was as though her mind was a thousand miles away.

"Camille."

She turned at the sound of his voice.

"Is something wrong?" Nicholas asked.

"No. Nothing."

"You're not a very good liar, you know. Tell me what has happened."

"I really don't want to get into it, Nicholas." She glanced at the clock on the wall and realized it was well past time for her to leave. "What are you doing here? You're not scheduled to work at the Center this afternoon."

"I had a late lunch with a client at a restaurant near here. I was on my way home when I saw your car in the lot and wondered what you were doing still here. I knew you were supposed to leave at twelve today."

"I had a few progress reports to finish." She stood up and groaning, massaged her aching neck.

Nicholas stepped over to her and made her turn

around so he could take over the job.

"Oh, that feels wonderful." She moaned her pleasure. "Your touch is firm and yet comforting at the same time."

"Thank you, Madame. Any time I can be of service."

She eased away from Nicholas and turned to face him.

Their eyes met.

"Camille." Nicholas felt his heartbeat accelerate. He lowered his lips to hers and tasted her and groaning brushed his tongue across them. Camille opened her mouth allowing him entrance.

Nicholas wove his fingers in her hair, massaging, stroking her head. Camille closed her eyes enjoying his touch and his lips, as his tongue caressed hers.

His hands moved as if with a life of their own down her throat to her full breasts. He felt Camille's nipples harden and peak beneath the thin material of her dress. When she let out a low blissful sound, he slipped his fingers inside her bra and caressed the taunt peaks. He soon left them, moving both hands around to her back and down to the firm slope of her buttocks and squeezed gently.

"Oh, Camille, what you do to me. I want you so

much."

"And I want you. We can go to my house."

"Your mother and brother."

"I have a house of my own."

"Are you sure you want to do this, Camille?"

"Let's go."

He swallowed past the lump in his throat. "As much as I want to make love to you, I want you to be sure this is what you really want. Once I make you mine there will be no turning back."

What would it be like to belong to Nicholas, to truly belong to him, she wondered. The attraction between them was magnetic and so completely overpowering. Yet there was more to it than just chemistry. They were on the brink of sharing something more important than just their bodies, something as precious as the children they had created. Was it love?

Nicholas studied the emotions as they ebbed and flowed across her face as he waited for her answer.

She touched her fingers to his lips. "I want you, Nicholas."

He relaxed and smiled. "Your wish is my command."

He kissed Camille again and again each kiss sweeter than the last until they were both weak and breathless with need.

"I think we'd better go right now while I can still drive in relative comfort," he said moving a few steps away from her. The brush of his pants against his responsive flesh was almost painful.

Camille had felt the ridge of his arousal against her stomach. She could feel the dew from her womanhood seep onto her panties, attesting to her own state of arousal.

"I agree, we should."

* * *

Twenty minutes later Camille let herself into her house in Treme. Nicholas was right behind her and immediately closed the door, pulling her body flush against his.

"You're so soft and so beautiful you take my breath away, Camille," he whispered in her ear and then kissed it.

Camille shuddered, her mind taking in his words and her body glorying in the contact with his.

Nicholas unbuttoned Camille's dress and peeled it and her slip down her body, ardently kissing her shoulders and bare back as he did so. She whimpered when he undid the clasp of her bra and his fingers grazed a nipple. He tossed the bra to the floor. Then he dragged her panties down her thighs and she stepped out of them.

Eager to feel her, Nicholas slipped his fingers around to the juncture between her legs and delved two of them inside her and caressed the bud of her desire with his thumb.

Camille nearly melted against him. "Oh, Nicholas." she gasped.

"Yes, my darling." He moved frenzied fingers in her desire-dampened passage. Nicholas groaned when he felt her essence creamed over his fingers. He stroked and circled her sensitized kernel of flesh repeatedly until her breathing came in ragged, jerky gasps as the pleasure escalated to the fever pitch.

"Nicholas, I want to feel your naked skin against mine."

"Soon, my darling. I want to please you."

"Oh, you are. You are." Then all thought was suspended when the next movement of his fingers brought her to climax. As Camille reveled in wave after wave of sheer enjoyment, Nicholas quickly undressed.

When she turned and saw his hardened male strength rise upward, Camille's breath sucked in and she slid her fingers around him.

"You are magnificently made, Nicholas Cardoneaux," she said worshipfully.

At her words he tenderly kissed her lips.

"Camille, I love you so much."

"Oh, Nicholas, do you? Do you really or is it - "

He hushed her words with another kiss and said. "I love you." And lifted her in his arms. "Where is your bedroom, my darling?"

She looped her arms around his neck and instructed him where he would find the place he sought. Nicholas shouldered the door open and carried Camille inside, then lowered her onto the bed, and joined her.

Nicholas moved Camille onto her back and himself between her thighs and with a slow tunneling motion delved his hardened male organ deep inside her. Camille arched her hips upward almost off the bed as rapture undulated through her femininity.

"Nicholas, oh, Nicholas."

He was momentarily lost in a sea of pleasure that he'd never experienced before with any other woman. He kissed Camille deeply, then delivered little nipping kisses to her face and throat. Camille rubbed her face against his lips and placed equally fervent kisses on his throat.

Nicholas growled and moved her hips against his, being careful not to put too much weight on the swell of her stomach. Again and again he stroked and withdrew, stroked and withdrew, each time building the pleasure a little higher. He eased a little away and rubbed her essence-slick pearl of passion with his fingers.

Camille cried out as the fire ignited and the erect nodule just beyond the damp folds of her womanhood began to pulsate. Deep inside her feminine passage a quivery sensation reverberated with each thrust Nicholas employed. Pleasure began to rise like a huge wave until it reached wild tide shattering proportions and washed over her body. She had never felt such complete fulfillment before.

Nicholas felt her throbbing flesh pulse against his shaft as he delved deeper.

"Camille, oh, God, yes. Yes, oh yes," he shouted in male triumph and closed his eyes as his climax exploded and flung him into a sensuous universe.

His voice unsteady and his breathing labored, he rasped out. "You have given me more than anyone ever has. Not just physical satisfaction, it goes beyond that. You're giving me two beautiful babies besides your own sweet self. Camille. You are mine now and forever."

"As you are mine, Nicholas. And I love you."

* * *

As they lay still entwined, Camille fell asleep with a smile on her lips. Nicholas traced a finger down her nose and over her lips. Then kissed a path down her throat, to her breasts and finally her stomach and in that next moment one of the babies pushed against his mouth, proof that their children flourished inside the woman he loved.

What he held in his arms was more precious than anything in his life.

Nicholas caressed Camille's stomach, then moved his fingers lower delving inside her moist cavern, gently awakening her from sleep. A soft murmur left her lips and she parted her thighs allowing him better access to the place she wanted him to touch. He drew a shuddering response from her and she climaxed. While she was floating in euphoria, he moved in front of her and resting back on his heels eased Camille's hips forward, splaying her thighs over his. He buried his throbbing flesh deep within, moving forward and then retreating once and then again, relishing the slid in and out of her. Again and again, and yet again he repeated the action. He felt his seed leave his groin. Seconds later his essence shot free, splashing against Camille's womb.

"I love you, Nicholas."

"I love you more, my sweet wonderful darling."

They fell into a deep sleep, Nicholas's arms protectively wrapped around Camille's stomach.

* * *

Camille opened her eyes. The room was dark which meant it was probably very late. Her mother and brother would be worried. She had left her cell phone at home that morning. Nicholas's phone was in his car. She eased out of his embrace and off the bed, padded across the room and stepped out into the hall to the linen closet and retrieved a towel and a candle.

Nicholas awoke to find himself alone in the bed.

"Camille."

"I'm here. We need to get dressed. My mother will be wondering what happened to me. I hadn't intended to stay so long. There's no electricity, our only light is this candle. We'll have to feel our way around to find our clothes."

"You're not sorry that we made love, are you?" he asked.

"No, never. I meant it when I told you I loved you."

"I'm so glad to hear you say that, Camille." He pulled her into his arms and kissed her.

"Nicholas, stop," she murmured, but the tremor in her voice belied the meaning of her words.

"I want to love you one more time before we leave."

As he caressed her breasts Camille melted. Nicholas laid her on the bed and made slow sweet love to her.

* * *

"We have to go now, Nicholas," Camille said when she could catch her breath.

"I know. Your brother is liable to call out the National Guard if I don't get you home."

As he drove, Camille called her mother on Nicholas's cell phone.

"I'll be home in a few minutes, Mama. All right. Bye."

"What did she say?"

"She was relieved that I was all right. Jamal was just about to go out looking for me. And guess where he was going to begin his search."

"My house, which means he's going to demand explanations."

"I'm not a child. He wouldn't."

"I think it doesn't matter to him that you're the eldest. You're his sister and he's protective of you."

Minutes later, Nicholas parked in front of the Parker house, the porch light came on and Jamal strode out the front door, Hazel following close on his heels.

"Are you really all right, sugar? Where's your car? You didn't have an accident or - "

"I left it at the Center. And no I wasn't in an accident. As I told you on the phone, I'm fine, Mama. I was with Nicholas."

Jamal's eyes narrowed as he took in Camille's wrinkled dress and slightly tangled hair and kiss-swollen lips and Nicholas's shirt collar smeared with lipstick stains and minus his tie.

"I don't have to ask what the two of you have been doing. I can already guess."

"I love her, Jamal."

"No, you don't. You just want the babies and you'll do or say anything to get your way."

"That's not true, Jamal," Camille cried.

Jamal took a step toward Nicholas.

Camille put a hand on her brother's arm. "Jamal, I'm a grown woman."

"Meaning, you wanted him to -"

"Make love to me? Yes, I did." Camille turned to Nicholas. "I think you'd better go. It's getting late and I have to be at the Center early in the morning."

"I'll drive you there. Camille, I - "

"Please, Nicholas. We'll talk tomorrow."

"All right." To Jamal, he said. "I didn't plan this."

"Tell me anything."

"Jamal," Hazel chided.

"I'll see you in the morning, Camille." Then he strode to his car.

"Don't say anything, Jamal. I don't want to hear it. If my being with Nicholas bothers you, I can move back to my own place."

"I don't want you to do that."

"Then back off. Let me and Nicholas decide what we want to do with our lives."

"I hate to see you get hurt, Camille."

"Nicholas would never hurt me."

"I hope you're right and that you know what you're doing." Jamal left his mother and Camille on the porch and went inside the house.

"You love him, don't you, sugar?"

"Yes, I do, Mama."

"It's not going to be easy."

"I know."

Chapter Seventeen

Just as Nicholas was passing his mother's bedroom on the way to the west wing, she opened her door.

"You've been with *her*, haven't you?"

Nicholas sighed. "If you're referring to the mother of my children? Yes, I have. And?"

"You've become so disrespectful to me, your own mother, since getting involved with that woman. You won't be satisfied until you've destroyed your life. Will you? She's not worth it, Nicholas."

"Mother, I'm going to ask Camille to be my wife."

"What? You don't know what you're saying!"

"But I do. I love her."

"You only think you do. It's not her you love. It's the babies you want. And you've convinced yourself, that in order to have them you have to love their mother. But they are not yours, Nicholas."

"We've had this conversation before and I don't intend to get into it again. I was willing to give you until my children were born to adjust." Nicholas quirked his lips into an angry line. "But I've changed my mind. I'll be packed and out of here as soon as I can, Mother."

Suzette stretched out her hand to her son. "No, Nicholas, you can't just leave. This is your home."

"It hasn't felt like it lately. As soon as I've made all the arrangements for the ceremony, I'll let you know. I hope you'll come to my wedding."

"You're asking me to be a party to helping you ruin your life! Well, I won't do it."

"All right, fine. If that's your choice, Mother, so be it." Nicholas continued on down the hall to his apartment.

Once inside his bedroom, Nicholas leaned back against the door and closed his eyes. He'd hoped that it wouldn't come to this. He realized now that he'd been living in a fool's paradise to think otherwise. With a heavy sigh, he opened his eyes and moved away from the door and headed for the bathroom to shower.

As he slipped between the sheets fifteen minutes later, his thoughts were on Camille and what they had shared. She was everything he'd ever wanted and dreamed of in a woman. She was not only beautiful outside, but inside as well. Camille was sexy, passionate, loving and giving. And he was proud that she was the mother of his children and the recipient of his love.

At the thought of how passionately she made love turned his male organ hard as granite. God, he wished she was there beside him. Or better still beneath or on top of him. He replayed the moment they'd reached fulfillment together that last time.

He wanted to ask Camille to marry him. He wondered what her answer would be when he did? She'd said that she loved him.

That doesn't mean that she'll agree to marry you.

She had to. He loved her with all that was in him. And it wasn't just because of the babies. Camille was a beautiful person. She had to say yes.

What if she doesn't? What then Cardoneaux?

* * *

Nicholas picked Camille up the following morning and they stopped at Cafe du Monde on their way to the Center and ordered orange juice and beignets.

"What happened between us was beautiful and so special, Camille."

"Yes, it was," she sighed, smiling dreamily.

"It doesn't have to end. Marry me, Camille."

Her smile faded and she kneaded her bottom lip with her teeth.

He frowned. "Don't you want to marry me? You

said that loved me."

"I do, but marriage... I don't know, Nicholas. I - I didn't expect you to ask me to marry you because we made love."

"It's not for that reason I'm asking you to be my wife."

"For the sake of our babies, then?"

He took her hands in his. "No, my darling. Listen to me. It's because I love you and for no other reason."

Camille gazed into his eyes. "Are you sure, Nicholas?"

"I'm positive." He beamed his bone-melting smile on her.

"If not for my pregnancy we might never have met."

"Probably not, but we have met."

"Yes, we have." Camille eased her hand away.

Nicholas quickly reclaimed it. "You did mean it when you said that you loved me, didn't you?"

"Oh yes, never doubt that, but..."

"But what?" He rubbed his thumb across the back of her hand. "What about your mother and my brother, Nicholas?"

His brows crinkled. "What about them?"

"I know you said we shouldn't let what they think

influence our decisions, but how can we not. They are our family." Camille paused before going on. "Does your mother know how you feel?"

"Yes, I told her last night that I planned to ask you to marry me."

"And what was her reaction?" She didn't wait for his response. "It's okay. You don't have to answer. I can see it in your eyes. She's never going to accept me, Nicholas," Camille said sadly.

"In time - "

She shook her head. "No. I don't think time will help, Nicholas. She's always going to hate me."

"I'm sure she doesn't hate you. She just - "

"Nicholas, don't make excuses for her. She sees me as some kind of threat to her family. An enemy."

"Whatever she sees you as, it doesn't matter. Nothing is going to make me stop loving you, Camille. Will you marry me?"

"I need time to think."

"Will time change how you feel about me?"

She lowered her eyes. "No."

"Look, I don't want to pressure you."

"You're not." Camille brought his hand to her lips. "You're just expressing your feelings. I have to be true to myself, Nicholas. I have to be sure I'm doing the right thing for the right reason."

Disappointment jabbed him like the sharp point of a needle. But he wasn't giving up on her. If she needed time then he'd give it to her. Nicholas only hoped it wouldn't take too long and her answer would be yes. He wanted Camille for his wife and he wouldn't settle for anything less than marriage. He'd convince her somehow before the babies were born. He wanted all four of them to be a family. If he had anything to say about it they would be that and soon.

* * *

For the rest of the day Camille found it hard to concentrate on her work and her students. She knew that she loved Nicholas, but marriage...

Instead of going straight home after leaving the Center, Camille called her mother to tell her she'd be late. Next she stopped at a florist shop, then drove out to the St. Louis Cemetery. She got out of her car and walked up the incline to her father's grave.

"Oh, Daddy, I miss you so much." She knelt down and placed the flowers on his grave. "God knows that I need you more now than ever. I know it was your dream that I become a famous jazz pianist and I disappointed you and mama when I decided to give it all up to marry Elroy and teach instead."

Camille rose to her feet. "Daddy, I want you to know that I don't regret my decision. About teaching anyway. Teaching is what I've always wanted to do."

Camille splayed her hands across her stomach and smiled. "I'm carrying your grand-children, Daddy, a girl and a boy. I'm going to name the boy after you. I wish you could be here when they're born to love and spoil them rotten.

"Right now I have a hard decision to make and I so wish you were here to advise me. I love Nicholas, but I wonder if I'd be making a mistake in marrying him. He says that he loves me and I believe that he believes it, but considering the circumstance under which we met, I can't be sure.

"Daddy, he's wanted a child so badly for so long. And now that his wish is so close to coming true, I can't help wondering if he's not confusing his love for our babies with what he believes he feels for me.

"Marriage is a big step. I hurried into it with Elroy and thought later that maybe I should have waited."

Camille's eyes came to rest on her late husband's headstone. He'd been dead for over a year, and although she was sorry that he had died, she was also relieved to be herself again. Surely that didn't make her disloyal or a bad person.

She sighed. This was a question only she could answer. No one else. She turned and left the cemetery and headed for home.

Camille went to her house in Treme and sat down at the piano and played a tune that in the past seemed to always have a calming affect on her frazzled nerves whenever the pressure from performing had become too much.

Her babies squirmed around inside her for a few minutes before settling down. It was as if the music was a tranquilizer and had the power to calm them. She wished that it the same effect on her.

* * *

When she pulled up in front of the house, Camille saw Deja sitting on the porch with her headphones on, listening to music. She pushed them down around her neck as her friend approached.

"You look like you're carrying the weight of the world around on your shoulders, girlfriend."

"I feel like it, too."

"So what's up with you?"

Camille sat down beside her. "Nicholas has asked me to marry him."

"Say what? You told him yes, I hope."

"No, I didn't."

Deja's eyes widened. "Surely you're not going to

turn him down!"

Camille didn't answer.

"He's one gorgeous hunk of man. If you haven't noticed."

"Believe me, I've noticed."

"And?"

"Deja, please."

"Please what? The man must really care for you to ask."

"I'm sure that he does. After all I'm pregnant with his babies."

"Babies? You're having more than one!"

"You didn't know? I'm having twins - a boy and a girl.

"That's off the hook!"

"A boy and a girl. Isn't it wonderful."

For the first time in her life, Deja was speechless.

"Jamal knows. He didn't tell you?"

"He certainly did not."

"I'm not surprised considering, how he feels about Nicholas and the whole situation.

"That shouldn't matter. It's how you feel that counts. It's your life. If he can't accept that then oh well."

"Jamal isn't the only obstacle. Nicholas's mother hates me and doesn't believe the babies are his."

"Nicholas does though. Right?

Camille nodded.

"Then forget about what she thinks or believes. Twins, huh? Well you go girl! How about that!"

"I wish it were that simple."

"The way I see it, it is. You love Nicholas. Don't try to deny it. It's in your eyes when you look at him and I've heard it in your voice whenever you talk about him."

"I'm not denying it. I do love him. And because I do - oh never mind."

"If you love him, marry him."

"He's asked you to marry him, Camille?" Jamal demanded from behind the screen door before he walked out on the porch with two soft drinks in his hands.

"Tell me you didn't say, yes!"

Deja rose off the swing. "Jamal, she loves him."

"You need to stay out of it."

"You're the one who needs to back off, Jamal."

"Please, you two, don't argue. Jamal, I haven't given him my answer."

"But you're thinking about saying yes. Right? You're asking - no begging - to be hurt and humiliated, Camille. That mother of his can hardly wait to heap it on you."

"I won't be marrying her, Jamal."

"Wake up, sister girl. You'll be marrying into her family. Same thing."

What Nicholas had said to Camille about not letting other people dictate their relationship came back to her. He was right. It was up to them to decide what they wanted to do.

"Whether I marry Nicholas or not will be my decision, Jamal. Not yours. Not his mother's. I'm going in the house. I'm tired."

Chapter Eighteen

From the second-story loggia outside of his bedroom in the west wing, Nicholas stood looking out over Magnolia Grove. This house had been home to him all his life and now it somehow felt strange, foreign.

He walked over to the outside staircase and down the steps. It was the beginning of summer, the night was warm and humid, and the sweet smell of magnolias, oleanders, azalea's, moist earth and the Mississippi river surrounded him. The house was only half a mile away from the river, and he could see it from here. Built by his great-great-grandfather in the early 1700's, it hadn't changed that much over the years. But the Mississippi had reclaiming a little more of the land as time moved on.

This place was a part of his, his brother's and their future children's legacy. It hurt even considering leaving it, but he would do whatever he had to for a life with Camille and his children.

It's not a sure thing that she'll say yes.

No, it wasn't. Even if she turned him down, he would still leave Magnolia Grove because he refused to subject his son and daughter to his mother's prejudices.

Earlier he'd talked to the head of the real estate department at Cardoneaux Construction about the last house the company had completed.

"You were awfully quiet at dinner, Nick," Phillip said walking up beside his brother.

"I didn't have anything to say. I've asked Camille to marry me."

"Why, that's wonderful!" He laughed and then was quiet. "She didn't turn you down, did she?"

"No, but she didn't say yes either. And she might not."

"Mother?"

"And her brother."

"Surely she's not going to let them influence her decision!"

"I hope she won't, but there is that possibility."

"I saw the maids packing your things. You're really serious about moving out, aren't you?"

"You thought I wasn't?"

"I was hoping..."

"That mother would change her mind? Or I'd change mine? You know me better than that. Once I've made up my mind - "

"What you say is chiseled in stone. That's that, then. Judging from the set expression on mother's face she's not going to budge or bend."

"I figured as much. I don't think that even finding out the babies are mine will make any difference. Sometimes I just want to shake her. Make her realize - what's the use?"

"It's something she has to come to grips with, Nick. If she doesn't accept Camille into the family everyone will suffer, especially the children."

"She doesn't seem to care. And that worries me. What will I tell my children when they're old enough to ask questions?"

"That's a hard one, Nick. I don't envy you, man."

* * *

Camille came down to breakfast and found her mother sitting at the kitchen table enjoying her morning coffee.

"Where did you go after leaving the Center yesterday, sugar?"

"Out to the cemetery," Camille said, taking a seat across from her mother. "I wanted to be close to daddy. I miss him so much."

"I know you do. So do I. I really loved that man."

"I always wanted a marriage like yours and daddy's."

"And it wasn't like that between you and Elroy, was it? Don't look so shocked. I knew you weren't blissfully happy with him, although you tried hard to keep me from finding that out."

"Mama, Nicholas has asked me to marry him."

"From your expression I take it you haven't said yes?" She said sipping her coffee.

"No. I love him, but... Nicholas is willing to give up his home for me and our babies not to mention his relationship with his mother."

"And you're not sure you want him to?"

"What if he eventually grows to hate me because of it?"

"I don't think that'll happen. The man has his priorities straight. He knows what's important. It's you and his children. The Bible says a man will leave his mother and become one flesh with his wife." Hazel smiled sympathetically at her daughter. "I'm sorry I can't tell you what you should do, sugar. If you truly love him you'll find the answer that's right for you."

* * *

Nicholas, Camille, Jolie and Henri went to the Greek Festival together the end of May. Then the first weekend of June they went to the Tomato Festival and watched the cooking demonstrations, tasting and listening to the music performed at the French Market. And they also went sailing on the Creole Lady. During that time Camille still hadn't made a decision. She recalled her grandfather saying that indecision was the thief of time.

Today they were at the park and Jolie and Henri had brought their two children, Brian and Crystal. Nicholas and Henri had taken the children and had gone to get Camille and Jolie lemonades from a near-by refreshment stand.

"You seem preoccupied, Camille. Is anything wrong?" Jolie gave her a smile that encouraged confidences. "I am a good listener."

"Yes, you are." With a world-weary sigh she said. "Nicholas has asked me to marry him."

"I see. I won't ask if you love each other. It's obvious from the looks that pass between you two. Does Suzette Cardoneaux have anything to do with why you haven't said yes?"

"Partly. There is so much to consider, Jolie. I wanted to ask you something."

"Ask away."

"I don't know how to ask this."

Jolie smiled. "You're worried about what your

children will have to face coming from an interracial background. You know that my father is white and my mother is black and Spanish."

"Yes, I do. Nicholas told me. You don't mind my asking, do you?"

"Of course not. I can tell you this. It wasn't easy for my parents, especially back a few years ago. You see I'm darker than my brother and sister who look exactly like our father. It was harder for them than for me because they were tempted to pass for white. They thought they'd be accorded more respect and treated better.

"Then again, they sometimes felt out of place and envied my darker skin. My mother and father helped them see that it wasn't what color they were on the outside, it was the kind of person they were on the inside that mattered. They encouraged all of us
to be our own person and be true to ourselves. And that's what you're going to have to do. Your children are going to need both you and their father to help teach them to be proud of both sides of their heritage."

"You sound so sure that I'm going to marry Nicholas."

"You love him, don't you?"

* * *

During the ride to her house, Camille was

uncharacteristically quiet. And just before they got to the corner of her mother's street, she turned to Nicholas.

"Would you mind if we went to my house first?"

"Your house. Which means that whatever you have to say you don't want to say it in front of your brother. Right?"

"Nicholas, please."

"All right."

When they arrived at her house, Camille led Nicholas through a side gate that opened into the rose arbor. To the right there was a wrought-iron bench beneath an old oak tree.

After both had sat down, Nicholas asked. "Have you - Are you going to marry me, Camille?"

Camille saw the anxious look in his eyes and realized how hard this had been on him. She took one of his hands in hers.

"The answer is yes, I'll marry you." She smiled. "That is if you still want me."

"Still want you! Oh, Camille, you've made me the happiest man on the planet. I love you so much, my darling." He drew her into his arms and kissed her.

After Nicholas finally freed her lips, Camille asked. "When do you want to get married?"

"As soon as it can be arranged." He started kissing her again. He couldn't seem to get enough of the sweet taste of her mouth. He cupped her breasts, then caressed her stomach and next gently squeezed her buttocks. When he felt himself harden, he groaned.

Camille's legs felt the consistency of jelly when she stood up. She urged Nicholas toward the summer porch in back of the house. It was blacked out, screened in and private. She led him inside and over to the double bed.

"I want you so much, Nicholas."

"Not as much as I want you." He began to slowly undress her, kissing every inch he uncovered. He smiled as he looked at her stomach and gave it an extra kiss. Then he quickly undressed himself. He turned Camille onto her side, her back against his front. Raising himself up on an elbow, he lifted her leg with his other hand, and slid his manhood between the damp folds of her femininity. A low sensual moan of ecstasy left her lips when he entered her. Nicholas began a slow steady gliding motion, in and out again and yet again.

Camille cried out as the friction-rubbing slide of his hardened flesh moved inside her and Nicholas built the fire hotter and higher.

"Oh, yes, Nicholas. Baby, yes," she murmured.

He continued his addictive rhythm as they moved

closer and closer to climax. Each time his maleness delved it was deep and true, touching her passion-swollen pearl, now throbbing with pleasure, eager to find rapturous release. When it came, Camille felt herself fly apart and soar to the heavens.

Nicholas was right with her, enjoying every nuance of fulfillment.

"I must say the future Mrs. Cardoneaux certainly knows how to put a seal on a marriage proposal," Nicholas teased.

"You aren't so bad at that area yourself." Camille was touched by his consideration for her burgeoning belly, by making love in a position that wouldn't put any pressure on her stomach.

"I love you, Nicholas Cardoneaux."

The next time they made love she went up on all fours and he entered from behind, once more giving her exquisite pleasure and ultimate satisfaction.

It had begun to grow dark when they left the house in Treme.

* * *

"Mrs. Parker, and Jamal, Camille has consented to be my wife," Nicholas proudly announced when they arrived at her mother's house.

Jamal's jaw tightened. "Are you sure you want to

do this, Camille?" he asked.

"Yes, Jamal. I love Nicholas."

"I think you're making a huge mistake, but I know you're not going to take my advice," he said and strode from the living room out the front door.

"Don't mind him, sugar. I'm happy for you both." Hazel looked to her daughter. "I believe you've made the right decision for you both and the babies." There were tears in her eyes. She shifted her gaze to Nicholas. "You'd better make my baby happy."

"I intend to, Hazel. Since I love her, I can wish to do nothing else." He kissed the older woman's cheek. Then turned to Camille. How does the fourteenth of July sound?"

"It's my birthday."

"And it will be the birth of a new life for both of us, my darling."

Camille frowned. "What about your mother?"

"She won't be coming to the wedding. We don't need her." Camille hoped he still felt that way down the road.

"We'll have plenty of people around who will support us. They'll be only too glad to help us celebrate our happiness."

"Sugar, play something for us," Hazel urged her

daughter.

"Mama, I - "

"Please, Camille," Nicholas said with an irresistibly beseeching smile.

"All right." She sat before the piano and played a tune she'd written. Nicholas was completely captivated by her as well as her music.

When she had finished, he clapped. "Encore. Encore."

"Nicholas."

"We want to hear more, right, Hazel?"

"Just one more, sugar."

Caught up entirely in her music, Camille didn't see the look of longing in her mother's face, but Nicholas saw it. He was reminded of a similar look he'd seen on his mother's once. He recalled how much she'd wanted him to pursue a career as an artist. It made him sad to be at odds with her, but he wouldn't give in on this. Camille was too important to him. It was time his mother put her prejudices in the past and looked to the future.

He was sure there was a deep-seated reason for her attitude apart from anything he'd ever expect. His mother was full of contradictions. He wondered if he would he ever really understand her.

* * *

An hour later Camille walked Nicholas out to his car.

When they stopped in front of it, he placed his hands on her shoulders and smiled at her. "You have no idea how happy you've made me, Camille." He bent his head and kissed her. "I want you to know how much you mean to me. And I intend to continue telling you and showing you the rest of our lives."

"Oh, Nicholas."

He drew her into his chest and just held her.

"Pretty soon my stomach will be in the way and you won't be able to hold me like this. So you'd better take advantage of the opportunity while you can."

Nicholas grinned. "I love hearing you laugh, Camille." He cupped her face and placed a long, emotion-packed kiss on her lips. "I can hardly wait to make you my wife. You'll belong to me, heart, body and soul."

"I already do."

"I hate leaving you. July 14th can't come soon enough for me. On that day we'll make our commitment official."

"As far as I'm concerned it already is."

"I love you so much, Camille."

"As I love you."

Chapter Nineteen

"Judging from the look on your face you've convinced the King woman to accept your proposal," Suzette said as Nicholas entered the living room at Magnolia Grove.

"Yes, Mother, she has."

"Well that's that."

"I refuse to let your attitude bring me down. If you can't be happy for me there's nothing I can do about that."

"You're my son and I love you. Don't you think I want your happiness more than anything? I know it doesn't lie with this woman."

Nicholas's jaw clenched. "Can't you even say her name, Mother? It's Camille."

"Whatever, Nicholas." Suzette walked out of the room.

Nicholas let out a tired breath and strode over to the bar and poured himself a brandy. He'd said that he wouldn't let his mother get to him, but she and her attitude had gotten under his skin anyway. He never dreamed they would ever be at odds about something they'd both wanted for him for so long.

"Nick."

"Phillip."

"Camille turned you down," he said entering the room. "And that's why you're drinking."

"No." Nicholas took a swallow of his brandy. "On the contrary, she said yes."

"Then?" Phillip hunched his shoulders in bewilderment.

Nicholas took another sip. "I let our mother get to me."

"I take that to mean she knows and disapproves big-time."

"She knows all right and she more than disapproves. She's dead set against it. She believes my marriage to Camille will end up ruining my life."

"That bad, huh?"

Nicholas nodded. "But then we knew it would be."

Phillip walked over to his brother and squeezed his shoulder. "I don't know what to tell you, man."

"There's nothing anyone can say," he replied, swirling his brandy around in the glass. "Somehow, some day I'm going to find out what made mother this way." His mouth suddenly eased into a smile. "Camille and I have decided to get married on July 14th. You know who I'll want; you for my best man."

"You got it." Phillip answered, then gave his brother a big bear hug.

* * *

"You think you can have my wedding dress finished by then?" Camille asked Deja several days later while they were eating lunch at a sidewalk cafe.

"You said yes to the hunk. Well hallelujah! You'd better believe I'll have it ready. I'm so happy for you, girl."

Camille smiled at Deja's enthusiasm. Her friend worked as a seamstress for one of the exclusive bridal shops in New Orleans.

Deja's eyes lit up. "I have a few designs of my own I've been working on for when I open my own shop. I want you to see them."

"That's exciting, Deja. I'd love to."

"I'm curious, Camille. What made you decide to marry Nicholas?"

"I realized that I was wasting time I could be spending with the man I loved. And where love is concerned there are no guarantees. The perfect time or situation doesn't exist. If you truly love someone you have to be willing to take a chance. I'm ready to take that chance on Nicholas."

"What about his mother? And Jamal?"

"They're entitled to their opinions. I know one thing, I can't live my life according to their likes and dislikes. This is my life and Nicholas's. We deserve to be happy. Our babies deserve to be raised by parents who love them and each other."

"You go, girl."

"I'm meeting Nicholas later this afternoon. He says he has a surprise for me, but wouldn't even give me a hint as to what it
could be."

Deja looked at Camille's hand. "He hasn't given you a ring yet. Maybe that's it."

Camille smiled. "Could be."

"I love seeing you like this. Your face lights up when you talk about Nicholas. Did you know that?"

"He lights up my life. You remember that song?"

"I remember. I used to think that about your brother."

"Used to?"

"All right I still do," she admitted, "but don't tell him that. It'll go to his head. And trust me, it's big enough already."

"He doesn't realize how fortunate he is to have you."

"He will in time. I intend to make sure of that." She grinned.

And with that they began to harmonize: "You-light-up-my-life..."

* * *

"Nicholas, where are you taking me?" Camille asked, sitting next to him in the car with her eyes closed as he drove. The traffic sounds had changed. First lowering, then going quiet. A few minutes later she smelled flowers.

"We're almost there, but don't open your eyes yet. Keep them closed just a little while longer." He could hardly wait for Camille to see his surprise. He hoped she liked it. He stopped the car. "You can open your eyes now."

When she did, he asked. "Well, do you like the house?"

Her eyes widened in wonder. "You bought this?"

"Well not exactly. I designed it, though. It's one among many my company has built. We can move in as soon as possible. That is if you want to." Nicholas watched Camille's face, gauging her reaction. He saw how her eyes twinkled with excitement.

As he drove through the magnificent alley of newly planted tree Camille was reminded of the alley of oaks leading up to the to the Cardoneaux mansion at Magnolia Grove.

Nicholas pulled up in front of the house, got out and walked around to the passenger side to help Camille.

She recalled as a child how her father had driven their family through the Lafayette District on Sundays. As she observed some of the neighboring houses it was like watching a scene from the past suddenly come to life. She found it hard to believe that she might actually live and raise her own family in this exclusive area.

Nicholas reached for her hand and gave it a little tug. "Come on, let me take you on a tour."

Camille knew in that moment how important she was to him. He was willing to leave Magnolia Grove and move into this house with her and their babies. She knew what a sacrifice he was making for her and she intended to make sure he never regretted his decision. She was going to be the best wife he could ever wish for.

The similarity to Magnolia Grove stopped with the alley of trees. The elegant aquamarine painted, two-story house was unique. It was built on a slope, nestled perfectly into the side of a hill.

"I don't know quite what to say."

"The house should be ready to move into before our wedding. Though we won't get to enjoy it until after we get back from our honeymoon"

"Honeymoon? Nicholas."

"But before I show you around. First things first." He took a small square box from his pocket, opened it and lifted out a three karat, diamond ring with sapphires encircling it and placed it on her finger.

"Oh, Nicholas, it's exquisite." Camille gasped and happy tears spilled from her eyes. She threw her arms around his neck. "I love you so much. It's hard to believe that in just six weeks I'll be your wife."

"Yes, you will. It's too late for you to change your mind."

"Change my mind? Not a chance, mister." Her expression turned serious. "The house is wonderful, but-"

"I'm all right with the move, Camille."

"Are you sure?"

"More than anything I want to be with you. It's not possible for us to be happy living under the same roof as my mother. I'm looking forward to having you all to myself."

"So you can have your wicked way with me?"

"Most definitely. I intend to be an extremely devoted husband and," he lowered his eyelids, "an exceptionally wicked lover. I may just tie you to the bed until time for you to give birth."

"Sounds kinky." She giggled. " And what other interesting diversion do you have in mind for our honeymoon. Now you've got me curious about our destination."

"Make that destinations, my dear lady." He grinned.

"Destinations. Ooh!"

"How does a two week cruise on board the Creole Lady sound?"

"Oh, Nicholas. It sounds fantastic."

When he drew her into his arms, Camille closed her eyes. She was so happy at this moment, she felt the urge to pinch herself to make sure it was real. Reveling in the warmth of his embrace and the comforting solidity of his presence, she knew that in his arms was where she belonged.

* * *

The next weeks found Nicholas and Camille caught up in preparations for the wedding and decorating their new home, picking out and ordering furniture, choosing color schemes. Nicholas left the choice of linen, silverware and appliances to Camille and the decorators.

But he surprised her with the plans he'd drawn

up for transforming the bonus room into a music room for her, which included a huge circular window to let in the daylight and give an added dimension to the room. French doors would open into the garden. Nicholas even purchased a Steinway grand piano and a floor-to-ceiling music étagère to display her awards, plaques and sheet music. Glass cabinets on two walls to house their CD collections.

The circular window scheme started in the living room. The recessed center of the room allowed for an area couch/easy chair/loveseat set. This room had a grand piano.

The master bedroom really impressed Camille. She loved Nicholas's unrestricted use of windows; they were what made the house feel more welcoming. She got to see how exceptionally talented her husband-to-be was. The corner windows were designed up against the ceiling without frames making the space allowed for the window seat to look larger.

Camille saw and had to have a king sized, cherry wood sleigh bed. She had the walls painted a rich burgundy, the moldings were cream. The carpet was a thick plush creamy beige.

The bathroom had the look of a Roman bathhouse. Lighted marble steps led into a bathing pool and the windows in there were made from a material that could change with the touch of a button from clear to opaque. Nicholas explained how the windows could in summer with its solar energy properties cool the house. And that in winter hold in the heat. It was an innovative feature he had added to all the houses he designed.

Camille loved Nicholas's art studio and helped him decorate it. Together they decided on a mint green color scheme for the nursery. They left the other two bedrooms and the guest bedrooms to be decorated at a later date.

The grounds were like a paradise with the many flowers and plants and banana trees. Nicholas had designed a retractable awning to cover and heat the pool during winter. The same awning could be used for shade during the summer months.

"I had no idea of the extent of your genius, Nicholas."

"Hardly genius."

"Don't be so modest. I see now why you didn't pursue an artistic career. Your paintings are awesome, my love, but you are an architect first and foremost."

"Flattery will get you just about anything," my dear.

"Only just about?" she said, flashing him a coy

smile.

"Oh, Camille, you're priceless."

"And you, Nicholas Cardoneaux, have no idea how much you mean to me."

"You're going to show me, though, right?" He smiled, then suddenly, he looked into her eyes. "We're going to have a beautiful life together, my darling"

* * *

Deja pulled the dressmaker's pins from Camille's bridal dress. "At the rate you're increasing we'll have to have at least a dozen more fittings before the big day," she quipped.

"That's not even funny, Deja."

"I couldn't resist."

They had decided on a classic floor length, empire-waisted design in ice blue satin. The open sweetheart-shaped neckline and sleeveless bodice drew attention to her delicate collarbone. Deja commented on how the dress made her skin glow. Or maybe it glowed because Camille was in love.

The glow faded when Jamal walked past Camille's room without saying a word.

"Sometimes that brother of yours..."

"He can't help the way he feels, Deja. I'm sure he doesn't like this distance between us anymore than I do."

"You're right he doesn't. He admitted to me the other night how it was tearing him apart."

"But he won't change his mind about coming to my wedding."

"No. How about Nicholas's mother?"

"No change there. She still hates me and is resentful that I dared aspire to become a member of her family."

"She'll get over it."

"You would think so, but I wonder if she ever will."

"She doesn't have a choice if she wants to ever have any kind of relationship with her son and grandchildren."

"That's just it, she doesn't believe they are her grandchildren. She suggested I have a DNA test."

"She's hardcore."

"Well I'm not going to let her spoil things for me and Nicholas. I'll agree to the test if Nicholas ever wants one. So far he hasn't even mentioned it."

"I don't think he cares one way or the other. He loves these babies already. And he certainly loves you, Camille."

"And I love him."

"That's all that matters."

Camille could only hope her friend was right.

Chapter Twenty

"Don't move, Camille," Nicholas said applying another brush stroke to the portrait he was painting of her.

"I don't know why you insist on painting me while I'm in this condition," she complained.

"I happen to think you look absolutely adorable in this condition." His smile turned into a frown. "You're not getting too tired, are you? We can stop for today."

"No, I'm not tired."

"There's only one more week before our wedding and I want to be finished by then. Three more sittings should do it."

"Can I see how it's coming along?"

Nicholas gave it a critical scrutinizing glance. "No, not yet. It's too soon."

"Nicholas."

"Camille."

"Ouch," Camille yelped, rubbing her stomach.

The teasing light went out of Nicholas's eyes.

"Are you all right? "

Camille laughed. "Yes, I'm all right. It's just that our children seem to have moves like a professional soccer player."

Nicholas saw Camille's stomach change shape several times, and he was fascinated. "Does it hurt?"

"Not exactly. It's a feeling I can't quite describe."

He smiled. "Motherhood agrees with you. You have a - "

"Glow? I know. Mama and Deja said the same thing."

"They're right. It's what I hope to capture in my painting. There is an aura about you, Camille."

Nicholas put down his paint brush and walked over to her and kissed her. "I don't know what I did to deserve you, but I'm not going to look a gift horse in the mouth. I would love to ravish you at this very moment, but I'd get paint all over you."

"So what's a little paint?"

"Actually I want to paint a while longer. You keep looking at me like that and I'll never get any work done."

"Oh and why won't you, Mr. Cardoneaux?"

"Saucy wench. You want me to show you?"

"Later. Anticipation excites the heart."

"And arouses the loins."

"You're bad."

"But you love me."

"Yes indeed I do." Camille moved back into her pose. "I'm ready."

Nicholas mixed the paint for the delicate shade of turquoise of her dress. The color highlighted the toffee-brown color of her skin. He could go on all day, but he knew Camille couldn't.

"There that should do it," Nicholas said twenty minutes latter as he applied one last stroke. "That'll be all for today, my darling."

She stretched her arms and swiveled her neck around. "Hurry and clean up. I'll be waiting for you in the music room."

* * *

Camille was sitting on the piano bench when Nicholas walked into the room.

"Play for me?" he entreated with his killer smile.

"What would you like to hear?"

"How about,' Give Me the Simple Life.'"

"That's an old tune, but a good one."

Nicholas sat mesmerized as Camille wove her spell on the keys. Her eyes were closed and she was one with her music. When she finished he was quiet for a moment.

"You are awesome, Camille."

"I wrote a song just for you. Want me to play it for you?"

"Definitely."

"I wanted to express with my music how I feel about you. Something I never seem able to do with words."

Camille began to play, becoming lost in her own world.

Nicholas tried to blink away the moisture pooling in his eyes. The sound floating up from the piano as her fingers fluttered across the keys was so ethereal that a long time after she had finished playing it was as if he could still hear the melody echoing through his head. In that moment Nicholas knew the depths of her feelings for him.

He pulled Camille to her feet and into his arms. And just held her for a long moment before lowering his head and kissing her tenderly on the lips, then again and again as if tasting and savoring wasn't enough.

He smoothed his hand over her hair. "I can hardly wait for you to move into this house with me. That week is going to seem like a month."

"For me, too."

Later he turned off the lights and locked the door

and he and Camille left their home. It was like leaving a sanctuary to go out into the reality of the everyday world. He longed for the time when they would enter this house as husband and wife.

* * *

Nicholas finished the painting two days before the wedding and on the afternoon eve of their marriage he picked his brother up at the hospital. He called Henri and Jolie and had them meet him at the Parker house for the unveiling of Camille's portrait.

Hazel had insisted that Jamal be present. Camille wondered if that was such a good idea. Deja would be there. Maybe she'd have a calming effect him. He didn't want to do anything to upset Deja since they had so recently gotten back together. The knowledge that it didn't seem to matter whether he upset his sister hurt. She and Jamal had been close all their lives and now to be at odds like this... At least it gave her insight into how Nicholas must be feeling about the strain between him and his mother.

Phillip helped Nicholas set up his easel in the center of the living room. Hazel turned on the overhead fanlight giving the room more light, then she, Jamal and Deja stood to one side while Jolie and Henri sat on the couch. Camille stood next to Nicholas. No matter how much she had begged and wheedled, he hadn't let her look at the portrait. Now she was eager, more than eager, to see his artistic perception of her.

Phillip uncovered the painting.

Nicholas monitored everyone's reaction starting with Camille's. She seemed stunned but pleased. A tender loving expression came into her eyes when they met his. He moved on to her brother's, they narrowed and for a moment Jamal seemed to be reassessing his opinion of him. Nicholas hoped he wasn't over-projecting because he wanted to get along with him. He shifted his gaze to Deja who smiled at him and Camille, then gave him a nod and a thumbs up. She was a down-to-earth woman, not judgmental in any way. He liked that about her.

Then he focused on Hazel. There were tears in her eyes.

"You've captured my baby perfectly, Nicholas."

"I have to say, Nick," Phillip commented, "I didn't know you had it in you. It's so real you expect Camille to step out of the canvas at any moment."

"I feel that way too," Jolie added.

Henri stood up and walked over to the painting and reached out as if to touch it, but refrained.

"You must let me display this masterpiece in my gallery, Nicholas. This is the best thing you've ever done.

It is simply magnificent. The love you feel for this woman shines through."

"That's praise coming from you."

"I'm not that critical. Am I?" he said looking to his wife.

"You can be at times, dear," she answered with a smile.

Nicholas had eyes only for Camille. "What do you think? Is it all right with you to display it at the gallery?"

"I can hardly believe that's me. You think I really look like that."

"I tried to capture your vitality and unique beauty."

It touched Camille that he thought she was that beautiful.

"So you can paint. It doesn't mean I want you as a husband for my sister. I think she deserves a lot better than you."

"Jamal," Deja warned.

"Let him have his say. Is it because I'm white you feel this way? I might not deserve her, Jamal, but she has chosen to be with me. Tomorrow she will become my wife. I think you'd better face that fact."

"It's not as though I have a choice."

Camille walked over to her brother and put a hand on his arm. "I need somebody to give me away."

For a moment his face lit up, then the light went out and he said.

"You're my sister and I love you. Don't you think I want to do this for you." A tear slid down his cheek. "But I just can't."

"Jamal," Hazel pleaded.

"I'm sorry, Mama. I just can't."

Camille turned to Henri. "Will you give me away?"

"I would be happy to, Camille."

Jamal brushed the tear from his face and turned around and walked out the front door.

"I'll talk to him, Camille," Deja promised.

"No, please don't. I've noticed lately that he's really been struggling with his feelings."

"That may well be true, sugar, but as far as I'm concerned there can be no excuse for his behavior this evening."

"Miss Hazel is right, Camille."

"Don't come back at him about it, Deja. Okay?"

"But - all right. I won't. He can be so pig-headed."

"I know." Camille smiled. "He wouldn't be Jamal

if he were any other way. You go after him. He needs you."

Hazel invited Phillip, Henri and Jolie to eat gumbo in the dining room.

"We need you at the restaurant, Hazel," Jolie complimented. "This gumbo is fabulous. Undoubtedly the best I've ever tasted. What's your secret?"

"It's my grandmother's recipe," Hazel said proudly. "You season the ingredients to taste."

"In other words it's a pinch of this and a dash of that. Just the way my grandmother cooks." Jolie smiled. "I might have known."

"We'll have to be going," Henri said. "Our sitter has a class this evening." Winking at Nicholas he said. "And I have some place to go later."

Camille intercepted the signal passing between them and looked from one to the other wondering what was going on.

"We'll talk about displaying the painting later, Henri," Nicholas said.

"We'll drop Phillip off at the hospital."

While Nicholas walked Phillip, Jolie and Henri out, Hazel studied the portrait.

"That man really loves you, sugar."

"Yes, he does, and the feeling is definitely mutual, Mama. She sighed. "I just wish that Jamal would see that and stop thinking of Nicholas as the enemy and come to my wedding."

"Maybe he'll change his mind."

"I can only hope, Mama."

Nicholas returned and put an arm around Camille's shoulders. "Tomorrow is the big day. Your last chance to back out."

"Back out? I don't think so. I have very special plans for you, mister. Camille Cardoneaux, I like the sound of that."

"I have to admit that I do too."

Hazel smiled knowingly. "I'm going upstairs so you two can be alone."

As she took her leave, Nicholas couldn't help admiring his future-mother-in-law. And couldn't help wishing his own mother was more like her.

"She'll come around, Nicholas."

"How did you know I was thinking about my mother?"

"I'm psychic. That look in your eyes said it all. I've come to know you pretty well, sir."

They walked out on the porch and sat in the swing. The moon silvering the lawn and trees lent an intimate tranquility to the night.

"You've made me so happy, Camille."

He took her hand and they swung for a while in silence.

Nicholas said at last, "You and the babies are my life."

"As you and they are mine."

"We're going to have one fantastic marriage." Nicholas placed a tender kiss on Camille's forehead.

Camille brought her arms around his waist, then laid her head on his chest.

"We are so lucky to have found each other, Nicholas. What are the odds of something this wonderful happening to us?"

"Probably a million to one." He pressed a gentle kiss on her forehead. "You're my one in a million."

"Other people wish for what we have."

"If only my mother could see that and not consider race or social position as a yard stick to go by."

"Hasn't she ever discussed why she feels the way she does?"

"No."

"Maybe she will in her own time." Camille reached up and touched his cheek and smiled. "But tomorrow is our special time."

"Yes, it is. We start a whole new life. You and I

and our children," he said moving his hand across Camille's stomach." He laughed when he felt a strong kick. "Do you think our little restless natives are as excited about it as we are?"

Camille laughed. "It sure feels like it. I can hardly wait until they are born."

"Me either. I'd better be going. Phillip, Henri and a few friends are throwing a bachelor party for me."

"So that was what all those eye signals were all about. Just make sure you're in shape to show up for the wedding."

"That's one event I definitely won't be late for."

Chapter Twenty-one

"Hold still, Camille, so I can zip up your dress." Deja sighed in frustration.

"I wonder if Nicholas is at the chapel," Camille said worrying her bottom lip with her teeth. "I called him at home earlier and was told he nor Phillip was available."

"If he isn't at the chapel this very moment, he will be by the time you get there. Relax, sugar."

"You don't really know that, Mama. What about that wild bachelor party last night?" Camille looked to Jolie.

"Henri said he made sure Nicholas left at a reasonable hour. I don't remember what time Henri got home because I was asleep, but it must have been as he said."

"Who knows what reasonable is when it comes to men and bachelor parties. One o'clock? Three? Or even six may seem reasonable to them?"

"Everything is going to be all right. You're just suffering from a case of bridal jitters." Jolie smiled sympathetically at Camille. "I've been there and survived them and so will you."

Camille should be able to say the same thing since this was her second marriage. But she couldn't remember feeling this way the first time around.

"Look, if you don't cool it, you'll turn yourself and the rest of us into basket cases," Deja said shaking her head. "I hope this doesn't happen to me on my wedding day."

Camille's face relaxed at the change of subject. "Have you and Jamal decided on a date."

"Ah, no."

"Your decision?"

"Kind of. He's too stressed to think about that right now."

"You mean too obsessed with my relationship with Nicholas. If you're hoping the tension will ease after we're married, that may never happen, Deja."

"After the babies are born and Jamal sees how truly committed and happy you and Nicholas are, he'll accept your marriage."

"I hope so, but if he doesn't I want you to go ahead with your marriage plans. Okay? I want your promise."

"All right, I promise, but in the meantime I'm

going to work on him."

"I wouldn't expect anything less since you're in love with the impossible man."

"It's time to put on your tokens, sugar."

Deja handed Camille a blue garter, her something blue. Jolie gave her a penny to slip inside her shoe, her something borrowed. Her something new was the wedding gown Deja had made for her. Her mother slid a small pearl ring that had belonged to her grandmother on the, her something old.

Camille hugged her mother and her friends. She was so choked up she couldn't speak for a few moments.

"This is the happiest day of my life. I'm marrying the man I love and expecting his babies."

"You're a lucky woman all right," Deja agreed.

"So are you. My brother is a good man. Just be patient with him."

"After the way he's been acting toward you lately how can you not be upset with him."

"Because I love him, Deja. And so do you. Promise me you'll stick by him?"

"Oh, I will. Besides, what would life be without challenges? You have to admit that your brother is definitely one of those."

"I know what you mean about the male challenge," Jolie said sagely. "Henri took work and believe me he still requires continued maintenance. But in the long run I think he's been worth it."

Hazel's eyes misted with emotion when she looked at her daughter. "Xavier would be so proud of you, sugar."

"I wish Daddy could have met Nicholas and been here to give me away. Not that I'm not grateful for Henri, Jolie."

"I know you are," she smiled. Jolie turned to Deja. "I love the dresses you made for all of us, Deja, especially Camille's."

"Thanks, Jolie."

"And just think, I'll have that talent in my family one day soon." Hazel hugged Deja. "You've been like a daughter to me. I hope that son of mine realizes how rich he is."

"I'm sure he does, Miss Hazel," Deja assured her. "Trust me, if he doesn't he will in time."

The sudden peal of the doorbell intruded.

"That must be the chauffeur," Camille said. She and Nicholas had decided to marry at a small wedding chapel. Henri and Jolie insisted on giving them a reception when they returned from their honeymoon. Nicholas had insisted that she be driven to the chapel by chauffeured limousine.

Camille's heartbeat quickened. She recalled feeling this exact same way just before a concert.

Hazel kissed her cheek. "You make a beautiful bride, sugar."

"It's the gown."

"No. It's more than that, Camille. You're absolutely radiant," Jolie remarked.

"It's time to get this show on the road." Camille let out a shaky sigh. "Or else Nicholas will begin to wonder if I'm going to show up."

* * *

Nicholas glanced at his watch, then out the window of the upstairs dressing room at the chapel. From here he had a clear view of the front walk.

"She'll be here, man," Henri said in a reassuring voice. "Calm down."

"I know she loves me. I don't know what's wrong with me."

"You're just nervous."

"You have the ring?" he asked his brother."

"Here somewhere," Phillip said tongue in cheek, searching through his pockets.

"Oh, man. Don't tell me you - "

Phillip held up the ring and laughed. "Gotcha."

"One of these days, Phillip."

"The limo just drove up," Henri said glancing out the window.

Teddy, the minister's son came and informed them that everything was ready and they should come downstairs and take their places.

* * *

Nicholas and Phillip stood waiting at the altar. People who worked with Nicholas at Cardoneaux Construction were there along with a few old friends. Several of Camille's relatives besides her mother were present. It was disappointing that his mother and Camille's brother hadn't changed their minds and decided to come to the wedding. But he wouldn't let either one of them ruin this very special day.

* * *

When she heard a knock on her dressing room door, Camille knew it had to be Henri. Deja and Jolie had just left a few minutes earlier. Releasing a shaky breath, she opened the door.

"I'm ready, Henri." Camille gasped. "Jamal!"

"Yes, it's me, sister-girl."

Henri cleared his throat. "I'll be right down the hall. If you need me, Camille, just call."

"I will."

"I need to talk to you. Can I come in?" Jamal asked after Henri had walked away.

"If you've come here to cause trouble - "

"I haven't."

"All right. You can come in," she said and moved aside.

"After the things I said, you have every right to kick me out. But please hear me out. You don't know what it did to me seeing the pain in your eyes. Pain that I put there by refusing to give you away. We've been close all our lives, and I've never done anything to hurt you and would have hurt anyone else for daring to try.

"When I got home last night mama was up waiting for me. She told me that she was ashamed to call me her son. Her words hurt me to the bottom of my soul. I knew I couldn't live with myself or face her if I didn't come and tell you how sorry I was. And I am sorry, Camille. I may not think Cardoneaux is the right man for you, but that's my problem. You're my sister and I love you. I know I don't deserve it, but I'm asking you to forgive me, sister-girl?"

Camille walked over to him and cupped his face in her hands and made him look at her. When she saw the misery in his emotion-wet eyes, she caressed his cheeks with her thumbs and said. "Of course I forgive you. And

I still want you to give me away." She smiled, happy tears trickling down her cheeks. "You're my brother and I love you very much."

"Sister-girl..."

She silenced him with a reassuring smile, then squeezed his arm. "I think we'd better go downstairs before everyone starts to worry."

* * *

Soft wedding music began to play, as Deja and then Jolie marched down the aisle. Nicholas was stunned to see Jamal and not Henri marching in with Camille on his arm. He'd find out later how that particular miracle came about. But right now the woman he loved was his main focus. At the sight of her, his breath caught in his throat as she made her way toward him. Pride swelled out his chest when he glanced at her stomach. He had it all and his heart was full to bursting.

Camille gasped when she saw Nicholas standing at the altar. He looked so fine in his tux, she thought. The blue of his shirt made his eyes look an even deeper shade of blue.

The minister cleared his throat when both Nicholas and Camille stood before him.

"Nicholas and Camille have agreed to share

every aspect of their lives. Marriage is a serious undertaking. Not one to be entered into lightly. It's a lifetime commitment. They have an added blessing in their coming children..."

Camille didn't hear the rest of what he said. Before she knew it the photographer started flashing pictures as Nicholas placed the wedding ring on her finger.

"With this ring I promise to love you for the rest of my life. I never knew what my life was, until I met you. I want to spend the rest of my days on this earth with you."

As Camille slid a wedding band onto Nicholas's finger, she said. "With this ring I promise to love you until the end of time and beyond. My life was incomplete until the day you walked into it. Your love has made me whole."

"If there are no objections to this union..." The minister waited the obligatory seconds.

For a wild moment Nicholas expected his mother to intervene. He relaxed when it didn't happen and looked into his bride's eyes.

"I pronounce you husband and wife." the minister smiled and added. "You may now kiss your bride."

Nicholas swept the veil back and cupping her face in his two hands, he gently kissed Camille's lips.

Camille closed her eyes and the world seemed to

melt away. "I love you so much," she whispered.

"Enough of that you two," Phillip teased. "Leave something for the honeymoon."

Jolie handed Camille the bouquet of flowers. With a smile, she tossed them to Deja.

"It would seem that my fate is sealed." sShe said with mock seriousness, but her eyes were sparkling. Then she wrapped her arms around Jamal's. "I'm so glad you changed your mind, baby."

"So am I," he said in a low uncharacteristically humble voice.

Hazel smiled and nodded her approvable, then shifted her attention to Camille. "I have to say it again, sugar. You are the most beautiful bride I've ever seen. And I'm not just saying it because you're my daughter either." She sniffed and dried her eyes with her handkerchief.

"I agree, Hazel," Nicholas seconded. "She is."

"You and Camille don't need any rice. You have no fertility problems as far as I see," Phillip said glancing down at Camille's stomach and then at his brother.

"Phillip!" Nicholas warned.

"He's right, you don't," Henri chimed in.

"Not you too, Henri."

"What are friends for?"

Everyone laughed as the happy couple headed up the stairs to their dressing rooms.

After quickly changing his clothes, Nicholas slipped into his new bride's dressing room and locked the door.

"Need some help?" he asked, giving her a hot look of desire.

"Yes, I do. The zipper seems to have gotten stuck," she said in a low sultry voice.

Nicholas unzipped the wedding gown and pushed it and her slip down her body, watching as it slid to the floor. He splayed his hands over her stomach.

"God, you look scrumptious."

"Even with this stomach."

"Because of this stomach." He lowered his head and placed a kiss there. He moved his hands upward and cupped her breasts, then caressed her nipples through the lacey material of her bra with his thumbs.

Camille moaned. "Oh, Nicholas."

At the desire-laced sound in her voice, his breath hissed from his throat, and the muscles in his groin tightened, and his sex hardened into a pleasure/pain erection. "I'd better help you into your- ah - other clothes."

Camille reluctantly agreed. Deja had made her a cool aqua cotton sundress with matching shortsleeve jacket.

Before she could put on the jacket, Nicholas kissed her bare shoulders and traced a path up her neck, kissing the sensitive area behind her ear.

She quivered with delight.

Nicholas turned her to face him, then kissed her lips. "What you do to me, Camille."

"No more than what you do to me, lover man," she said and returned the favor.

* * *

Phillip shot his brother a mischievous look as Nicholas and Camille descended the stairs, then said. "It's about time you two came down. What kept you?"

"Don't answer that, my friend, on the grounds that it might incriminate you, " Henri laughed.

"Give him a break, guys," Deja said.

"Yes, because the limo is waiting," Jolie reminded them.

Nicholas slid his arm around Camille's waist and ushered her out of the chapel. Despite Phillip's earlier comment about fertility, they were showered with rice and the photographer took pictures as they made their way to the limo.

Once inside Nicholas pulled Camille into his arms and kissed her as if there was no tomorrow.

"If we don't stop now our marriage will be consummated in this limo," Nicholas said breathing hard.

"You're right. I don't understand why you can't control yourself, Nicholas."

"Me? Can't control myself? Oh, lady, you're going to pay. You just wait until I get you on the boat."

Camille pulled his face down to hers and ravished his mouth.

"What were you saying about control?" Nicholas quipped.

"Oh, hush." Camille silenced him with another kiss. "You still haven't told me where we're going, Nicholas."

"It's a surprise."

"Nicholas."

"My lips are sealed. I will say this, you're going to have the time of your life, Mrs. Cardoneaux."

"Mrs. Cardoneaux," she said dazed by the sound of her new name. "Camille Cardoneaux."

"I think I'll keep you."

"You'd better." She rubbed her stomach. "Your children just tended their votes."

"Both of them at the same time?"

"Yes. Feel!" Camille placed his hand over the top of her stomach and also on the right side.

"Wow!" His eyes lit up. "How do you stand all that tumbling and rolling around inside you all the time?"

"Their movements reassure me that they're all right."

"But it has to get uncomfortable. And you have three more months to go. What will it feel like when, you're close to term?"

"I may not have that long to wait. Twins are usually born early."

"But not always, though. Right?"

Camille smiled at his look of concern. "Stop worrying. Everything is going to be fine."

"What about making love?"

"Janet told us it would be all right. Don't you remember? You're not wiggling out of making love to me, mister."

"That, my darling, never once crossed my mind."

Just then the limo pulled into the Southern Yacht Club parking lot.

Nicholas walked Camille down to the marina. Claude and crew were waiting to welcome them aboard the Creole Lady.

"I've set up things as you instructed, sir." Claude smiled at them. "I want to take this opportunity to congratulate you on your marriage."

"Thank you, Claude." Nicholas turned to Camille. "Are you hungry?"

"Always. Your children make their demands known quite often."

Nicholas carefully guided his new bride down below to the dining area.

Camille smiled when she saw the table. There were two lighted candles in silver holders, two long-stem, crystal tulip champagne glasses and silverware laid out on a white Damask table cloth. A lone red rose took center stage.

"This is wonderful, Nicholas."

Claude appeared with a camera, and had them sit while he snapped pictures. A tuxedoed-waiter brought an ice bucket and sparkling cider and placed it on the table, then left and came back with a tray and placed the covered dishes on the table.

The aroma steaming up from the plates teased their nostrils.

"The entrée, almond green beans. Main course, Tournedos Sautés Chasseur, Filet Steak with mushroom and Madeira sauce, monsieur, madam," the waiter told them. "And for dessert strawberry torte."

Camille giggled when her stomach growled as she sniffed the warm, crusty French bread slices generously laved with creamy butter.

Nicholas quirked his lips into a wry smile. "I think we'd better get some food into you, before our children start complaining." He nodded to the waiter and he uncorked and poured the cider into their glasses. Then he and Claude left them alone.

Camille adored Nicholas for providing sparkling cider as a pregnancy substitute for champagne. His thoughtfulness brought tears to her eyes.

"Tears," he said frowning.

"Happy ones, my sweet man. You make me so happy."

"I intend to continue doing so for the rest of our lives so you'd better get used to it." He lifted his glass.

Camille lifted hers.

"To our love, our babies and our future."

They clinked glasses. Nicholas offered her a sip from his glass. He drank from the place her lips touched. Camille offered him a sip from her glass and she drank from the spot where his lips touched the glass.

Watching her eat always fascinated Nicholas. She could really put the food away these days. Her groan of pleasure when she sank her teeth into the strawberry torte topped with whipped cream was priceless.

"You think we have sufficiently pacified our hungry little natives?"

"Must have because I haven't felt a complaint yet."

"You want to go topside for some fresh air?"

"I'd like that. Can we go for a walk too? I definitely need the exercise."

Minutes later they were strolling through West End Park, observing the Art Deco picnic shelters and WPA-era fountains. They met several joggers and three or four other pairs of walkers in the square. After they had walked for a while Camille started to yawn.

"You've had a pretty busy day, Mrs. Cardoneaux. I think its time you took a nap. I want you well rested when I have my wicked way with you."

"You must really think I'm going to need it.

"Oh, you are."

"Such confidence. And just how wicked are you planning to be, lover man?"

"Oh, extremely wicked," he drew the words out and started raining wet smacking kisses all over her body.

"Nicholas!" She giggled. "I think I'd better have that nap." Because I definitely don't want to be tired and miss out on any of your marvelous wickedness."

"Let's head back to the boat. The sooner you have that nap, the sooner you get your wish."

"So now it's my wish, is it?"

"Our wish."

"That sound's better."

"Somehow I knew you would think so."

"Nicholas Cardoneaux!"

"Yes, dear."

Chapter Twenty-two

Camille awoke to delicious sensations feathering up and down the entrance to her womanhood. She parted her legs for easier access. Her heart began to beat faster and her skin started to heat when she felt a thumb tease her sensitive nub and fingers delve inside her aroused femininity. That same nub began to pulsate and swell as the sensations mounted and built to the explosion point.

"Oh, Nicholas," Camille moaned arching into his fingers.

"You're finally awake," he whispered as he knelt between her thighs, his weight resting back on his heels.

"Oh, yes, I most definitely am that."

As Nicholas flexed his fingers more frenziedly within her, his manhood hardened and her pleasure became his. When he had worked her aroused woman's flesh until she was almost past sensibility, he removed them and lifted her thighs onto his. And grasping her hips, he pulled her body forward to meet his enormous erection, then eased the tip of his sex just a little way inside her, and slowly, inch by rapturous inch, incited her sheath to take all of him. At the sound of her low-pitched moan of ecstasy, Nicholas wrapped Camille's legs around his waist and initiated a barrage of long sensual thrusts deep inside her.

Camille's climax reverberated through her body like rising waves building to reach its peak. The sensations quickly arrived at that point and lingered, then when it started its downward spiral, Nicholas moved his hips in circular motions, building the intensity back up.

"Nicholas, what are you doing to me?" Camille whimpered.

"Giving you what I promised." With each movement, he delved and penetrated a little deeper, setting sensitive nerve endings on fire in his quest to give her unforgettable pleasure and himself mind-shattering release. As the friction of her heated passage sensuously massaged his throbbing flesh again and again and yet again he groaned. And when he heard Camille cry out and felt her tremors begin, it pushed him over the edge and he gave a loud male shout of satisfaction and poured himself into her.

"What a way to wake up from a nap," Camille murmured.

"You did say you didn't want to miss out on anything, didn't you?"

"I have to admit that I like your interpretation of wickedness, Mr. Cardoneaux."

"You want more?"

"In a little while."

"But right now you're hungry. Right?"

"It's not my fault your children are as demanding as their father."

"Flattery will get you everything. I'll be right back."

"Nicholas, you're naked!"

"We have the boat to ourselves until noon. I gave the crew the night and morning off. It's a good thing too."

"Oh, why?"

"Darling, you are kind of vocal when you come."

"Nicholas!" She threw a pillow at him.

"Well you are, but I don't mind. I love you anyway."

"Thanks a lot." Camille smiled as she watched her husband leave their cabin. She stared wordlessly at the sight of his strong arms, tight abs and lean muscular buttocks. She knew how gentle he could be when he was holding her.

She could picture in her mind's eye Nicholas lovingly cradling their babies in those arms.

The door opening brought her back from the future to the present. Nicholas had returned with a tray of buttered croissants, strawberries and sliced ham.

"Where did all this come from?" she asked.

"I had the restaurant prepare it and Claude put it in the fridge so all I had to do was heat up the croissants and ham in the microwave. Ingenious, huh?"

"Very," she said eyeing the fare greedily.

Later replete and lazy, Camille and Nicholas lay in bed admiring the sun dancing on the water through the portal. Then they made love and afterwards showered together, to conserve water Nicholas told Camille. But, while showering he took his time making love to his new wife.

* * *

They were up on deck when Claude and crew arrived to make ready to sail. As the Creole Lady left the marina Camille and Nicholas observed the ease with which she moved out onto the lake and later as Claude maneuvered her down the canal to the Mississippi river, into the Gulf of Mexico, then headed for the Caribbean Sea.

"We'll be stopping in Mexico, Belize, Costa Rica, Caracas, then on to our final destination: Barbados,"

Nicholas revealed.

"I always wanted to see Barbados as a visitor rather than a performer as I once did at the Paint it Jazz festival. It was the next to the last stop on my final concert tour. I never had a chance to enjoy the scenery."

Nicholas smiled. "Well this time with me you'll get that chance." He wrapped his arms around her and brushed the top of her head with his chin, breathing in the delicate fragrance of her hair and the musky woman's scent of her skin. "It's time for your nap."

"Under one condition."

"What condition is that?"

"That you join me. I like having you around."

"You do, huh?"

"Now, Nicholas, I didn't mean - "

"Yes you did. And I'm game," he whispered in her ear and grinned when he saw a rosy blush infuse her caramel cheeks. "You're bad, Nicholas Cardoneaux."

"Almost as bad as my new wife," he said guiding her down below.

When they made love, Nicholas muffled Camille's cries of pleasure with long mind-altering kisses. It really wasn't necessary though because the master cabin was soundproof, but she didn't need to know that. He smiled at her efforts to tamp down her responses to his lovemaking. After tiring her out with his demands, Nicholas let her sleep. While she slept he watched over her. He noticed that she splayed her arm across her stomach in a protective gesture. He enclosed her and the babies in his embrace and fell asleep.

* * *

They had dinner in Mexico and the following afternoon lunch in Belize.

In Costa Rica, Camille and Nicholas went on a tour of El Fernando Banana Plantation. When they arrived in Caracas, they spent the day viewing the city's ancient ruins. That night they crashed in a hotel instead of going back to the yacht.

The next afternoon Nicholas took Camille to see Central University where he'd spent a semester studying the Spanish influence on the city's architecture.

"We'll be leaving Caracas tonight and by tomorrow we should arrive in St. James, Barbados. You'll enjoy the magnificent beaches and interesting sights the town has to offer that you didn't have a chance to when you were here before," Nicholas said as they stood out on the balcony of their suite looking out over Caracas as they sipped glasses of sweetened lime juice. "I have a friend that owns a sugarcane plantation outside of Bridgetown. We'll be staying there the remaining days of our honeymoon."

"It's a good thing I like a take charge man."

"I can't help it. It's my primitive genes I have to thank, I guess."

"I appreciate your primitive genes. Or haven't you noticed?" Camille ran her fingers underneath his shirt and caressed his chest, then angled them downward to his waist where she slipped her hand inside his pants and stroked his manhood. His sharp intake of breath brought a smile to her lips.

"I've noticed," was all he could manage to answer. When she felt him harden, she undid the button on his slacks and pushed his briefs down, freeing his sex, then moved her fingers up and down his length, as it tightened and swelled even more.

With a sensual growl Nicholas moved Camille's fingers and lifted her into his arms and carried her inside to their bedroom and quickly undressed her and laid her on the bed and finished

undressing himself, before joining her there. And lying facing each other on their sides, he brought Camille's legs over his hip and slid his shaft inside her warmth.

"Oh, Nicholas, that feels so good," she moaned.

He slowly brought her to climax again before finding his own release.

Chapter Twenty-three

As the Creole Lady approached Barbados, Nicholas explained that the island, made up chiefly of coral limestone, was almost completely surrounded by reefs. He pointed out the sandy beach and flat, coastal lowland where the land rose and spread out into a series of terraces.

"When I came here before, I'd flown in and never got an opportunity to do any sightseeing. My flight was late and I barely made it to the festival on time. Then when it was over I had to fly on to Brazil."

"You'll have all the time you need this trip." He scorched her with a flaming glance.

"Will I? I wonder if you'll even let me out of the bedroom."

"There's always that possibility. But I did promise that you would enjoy all aspects of our honeymoon. Which means I can't make love to you, every waking moment." Nicholas turned his attention back to the island

and pinpointed Mount Hillaby in the distance. It was the tallest range above sea level, he went on to say as the Creole Lady sailed into the St. James marina. He had reserved a suite for them at the Coconut Creek Hotel, having chosen it because it was small and intimate, and many of the rooms were built on the cliff edge overlooking the sea.

After her afternoon nap they had lunch at the Cliff Club with its warm red, terra cotta tiles and Cora stonewalls. It was an open-air restaurant with an impressive four level dining room. Camille stared in wonder as they enjoyed Bajan food and Thai style shrimp.

"What do you want for dessert?" Nicholas asked.

"Dessert? You've got to be kidding."

"You mean I've finally managed to fill you up? I'll have to mark it down somewhere."

"Nicholas."

"Want to take a stroll down the beach? It's cool this time of the afternoon."

"I'd love to. As much as I love sailing on the Creole Lady, I'm glad to stand on a surface that doesn't sway and rock."

Holding hands they headed down the beach, stopping once to watch the waves wash over the sand.

"It's so beautiful here, Nicholas."

"You know what they say about tropical paradises?"

"No, what?"

"If you stay long enough you'll never want to return to civilization."

"I can understand why." The fragrance of the exotic flowers and plants filled the air. And the sway of the palm trees in the soft sea breeze added a rare serenity to their surroundings. All any honeymooning couples could ask for.

Later Nicholas and Camille watched as the orange-gold light of sunset gilded the water. Camille wondered how this same beach would look in moonlight as she and Nicholas made love on a blanket beneath its silvery glow.

"A penny for your thoughts, my darling."

"You don't need one."

Nicholas swallowed hard, mesmerized by the invitation in Camille's melting chocolate eyes.

"Let's go back to the hotel."

"I was thinking the same thing. They say that great minds work alike."

Nicholas grinned. "Greatness of mind wasn't exactly what I was aspiring to; it's the joining of bodies that interests me most right now."

"Just any body?"

"I'll answer your question when we get back to our suite."

"Your proving ground no doubt?"

Nicholas lifted Camille in his arms and carried her back to their suite. Along the way they received knowing glances from the staff and other guests.

* * *

"That feels so good, Nicholas. More, please," Camille moaned, closing her eyes.

Nicholas smiled and advanced his massaging hands from her feet to her calves and thighs and even higher. He enjoyed just watching his wife's freshly showered, naked body. He stopped the massage unable to resist reaching up and touching her sexy, cherry-sized nipples. His eyes dropped lower to her stomach and lower still to the dark triangle of curls beneath it. He moved his hand to that enticing juncture between her thighs and cupped her there.

Camille opened her eyes. "Nicholas?" she whispered. Then closed them again, when he eased her thighs apart and delved two fingers inside her and caressed the pearl of her desire with his thumb. Seconds later she surrendered to his expert ministrations.

"Now it's your turn," Camille said when her

heartbeat had calmed. She took his manhood in her hands and began her massage, starting at the base and working her way to the tip. When she heard his voice catch in his throat, Camille mounted her husband and lowered herself onto his erection.

Nicholas raised her hips up and down in a slow exciting rhythm as his tongue moved in and out of her mouth, imitating the rhythm going on below. Camille cried out when the delicious sensations of beckoning rapture began to overtake her. Nicholas moved her body against his, reveling in the euphoria of her flesh as it spasmed around him and then subsided into short intermittent eddies.

Camille sighed. "I love your massaging techniques and its - ah - extras."

"Does that mean I get to keep my job?"

"Oh, yes, definitely. I can't let a treasure like you work on anyone else but me."

* * *

Nicholas took Camille to the La Smarita restaurant that evening because they specialized in seafood.

"Nicholas, you keep this up and I won't be able to sail with you because the boat will sink beneath my weight."

"Darling, you're eating for three. Besides, I like

my women substantial."

"Oh, you."

"There's a local jazz group performing at Nico's Champagne Bar. Want to go?"

"Oh, yes."

"Does it bring back memories?" Nicholas asked Camille as they sat listening to the band.

"Yes," she answered her voice wistful.

When the band finished the set, a musician approached her.

"Excuse me for intruding, but I've often wondered what happened to you, Ms. King. My name is Enrique. You probably do not remember me. I played with the band that accompanied you when you performed at the jazz festival a few years back. You were so sensational. You had the magic touch on the keyboard."

"Yes, I do remember you. As I recall you played a pretty mean baby saxophone."

"You do remember!" he said obviously delighted that she had. "I am now teaching piano and music in New Orleans. I'm flattered that you remembered me, Enrique."

"I will never forget your unique take off on 'Piano in the Dark.' Do you not miss performing?"

"Sometimes," she said looking at Nicholas and

then moving her hand across her stomach. "But I'm happy doing what I'm doing."

"I am glad for you then." Enrique smiled and politely nodded before walking away.

"Are you sure you have no regrets, Camille?" Nicholas asked.

She smiled. "Yes, I'm sure. I could have resumed my career at any time. What I couldn't make Elroy understand is that although I was happy just being his wife and teaching music, more than anything I didn't want to wait to have a baby. It's only after his death and with you that I have finally realized my dream."

"Is that why - "

Camille put her finger across his lips. "No, it's not the reason I married you. I love you babies or no babies. You got it?"

"I got it," he said softly and placed her hand in his.

They listened a while longer to the band, then returned to the hotel. Tomorrow they would sail down the coast to Payne Bay, Brandon's Beach then on to Bridgetown to do more sightseeing. Then spend the last three days of their honeymoon on his friend's sugar plantation.

* * *

In Bridgetown Camille shopped at the Colours of De Caribbean, a shop on the waterfront, and bought several hand-painted Batik dresses for her mother and Deja and a necklace for Jolie. Later she and Nicholas went underwater sightseeing on a submarine that made several dives daily, and afterwards she and Nicholas stopped at a waterfront cafe called Bill Fisher II, owned by Captain Winston "The Colonel" White who told outlandish fish tales.

"Ready for a taste of plantation life?"

"After listening to Captain White's fantastic fish stories, yes I sure am. I think he made them up as he went along."

"Maybe not. He did sail the Caribbean for forty years."

"Is there anything you don't know?"

"I know all the important things," he said kissing her hand and then moving his lips up her arm.

Camille felt her insides quiver with longing. "I want you to pass on some of those important things to me."

"You do?"

"Umm." Camille rose from her chair and taking his hand urged him toward the door.

"The evening has only begun."

"You're right it has and I have special plans that involve you."

* * *

Camille liked Nicholas's friend, Paolo Estravez, on sight. He was part Spanish, black, Brazilian and white. He took them on a tour of his sugar plantation. Camille learned things about the growing and processing of sugarcane she never knew before. That evening she and Nicholas were royally entertained at an island cookout.

They spent the last two days of their honeymoon at what Paolo called his get away house on the edge of the plantation. He explained that once or twice a year he escaped to it. Their last night there they spread a pallet on the beach and made love beneath the stars. Then early the next morning they returned to the main house. Camille hated to leave Barbados. She didn't want this special time in her marriage to ever end.

* * *

Aboard the Creole Lady, headed back to New Orleans, Nicholas and Camille watched the beauty of the tropics recede as they left the Caribbean Sea. What would it be like when they got back home? Camille couldn't help wondering. They had a beautiful home waiting to start their new life. Would her brother and Nicholas's mother continue to shut them out? Or would they eventually come around and accept things the way they were?

"Let each day take care of itself, my darling," Nicholas said enclosing her in his arms.

"I've been meaning to ask you, what made Jamal decide to give you away, but other things," he grinned at her, "held my interest, like a certain beautiful, sexy pregnant woman."

"I was wondering when you would get around to asking. I had prayed that at the last minute he'd come. I know my brother pretty well. And I was convinced that in the end he would win the battle of conflicting emotions raging inside him, his distrust of you versus his love for me. I think he realized how much he'd be hurting me if he didn't put his misgivings aside. And the fact that Mama had practically disowned him didn't hurt."

Nicholas smiled nodding his head. "Your mother has a way of getting her point across, that's for sure. Jamal may have come around about giving you away, but it doesn't mean he's changed his opinion about me."

"I know, but I'm hoping he will in time."

Nicholas sighed. "I'm hoping time will work the same magic on my mother and her attitude toward you."

"If it doesn't it's not only their loss, but ours too. And more importantly our babies."

"You're right. I just wish there was something we

could do to bring them to their senses."

"So do I. We'll get through this. As long as we're together we can weather whatever storm fate has in store."

"I love you so much, Camille."

"And I you. Our love will see us through this."

Nicholas hoped that love would eventually wear down the walls his mother and Jamal had built to keep them out of their lives. Maybe not right away. But eventually.

Chapter Twenty-four

Nicholas called ahead and had his car waiting at the yacht club parking lot when he and Camille arrived back in New Orleans. And after she had called her mother to let her know they were back, Nicholas insisted that she take a nap before they started the drive to their new home. He also arranged for the boxes of souvenirs they'd brought back with them to be delivered there the following day.

Hours later as they entered their living room, the portrait Nicholas had painted of Camille greeted them.

"I didn't know you'd done this. I don't know if I can stand seeing an exact copy of myself day in and day out."

"You'll get used to it."

"It sounds like you intend keeping it here all the time. I thought you were going to let Henri display it at his gallery."

"Oh, I am, but later like maybe ten years from

now."

Camille laughed. "That wouldn't be fair. You can't do that to Henri."

"I know. I agreed to let him display it for a month starting next month. Maybe by then I will have resigned myself to letting it out from under my roof."

"There are fresh cut flowers on the coffee table and the windows are open." Camille smiled. "Which means my mother has been here."

Nicholas sniffed. "I smell fresh baked bread. I sense Jolie's fine hand in this, too," he said following the delicious aroma into the dining room."

Laid out on the table was a feast fit for a king. Grilled shrimp, dirty rice dressing, fried catfish, mustard greens, sweet corn, mashed potatoes and fresh baked French bread.

"After all the tropical food we've eaten the last two weeks this is a welcome change, not that the other wasn't equally delicious."

Nicholas smiled. "I know what you mean. I wonder if our babies' stomachs are growling. After all it has been four hours since their poor mother last had nourishment."

"Now that you mention it, I am getting hungry."

Nicholas went out to the kitchen and brought

back a pitcher of iced tea he'd found in the refrigerator. His mother-in-law and Jolie had thought of everything. For dessert peach cobbler sat on top of the stove.

* * *

Later Nicholas and Camille lay in bed, their appetite for food and each other satisfied. Nicholas placed his hand on her stomach. He could feel a strong rambling movement push against his palm.

"I wonder which one of our sweet little cherubs is settling down for the night."

"I wish they both would."

"I'll bet you do. I can only imagine what it feels like being constantly pummeled."

"You just think you can." She laughed. "But not to worry, my love, your time will come. There will be diapers to change and many nights spent walking the floor with babies who have gotten their days and nights mixed up."

"I'm sure you'll handle it."

"What!" She sat up, her eyes shooting daggers at him.

"I have every confidence in you."

"You what?" Camille picked up a pillow and started beating him about the head and shoulder.

He held up his arms. "Was it something I said?" he managed to slip in between blows and his own laughter. "Hey, watch it that hurts."

"I certainly hope so."

"I think you really mean that." He pulled her into his arms. "For your information I plan to be the best damn diaper changer and floor walker this side of the Mississippi. And the other side too. I would even help you with the feedings, but I'm afraid my equipment can't hold a candle to yours," he said caressing a nipple. "Now that I think about, I'm not sure if I'm ready to share."

"Aw poor baby." Camille laughed and patted his cheek, then laid her head on his chest and nestled deeper in his embrace.

For a while they lay in silence, then Nicholas lifted Camille's hand.

"Do you know what I especially like about your wedding ring?"

"No, what?"

"It's a no-trespassing sign."

"Whoa, that sounds pretty possessive, lover man."

"I'm a very possessive man." He was suddenly serious. "You're the most important thing in my life, Camille. As much as I love our children I love you more."

It was a balm to her psyche to hear her husband say those words. Camille knew how important having his own children was to Nicholas. And for him to say that...

"I don't know how Lauren could have ever walked away from you. But I'm glad she did because you're all mine now."

"Now who sounds possessive?"

* * *

Over the next weeks Nicholas and Camille settled into married life. True to their word, Henri and Jolie threw them a reception party at Antoine's. Jamal had come with Deja. He smiled and talked to Camille, but he said as little as possible to Nicholas. Suzette Cardoneaux hadn't shown up, making her absence conspicuously obvious. As Nicholas had predicted Jamal's appearance at the wedding and the reception hadn't meant that he'd changed his opinion about his sister's husband. Phillip, Jolie and Henri and their children, Camille's mother and Deja and Jamal came over for a family barbecue, and on another occasion ,a family dinner which Nicholas's mother also refused to attend was a deep source of disappointment for the newly weds. But it was something they had to learn to live with.

* * *

One afternoon as Nicholas was leaving the

office, headed for the Center, he received a phone call from his lawyer.

"How was the honeymoon?" Kyle Barnett asked.

"All right. If you have something to tell me, cut to the chase, Kyle."

He laughed. "You were never one to mince words, Nicholas. I need to talk to you about the Hadley Clinic."

"Why? Is there a problem?"

"You could say that."

"Kyle."

"When can you come to my office? I don't want to discuss this over the phone."

Nicholas glanced at his watch. "I'll be finished at the Center at 4:30."

"Will five o'clock work for you?"

"I'll be there."

Nicholas frowned as he cradled the phone. What about the Hadley Clinic? He'd had Kyle working on the legalities of the

case.

* * *

"Sit down, Nicholas," Kyle said indicating a chair in front of his desk.

"I'd rather stand if you don't mind."

Kyle sat in the chair behind his desk, picked up a file folder and opened it. "I think you need to sit down."

Nicholas had a sinking feeling in the pit of his stomach that he wasn't going to like what Kyle had to say, so he decided to take him up on his suggestion.

Clearing his throat Kyle began. "I've been in touch with the Hadley Clinic attorneys, Fletcher and Stedman. For the last month they've been evasive."

"Evasive, how? The clinic is guilty of carelessness. It's as simple as that."

"Nicholas, it's evidently not that simple or else they wouldn't be trying to avoid dealing with me."

"Well, what do you think is going on?" Curiosity and dread darkened his blue eyes.

"I believe there is more to this than just simple carelessness."

"What do you mean? They fired the person responsible."

"With most inseminations there is usually more than one procedure done. Am I right?"

"Well, yes."

"In Lauren's and Camille's case were there two done?"

"Yes." The implications of what his lawyer was saying hit Nicholas with the force of a knockout punch.

"What are you saying?"

"I won't know anything for sure until I get a copy of the Clinic's records and examine them. And then we can only hope they haven't been altered."

"Altered, in what way? They've already admitted to the mistake."

"There could have been more to it than they revealed, but we won't know until - "

"I get the message." Nicholas got up and walked over to the window, looked out, then turned. "How soon will you be able to get a copy of the records?"

"I don't know the answer to that. It depends on how soon the judge issues the writ. I've already started the ball rolling."

"How long have you suspected that all wasn't as it appeared to be?"

"Since before your wedding. I didn't want to spoil your honeymoon over something that might or might not be a factor."

"I appreciate that. I don't know how Camille is going to take this."

"You can't tell her until we know for sure what we're dealing with. I contacted her attorney, Martin Greenwood. Camille signed a paper agreeing not to sue the clinic before being fully apprised of all the facts. You were wise not to sign anything. I'll get back to you about this as soon as I can. I know that in the meantime it's going to be hell keeping this from your wife."

"You don't know the half of it."

Nicholas was in a daze when he left his lawyer's office. Could there possibly be another mistake they weren't told about? Oh, God, he didn't want to think about that possibility. His life was finally coming together after years of disappointment and heartache. He had two children on the way and he had found the love of his life. Surely fate couldn't be so cruel and take it all away.

* * *

Camille noticed how distracted her husband had been over the last few days and wondered what was causing it. At first she put it down to problems at the office or his frustration and disappointment over his mother's and her brother's continuing cold war attitude. But when his distraction seemed to hang on longer than it should, Camille called Phillip and invited him to lunch at a restaurant close to the hospital.

"Something is bothering Nicholas, Phillip. Has he said anything to you?"

"No," Phillip said thoughtfully. "But I had noticed that the few times he's been to Magnolia Grove. There's nothing wrong between you two? Is there?"

"Not that I'm aware of. He was fine, then two weeks ago I noticed the change in him. I don't know what could have happened between then and now. Whatever it is he won't talk to me about it."

"Give him time."

"I have, Phillip."

He took her hand in his. "Then give him a little more. Okay? Don't start obsessing until you have something to obsess about."

"All right." she smiled fondly at him. "When my own brother is not available, I think I'll borrow you."

He grinned, "Borrow away at any time, sweet lady."

* * *

Nicholas felt as if he would crawl out of his skin waiting for Kyle's call. He stayed late at Cardoneaux Construction catching up on work because he couldn't concentrate on it during his regular workday. He'd turned his class over to his assistant for pretty much the same reason. At times he felt the desperate urge to take Camille and leave New Orleans, but knew he'd only be running away from his problems and it just wasn't in his nature to do that.

This not knowing was slowly killing him, he

thought, pacing back and forth before the windows of his office. He already loved the babies his wife was carrying. Feeling them move inside her womb reassured him daily that he would soon become a father. Next to their mother the babies were the most important thing in his life. All three were his life. He didn't know if he would keep his sanity if he ever had to be without them. He'd lost four children before they were born and it had torn his soul apart. Then his wife had rejected and divorced him. How much was a man supposed to take without cracking up?

He knew that Camille suspected that all wasn't right with him by the concerned looks she gave him. He wanted to go to her and unburden himself, but he couldn't do that to her. He wouldn't tell her anything until he knew for sure...

Knew what for sure, Cardoneaux?

Nicholas raked his fingers through his hair. No matter what his lawyer found out, Camille and the babies belonged to him and always would.

Are you willing to accept them if they were fathered by an unknown man? Or heaven forbid, Camille's late husband? What if, as Jamal had said, there really hadn't been a mistake and Camille hadn't been inseminated with his sperm?

No, none of those possibilities could be it.

You don't know that.

No, he didn't, but he didn't care. He wanted to spend the rest of his life with Camille and the babies.

Are you so sure about that? You don't have any doubts about your ability to accept that your wife could be carrying another man's baby?

He loved Camille. And he would love her children whether they were biologically his or not.

That's noble of you Cardoneaux.

He wasn't being noble. He wasn't.

* * *

"Nicholas, what's wrong?" Camille asked when he got home late that evening. "Mr. Shelton told me that you had turned your class over to your assistant for this entire week."

"I've had a lot to contend with at work, Camille."

"Can't you share whatever it is with me? I'm not a fair weather wife."

He kissed her. "I know you're not, darling. It's nothing you can help me with. Hopefully everything will be resolved soon."

Camille sensed that her husband was keeping something from her that involved her. It wasn't at all like the Nicholas Cardoneaux she'd come to know and love to be so secretive. Was he having second thoughts about their marriage? Had he come to the conclusion that he wanted the babies more than he wanted her, and he was just putting up with her?

She shook her head. No, she had to stop torturing herself like this. He said he loved her and she believed him yet...

The phone rang. Nicholas rushed to answer it. He glanced at the Caller ID and then picked up the receiver.

"Kyle, what do you have for me?"

"I have the records. Can you and your wife come to my office first thing in the morning?"

"Yes."

"See you both at nine o'clock."

"We'll be there." Nicholas hung up the phone and walked over to the window and looked out.

"Nicholas, what is it? The look on your face..."

"That was Kyle Barnette, my lawyer."

"I remember hearing you speak about him. What did he want?"

"To see us tomorrow morning."

"About?"

"The Hadley Clinic. Evidently they haven't been completely open and above board with either one of us. Kyle got a court order demanding that the clinic turn over a copy of their files to him. He now has them and wants to go over them with us."

"But why, I don't understand."

"We both will tomorrow."

"Nicholas."

"Camille, please. Just wait until tomorrow."

"You know more than you're saying about why he wants to see us. Don't you? Tell me the truth, Nicholas."

Nicholas turned and walked over to her and pulled her into his arms.

"I don't know anything really. All I know is that Hadley's attorneys were being evasive and Kyle was suspicious."

"About what?" Frustration laced her words.

"They may not have told us everything about the mix up."

"What else could they - Oh, my God." Tears welled in her eyes and slid down her face.

"Darling, don't cry. Whatever he has to tell us we'll face it together."

"But what if -"

"Don't."

"I can't help it, Nicholas. Something could be wrong with our babies."

"I don't think it's anything like that."

"But you don't know that."

Nicholas felt Camille tremble and it wrenched his guts. Hadley would pay for this.

Chapter Twenty-five

Nicholas noticed the shadows under Camille's eyes when they sat down to breakfast the next morning. He knew she hadn't slept last night and her usually healthy appetite was gone. She only picked at her food. He put his hand over hers.

"Are you all right?" he asked.

"No."

"Try to eat something."

"I can't." She rose from the table and walked out of the breakfast room.

Nicholas followed her. She stood in front of her portrait staring at it, her eyes zeroed in on the huge rounded stomach.

"What if the babies aren't yours, Nicholas?"

"We don't know that."

"But what if - "

"It doesn't matter. I'll love them anyway."

"How can you say that?"

"I can say it because I love you. They'll be a part of you. How could I not love any child of yours?"

"I know how much having your own flesh and blood children means to you, Nicholas."

"I won't deny it. But you mean more. Your children will be my children."

Camille wondered if the love he felt for her wouldn't change if he found out her children weren't his children. The only reason they had even met was because of a mistake. He had believed the child she conceived was his. She remembered how possessive and determined he was to have that child in his life.

Nicholas saw the closed expression on his wife's face when she got into the car and it hurt. During the drive to Kyle Barnette's office she was quiet and distant. He hoped that she didn't doubt his love for her and his commitment to their marriage.

Camille's legs felt as though they wouldn't support her when she got out of the car. Oh, God, what did she have to face when she went inside. Every worst-case scenario she could think of raced through her mind.

Nicholas cupped Camille's elbow as they entered the law offices of Barnette and Robinson. The receptionist signaled for them to go on into Kyle Barnette's private office.

Kyle met them at the door and waved them inside.

"Have a seat."

Camille looked at Nicholas and then Kyle Barnette before sitting down.

"I know you're both on edge so I won't waste time."

"Yes, we are. What are we looking at, Kyle?"

"Camille you were inseminated January 4th?'

"Yes." She swallowed past the lump in her throat.

"And also on January 5th?"

Nausea roiled in Camille's stomach. She had forgotten that she'd undergone the procedure twice because those were her most fertile days. And evidently they had been for Lauren Cardoneaux, too.

"Before we begin - "

A knock at the door interrupted. Kyle instructed whomever it was to come inside. Dr. Hadley, and a man neither Camille nor Nicholas recognized, and a third man, who judging from the briefcase he was carrying, was probably an attorney.

Camille felt a heavy pressure on her chest that was threatening to squeeze the air from her lungs.

Nicholas frowned. "Kyle, you didn't say anything about anyone else joining us."

"I tried to call you, but I assumed that you'd already left the house because I got the answering machine. I dialed your cell phone and got your voice mail."

"I left the phone in our bedroom."

"Mr. Cardoneaux, I want to say again how sorry I am," Hadley said nervously.

"Let's get on with this," Nicholas said ignoring the man's apology.

Kyle asked Hadley and the other men to take a seat and he picked up the file folder and opened it.

"According to these records a second insertion procedure was performed the following day. Is that correct?" he asked Dr. Hadley.

He looked to his attorney and when he nodded he said. "Yes it is."

Kyle shifted his attention to one of the other men. "Are you the technician who delivered the vials?"

"Yes, sir, on the second day, January 5th, I was. My name is David Shaw."

"Explain to us exactly what happened."

"I - I brought one vial to Mrs. Lauren Cardoneaux's room. And the other to examining room 5, which was Mrs. King's."

"How did you know there had been a mix up with the two vials?"

"I had proceeded according to the numbers on the vials. It wasn't until I came to work the following day that I realized what had happened the day before."

"Why didn't you inform anyone about the mix up?"

"Well ah -"

Nicholas vaulted out of his chair and grabbed the man by the lapels of jacket. "Well what, man?"

"Nicholas," Kyle warned. "Please let me handle this."

Reluctantly he let the man go and sat back down. He glanced at Camille. She seemed frozen in a state of shock. She hadn't moved. He was worried about what this was doing to her. "Mr. Shaw, answer my question." Kyle demanded.

"I was afraid to say anything because Mrs. King was black and Mrs. Cardoneaux was white. And if the mistake ever came to light..."

"You were worried that you would lose your damn job. Is that what you were going to say," Nicholas roared. "I have news for you, your job is history."

"Nicholas! Stop brow-beating the man and let him finish," Camille finally spoke.

"Continue, Mr. Shaw. You haven't explained how it happened."

"The initial collection containers are labeled with a computer generated number. When the sperm goes to the lab for storage the technicians are responsible for transferring the identifying numbers onto the individual vials. Since both technicians must sign off on every step of the entire process, if a mistake is made it can be traced."

"And what you're saying is that you weren't the technician who put the label on the vials and signed off on January 4th, just the one who did the following day," Nicholas ground out.

"Yes, sir."

Nicholas glared at Dr. Hadley. "You said you fired the one responsible."

"And I did."

Kyle cleared his throat and asked. "What happened with the second insertion, Mr. Shaw?"

"I followed procedure and delivered the vials to the respective patients examining rooms as I've told you."

"What you're telling us is that Mrs. King was inseminated with her husband's sperm on the second day?"

"Yes, sir."

"Oh, my God," Camille cried.

"Dr. Hadley, when were you made aware of the

mix up?"

"When the pregnancy tests were positive for both patients, Mr. Shaw came to me."

"Why did you wait so long to inform Mr. Cardoneaux and Mrs. King?"

"Lauren Cardoneaux had miscarried as a result of a car accident."

"According to the records you were listed as Lauren Cardoneaux's doctor. And you had the pathologist at Queen of Angel's hospital perform a DNA test on the fetus, didn't you?"

"Yes, I did. You see Mrs. Cardoneaux had a history of miscarriage."

"But that's not the reason you wanted it done. Is it? You wanted to know whose baby Lauren Cardoneaux had lost. You found out it was Elroy King's and not her husband's, didn't you? Because Camille King had been inseminated with her husband's sperm in the second procedure you were willing to gamble that she had conceived her husband's child. Weren't you?"

"Yes." He bowed his head.

"When you found out from Dr. Broussard that Mrs. King was expecting fraternal twins, twins from two different eggs, you got worried because you couldn't pinpoint exactly when conception occurred."

"Yes," he answered uncomfortably.

"Knowing that the life of active motile sperms is 48 hours, there was no way you could be sure who fathered the babies. Either man could have fathered one or both because the two procedures had been done within that 48-hour period. That is the reason you instructed your attorney not to cooperate, isn't it? You don't have to answer, doctor. We all know the truth."

Camille felt as though she were on a stage watching a play unfolding not witnessing a scene from her life. One of her babies could be Elroy's child. Or they both might be his. They may not even be Nicholas's period. Or maybe one of them might be his. Which one? She stood up and moving like a zombie walked out of the lawyer's office.

"Camille, wait!" Nicholas called after her, but she seemed not to have heard him and kept on walking. He shot Hadley and his technician a look of contempt before heading for the door.

"Nicholas," Kyle said. "We need to discuss what you want me to do?"

"I'll get back to you. Right now I have to go after my wife."

"I understand. She looked to be in a state of shock. Just to be on the safe side, maybe you should take her to see her doctor."

"I agree." Ignoring Hadley's attorney, Nicholas glared at the doctor and spit out. "If anything happens to Camille or the babies you and your clinic are history."

Nicholas found Camille sitting on a bench in the park across the street from Kyle's office and sat down beside her.

"Whatever happens, we'll face it together, Camille."

"Will we? I wonder. I thought nothing else could happen to me. How wrong can one person be?"

"The babies are healthy, darling. We'll raise them together. I love you, Camille. It doesn't matter - "

"Don't say that. It does matter. It matters to me. It matters because I love you and wanted to give you children of your own to love after all you've been through," she cried, laying her head on his chest.

It was shades of deja vu for Nicholas. It was right after finding out Camille was carrying his child he'd taken her to Audubon Park to calm her. But this time there was no peace to be had despite their tranquil surroundings.

"I wish I could make this all turn out right for you, but I can't. The babies will be ours, Camille. We'll give them all the love we have to give."

Camille was afraid that he was just saying that

now. And that after the babies were born his feelings would change. If there was only some way to find out, right now today. The only other option was to have DNA tests done, but she couldn't right now. It was too dangerous for her babies at this stage of her pregnancy. The tests would have to wait. And she knew the waiting was going to be hell.

"We need to tell Kyle what we want him to do about Hadley and the technician."

"I don't want to think about that right now. I'm having a hard enough time as it is." Camille rose from the bench. "Just take me home, Nicholas. I can't take any more."

He hated hearing that pained miserable sound in her voice and the sad look in her eyes. She shouldn't have to go through something like this. But if not for the clinic's mistake she wouldn't be a part of his life. And she wasn't merely a part of his life, she was his life. He couldn't lose her now. He wouldn't lose her.

* * *

"What's up with you?" Deja asked Camille as they relaxed on lawn chairs in the garden. Deja had come to visit her friend on a day she wasn't busy teaching at the Center.

"When I called earlier, I heard the sadness in your

voice, Camille so I came over. Something is wrong, isn't it?"

"I really don't want to talk about it." Then Camille suddenly burst into tears.

Deja put her arm around her shoulders.

"What is it? You can tell me. That's what friends are for."

After a few moments Camille regained control of herself.

"The babies might not be Nicholas's."

"Say what?"

"We found out that because of the two insemination procedures that were done, there is a strong possibility that one or both of my children might be Elroy's. You see, on one day I was inseminated with Nicholas's sperm and on the second Elroy's."

"Oh, God, what you must be going through. How is Nicholas taking this?"

"He's being wonderful. He says it doesn't matter, but -"

"You don't believe him?"

"I think he believes what he's saying, but he won't know how he really feels until after the babies are born."

"I don't agree. If he says it doesn't matter, it

doesn't matter. The man loves you, Camille. He'll love any child or children that are yours whether they are his or not."

"I hope you're right. I don't know how I'm going to get through the next two and a half months, Deja."

"Love will see you through it. Have you told your mother?"

"Not yet."

"Don't you think you should? She'd want to know and help in any way she can. You know Miss Hazel."

"Yes, I do. You're right. Thanks for coming over. You've made me feel better."

"I'm glad. I'll probably be crying on your shoulder one day after I marry your brother."

"After? Have you two set a date?"

Deja held out her left hand.

"You're engaged!" Camille exclaimed. "When did this happen?"

"Last night. You could have knocked me over with a feather. He has money now that he's working for Allanby's."

"I'm glad he finally found a job."

"Me too. He's not going to be happy when he hears about the latest developments. Does Nicholas family know? More specifically, his mother?"

"No. I can just hear her telling Nicholas he should wash his hands of the whole situation and divorce me."

"He wouldn't listen to her or ever consider what she suggested."

"No, he wouldn't because he's too good and too honorable a person to do something like that. He has principles, Deja."

"It's more than that and you know it, Camille."

"Over the last few days I've felt a subtle distancing where I'm concerned. I don't want him to stay with me out of a sense of responsibility."

"I'm sure he doesn't feel that way. You have to keep the faith."

"Believe me, I'm trying, Deja. Why did this have to happen to us? We just started a new life together."

"Adversity makes you stronger."

"Or it can tear your life apart."

Chapter Twenty-Six

"I'm totally floored by what you've just told me!" Phillip exclaimed after listening to his brother's story. "How is Camille?"

"Not good." Nicholas frowned. "I'm worried about her. She doesn't sleep. She doesn't eat properly. Now that she no longer teaches at the Center, all she does is sit in the rocking chair in the nursery and stare into space. I've tried to reassure her that I love her and no matter who the father proves to be I'll accept it and be there for her and them."

"But she's still skeptical?"

"Not about my love. The babies are another story. She thinks that if they aren't mine, I'd only stay married to her out of a sense of obligation." Nicholas raked his fingers through his hair as he paced back and forth in the living room at Magnolia Grove. "I don't know what else to say to her."

"I guess there is nothing. Only time will convince

her. Are you sure you've really accepted the negative aspects of this?"

Phillip's eyes seemed to narrow as if he were studying him.

"Not you too. Phillip as far as I'm concerned, I'm the father. I love these babies and their mother. And I want to share my life with them."

A relieved sigh left Phillips lips. "I'm glad to hear you say that, Nick."

"I wish my wife believed as you do. From the moment I felt the babies move inside Camille's womb I was irrevocably connected to her and to them. The possibility that the twins might not be biologically mine doesn't bother me."

"It should, Nicholas," Suzette said from the doorway. "You've been duped by Camille King and that clinic. I tried to warn you not to trust either one of them, but no you wouldn't listen to me."

"Mother, I don't think you should -" Phillips began

Nicholas held up his hand. "It's all right, Phillip. Mother, Camille is my wife and a Cardoneaux. You will not say another derogatory word about her."

"You have to disclaim paternity now and divorce the woman," Suzette said baldly, completely ignoring his warning.

Angry and exasperated, Nicholas answered. "That I will never do. The babies are as much mine as their mother is."

"Even though they were in all likelihood fathered by another man!" she exclaimed in disbelief. "Her dead husband for God's sake. Or some unknown man! Nicholas, wake up and smell the coffee. That woman has played you for a fool. Can't you see that it's all a well thought out scheme. She and Hadley made up this story about her being inseminated with your sperm."

"For what purpose, Mother?" he demanded, his temper reaching the boiling point.

"Money of course. The King woman got you to marry her, didn't she? She now has access to your wealth and social position. It has opened doors for her that had previously been closed. I'm sure she is very grateful to Hadley for her windfall. And will no doubt reward him accordingly."

"Are you finished, Mother?" Nicholas ground out between clenched teeth. "Money and social position may be all that is important to you, but it's not to Camille."

Suzette flinched at the rage she saw flaming in her son's eyes. "Nicholas, don't look at me like that."

"How else am I supposed to look at you after the way you just trashed my wife's character." Nicholas shifted his attention to his brother. "It was a mistake coming here. And believe me it's one I won't make again. In the future I'll meet you at the hospital or at a nearby restaurant, Phillip. Or you can always come visit me and Camille at our home," Nicholas said heading for the door.

"Nicholas," Suzette came after him. "You can't just cut me out of your life. Leave that woman and come home where you belong."

"I belong with my wife and our children in our home. Good-bye, Mother."

"Nicholas!"

Ignoring her, he walked out of the house.

* * *

"Sugar, what can I say to you," Hazel said hugging her daughter.

"There's nothing anyone can say or do at this point. We'll have to wait until after the babies are born before we know if Nicholas is really their father."

"I thought you were so sure that he was," Jamal said entering the kitchen. "What's happened to make you doubt that he's the father?"

Camille didn't want to explain, but knew he would eventually find out anyway so she told him about the latest development.

Jamal walked over to Camille and took her in his

arms. "I could kill them for doing this to you."

"It wouldn't change anything, Jamal."

"Maybe not, but it would damn sure make me feel better. I can only guess what you're going through," he said gently. "Has Cardoneaux moved back to the mansion? Is that the reason you're here?"

Camille pushed out of his embrace. "No, he hasn't. We're closer than ever. It doesn't matter to him."

"Is that what he told you? And you believe him?"

"Yes. He loves me, Jamal, and I love him."

"That so called love will disappear soon enough once you've given birth to Elroy's babies."

"We don't know that they are Elroy's."

"And you can't be sure that they're Cardoneaux's either."

"As far as I'm concerned Nicholas is the father."

"You're living in a dream world, Camille. Come back to reality, sister-girl."

"Jamal, please," Hazel interjected, "Can't you see that you're upsetting your sister."

"It's all right, Mama. I'm going home to my husband. I should have known I wouldn't get any support from my brother."

"That's not true, Camille!" Jamal exclaimed defensively. "When the time comes I'll be there for you."

"I need you to be there for me right now. But you're not. I told you that I loved Nicholas and that he loves me, but you don't care about that. You've never given him a chance. Or even tried to get to know him. Because he's white you hate him. Because he has money you resent him. He doesn't hate you because you're black. Or resent you because you're poor. It's only you and his mother who are obsessing over this. You're both so steeped in your own prejudices, to hell with anyone who doesn't think and feel as you do."

"You have tunnel vision where Cardoneaux is concerned. As sure as I'm standing here, if those babies aren't his, he's going to walk."

"I don't happen to believe that he will. Nicholas loves me as much as you love Deja. You wouldn't hurt her any more than Nicholas would hurt me."

"That's different." Jamal threw his hands in the air. "It's no use talking to you about this."

"You're right, as long as you say things like you've said to me."

"Both of you stop it," Hazel cried. "You're brother and sister. Please, don't let this destroy your relationship."

"I'm sorry, Mama, I've been trying to accept this man into our family, but it's just not working," Jamal said and strode out of the room.

Tears spilled from Camille's eyes. She had thought that because Jamal had given her away that things would be different, but instead, the gulf between the men in her life had grown wider with each passing day. And it was tearing her family apart and there seemed to be nothing she could do to stop it.

"Oh, sugar, I hate to see you suffer so."

"It can't be helped. I'm going home."

"You don't have to leave. What about the things in the nursery? Jamal made you that beautiful cradle."

"He wanted me to have it when he thought I was carrying Elroy's child. Since there is a possibility that I may not be, he probably doesn't want me to have it."

"I'm sure that's not true."

"I'm going to leave everything where it is for now. I'll talk with you later, Mama." With that she left her mother's house.

* * *

When Camille got home, she found Nicholas sitting on the couch in the living room staring at her portrait.

"I think you should take it to Henri's gallery."

"I can't stand to part with it. Not yet." For some reason her suggestion felt like a rejection.

From the look on her husband's face, Camille

realized that she had hurt him. She examined the portrait. His love for her was evident in every single brush stroke.

Camille walked over to Nicholas and sat down beside him.

"I'm sorry. I never meant to hurt you."

He pulled her into his arms and held her close. "I know you didn't. It's this whole situation. It has us both on edge."

"We have another month and a half to go until the babies are born. Then we can have DNA tests done."

"I don't want them done." He moved his hand across her stomach. "These babies are as much mine as you are."

"But, Nicholas - "

"I mean it, Camille. I don't want any tests done."

"You're saying that now, but you'll change your mind."

"No, I won't," he said emphatically. "There will be no DNA tests. End of discussion. I don't want to hear anymore about it."

Camille wanted to say more, but saw the closed implacable expression on her husband's face and decided against it.

* * *

Camille lay resting on the bed with the lights off

when Nicholas entered their bedroom. The scent of strawberries filled the air and she heard the rattle of dishes, then a sudden flicker of candlelight illuminated the room. Camille's eyes widened in surprise when she saw that her husband was wearing a towel, that was arranged around his hips like a loincloth and it barely covered his manly endowments.

As Camille raised herself to a sitting position, she saw a tray table laden with fresh ripe strawberries, chocolate squares and a fondue pot.

"What is all this, Nicholas?"

He bent down to light the candle beneath the fondue pot.

"I'm your love slave tonight."

"My what? Nicholas."

"Yes, my queen, your wish is my command." He bowed from the waist. "If you'll allow me, great one, I'll remove your clothes so you can be more comfortable."

Camille didn't say another word - just watched as he undressed her. After removing her clothes, Nicholas left the room, then returned with a colorful array of throw pillows. He propped her back against them and kissed her and kept on kissing her until he'd aroused her passion to the fever pitch before returning his attention to the fondue pot. The chocolate in it had melted. He dipped a strawberry into the heated liquid and fed it to her, then another and another until she had her fill.

Next Nicholas gave her a body massage, starting at her feet and working his way upward. He paid special attention to her breasts, kneading them until the nipples stiffened into twin identically aroused peaks. And by the time he finished the massage, the oil he'd applied to her body had left her skin warm and glowing and sensitive to his touch. He smiled when she let out a soft moan of pleasure when he rolled her nipple between his thumb and forefinger.

He then gently positioned Camille crossways on the bed and eased her bottom to the edge and spread her thighs apart. He reached for a pillow beside the bed. It was high enough so that when he knelt on it his groin was level with the juncture of her femininity.

Camille raised her head, craning her neck, so that she could see over the large rounded mound of her stomach. "I'm so huge, Nicholas," she complained.

"Yes, you are." He grinned. "The term is 'great with child.'" At the rate your body is blossoming, this'll probably be the last time we'll be able to make love with abandon before the babies are born. If you're too uncomfortable we won't do it."

"I'm not uncomfortable. I want you to make love

to me. I see you've found yet another way to bring us both pleasure without harming the babies."

Nicholas kissed his way from her stomach to her breasts and stroked her nipples with his tongue until she whimpered. When he began to trail kisses up her throat, she closed her eyes. He finally reached her mouth and thrust his tongue inside, thoroughly seducing it. At the same time he brushed his fingers over the sensitive areas of her skin, behind her knee, then up her inner thigh.

Camille moaned. "Please, Nicholas, baby, I can't stand it. I want you inside me."

"Soon, my darling, soon." He kissed her deeply and slid his fingers over the large curve of her stomach to the delta beneath. He felt her shudder when he petted the little bud between the folds of her womanhood. She gasped when he inserted a finger and then a second inside her. Her breathing grew ragged as he teased her pulsing nub with his thumb.

"That feels so good, Nicholas."

"I intend to make you feel even better." He eased his fingers away and removed his towel. Instead of returning them to her woman's flesh, he slowly tunneled his desire-swollen sex into her waiting heat.

"Can you feel how much I want you?" Nicholas rasped as he began to move in and out, his shaft brushing against her ultra-sensitized bud of desire, turning the pleasure a notch, higher and then higher still. As they neared that wondrous pinnacle of rapture, he grasped her hips and made one more deep thrust. Then they tumbled over the precipice into ecstasy together. Moments later he collapsed on the bed beside her.

"You were spectacular, Nicholas."

"So were you. Is there anything else your love slave can do for you?"

"Oh, I don't know. The night is young and the possibilities are endless."

Chapter Twenty-seven

Nicholas watched over Camille as she slept. To him she seemed to grow more beautiful with each passing day. He licked the smear of chocolate from her bottom lip. Then placed his hand on her stomach and moments later felt a kick that was strong enough to make Camille squirm, but not enough to wake her. He smiled. The doctor had said the babies were healthy and the pregnancy was proceeding normally. She had told them that the twins could come early and to be prepared just in case.

He eased her out of his arms and got out of bed and walked over to the window. He could see and hear the droplets of rain as they pelted the leaves on the Magnolia tree outside their bedroom window. After the downpour had stopped, the moonlight shining on the rain-drenched shrubbery gave the night a magical sparkle. He couldn't help wishing that magic extended to their situation.

Camille was right. He did want his own flesh and blood children. He'd wanted that for years, but had been continually denied that miracle. Now when he thought that miracle was within his grasp... If these babies weren't his, then the next ones would be. But he wouldn't treat them any differently. As far as he was concerned the twins would be his firstborn.

Nicholas slid into bed beside Camille and held her close. He had to be honest with himself; it did bother him that she could be carrying Elroy's babies. He was only human. He couldn't help hoping and praying that they would turn out to be his.

* . *

The next three weeks were filled with activity for Camille, and she left her doldrums behind. The first thing she did was to sell the house Elroy had left her. If things didn't work out between her and Nicholas, she knew she could never live in it again. She gave most of the furniture to Deja. And also helped her friend find the perfect place to start her married life with Jamal. It hurt Camille that she and her brother hadn't spoken since that day at her mother's house.

She soon became caught up in buying double everything for the nursery. Luckily, the room was large enough to accommodate the extra furniture. As she was hanging the curtains in the nursery, she heard the doorbell and went to answer it.

When she opened the door, there stood Suzette Cardoneaux. Hope rose inside Camille. Could her mother-in-law have come to mend fences? She smiled and invited her inside and waved her into the living room.

"I won't mince words. How much will it cost to get you out of my son's life?"

Camille's smile faded. "You don't have that much money. Why do you hate me so much, Mrs. Cardoneaux?"

"Because you're ruining Nicholas's life."

"How am I doing that?" Anger exploded through Camille. "I love him."

"If you do then prove it."

"How? By leaving him? It won't change the way we feel about each other."

"If the children you're carrying aren't his, what do you think will become of this so called love. It'll grow into bitter resentment and eventual hatred."

Camille observed the look of desperation on Suzette's face and frowned. What was driving the woman? Fear? Fear of what?

"You see our relationship as some kind of threat to you, don't you?"

"No, I don't. I just want you out of my son's life."

"It doesn't matter to you that he loves me and is happy with me, does it?"

"He only thinks he loves you because he's convinced himself that the children you're carrying are his."

"You don't know that they aren't his. But you don't care. Why is that?"

"How much, Mrs. King?" Suzette said bringing out her check book.

"The name is Cardoneaux the same as yours. You can put that away. I think you'd better leave." Camille headed for the door.

Suzette advanced on her, grabbing her arm. "I'm trying to protect my son."

"From me? I love him. I'd never hurt him. He wants to be with me and our children. You had better learn to accept it." When Camille jerked out of Suzette's hold, the burgeoning weight of her pregnancy tilted her off balance and she stumbled. Her body momentum sent her slamming into the door. She doubled over in pain and fell to her knees.

"Call Nicholas!" Camille cried.

Suzette stood frozen to the spot.

"Please." Camille bit her lip. "Help me." Then she felt a sudden gush of warm water run down her legs.

"Oh my God." Suzette's eyes widened and she cried. "Your water has broken. You can't be having the babies now! It's too soon."

"It looks like I am. Please help me."

They heard a key turn in the lock.

Nicholas entered. Taking in the situation at glance, he reached inside his jacket pocket for his cell phone and called Camille's doctor, then alerted the hospital. He knelt down beside his wife and looked up at his mother.

"What happened? What are you doing here? You didn't - "

"It was an accident, Nicholas. I swear to you," his mother pleaded. "We were talking and she lost her balance."

Nicholas's nerves screamed. He recalled seeing Lauren writhe and moan in pain when she started to miscarry. And fear gripped his heart. He lifted Camille into his arms.

"Open the door, Mother. We have to get her to the hospital right away."

* * *

Nicholas held Camille's hand as she rode out yet another contraction.

"How long, Dr. Broussard?" he asked, his voice shaky with worry. "She's been in hard labor for hours.

The doctor smiled at him. "It won't be long now, Nicholas. I know you're worried."

Just then Camille moaned as another contraction twisted through her.

"Do you feel the urge to push, Camille?" the doctor asked.

"Oh, yes. God, yes."

"Bear down with the next contraction."

Nicholas counted to ten as Camille pushed and groaned.

"I see the head. One more big push. Push, push, push. That's it, Camille," she encouraged.

"The baby is coming, darling," Nicholas said, holding her leg while a nurse held the other.

A head popped from between Camille's legs. With the next contraction Camille pushed her baby out into the doctor's waiting hands.

"It's a girl," Dr. Broussard informed them.

Out of breath Camille managed a smile when the doctor held her baby up for her inspection. The baby's hair was a mass of midnight black curls like her father's. Before she could examine her further a nurse handed Nicholas a pair of scissors so he could cut the cord. Then her daughter was wisked away and weighed.

"5 lbs 3 ounces." The nurse called out.

Before she could relax a pain streaked through Camille and she cried out.

Dr. Broussard was seated between Camille's legs awaiting the next birth.

"Push, Camille. Push, push, push."

Nicholas counted again. With one final push their son slid easily from his mother's body. Dr. Broussard laid him across Camille's stomach. He was screaming bloody murder, complaining at being taken from his warm haven into the cooler air of the delivery room. He had a crop of brown hair and after his lungs filled with air his skin changed from gray to brown. Camille looked at Nicholas for his reaction, but all she could see was love shining in his blue eyes as he cut the cord.

The baby was wisked away to be weighed.

"6 lbs. and 6 ounces," a nurse announced.

Camille watched as her babies were cleaned up, wrapped in blankets and their heads covered with cute little beanies, pink for the girl and blue for the boy. Nicholas held a baby in each arm, a grin spreading from ear to ear. He walked over to his wife and kissed her lips.

"You've made me the happiest man on earth, Camille. I have my beautiful wife and our two beautiful babies."

It was love at first sight when Nicholas saw the babies and heard their cries as they filled the delivery room. He finally had the family he'd dreamed of for so many years.

* * *

Later outside the nursery window, Nicholas studied his children. He and Camille had decided on Xavier Jacques for their son's name. After her father and his. Their daughter Solange Denae. There was no question that Solange was his child. She had his blue eyes and her skin was a shade darker than his. Xavier's skin was the same shade as Camille's. A twinge of uncertainty stabbed through him, but only for a moment. Xavier might not be the son of his loins, but he was the son of his heart and always would be.

But you don't know for sure that he's not yours. A DNA test would confirm it.

He didn't want to know.

Are you afraid of what you might find out? Is it any better not knowing?

No, it wasn't, but—no, he wouldn't have the test done.

You would rather stay in blissful ignorance.

He shook the idea away. Xavier was his son.

* * *

Camille brushed her son's hair away from his face and kissed his forehead as he nursed at her breast. He certainly had a healthy appetite unlike his sister who drank very little and mostly used her mother's nipple as a pacifier. Solange had fallen asleep a few minutes earlier and Camille had laid her in her crib and picked up her son.

Tears slid down her face. Whereas they were sure that Solange was Nicholas's daughter, they weren't about Xavier. It was hard for Camille to comprehend and accept that uncertainty. It didn't seem to faze Nicholas. He would sit in the rocking chair in the nursery rocking Xavier to sleep every evening when he got home from work. And in so doing often ended up falling asleep himself. He seemed truly fascinated by the babies and helped out any way he could with their care.

She and the twins had been home from the hospital two weeks. Every time Camille looked at her son she thought she saw several of Nicholas's traits in his face and body, but knew it was probably wishful thinking.

You don't know that, girl. The only way you'll ever be sure is to have a DNA test done. If not for Nicholas's peace of mind, then for you own.

Solange's eyes had deepened to the cobalt blue of her father's and her skin had darkened to a light cafe au lait. Xavier's skin had also darkened to another deeper shade of brown. He was absolutely beautiful. He had deep dimples in both cheeks—like Nicholas's, she thought hopefully. Her hopes sank. Elroy also had deep dimples.

Her son had inherited hers and her father's chocolate brown eyes. His hair was wavy and the same cinnamon brown shade as Camille's.

Since the birth of the twins they'd heard nothing from Nicholas's mother.

Nicholas had told her he'd seen his mother standing outside the hospital nursery, but that she'd left without saying a word to him. Camille wondered if it had given her any satisfaction to know that she might be partially right about Nicholas not being the father of one of her babies.

Maybe she was and maybe she wasn't. Insist on a DNA test, the voice of reason urged.

Jolie and Henri had brought gifts. Deja and Jamal and their mother had come to visit. She was sure that Deja had talked him into it. Her brother hadn't said anything, but she saw the speculation in his eyes when he looked at his nephew. Camille wanted to shout at him that Xavier was Nicholas's, but she couldn't because she didn't really know herself whether that was true or not and that frustrated her no end.

Nicholas should have been the one eager to have a DNA test instead of her. But he had refused to discuss it whenever Camille brought up the subject.

The babies were two months old when Camille

and Nicholas took them to the pediatrician for their check ups. Nicholas was everything a woman could ever want in a man. He was an exemplary father and a passionate, loving husband. He was calm and patient amidst the chaos that often arose with two small newborn infants to care for. It was Camille who was the wreck. She'd wanted everything to be perfect - her life to be free from doubt - but it wasn't.

Camille noticed a gradual change come over her brother. When he was around, he would watch Nicholas closely when he interacted with the twins. It was as if he was waiting for something to happen and it never did.

Nicholas was aware of his brother-in-law's scrutiny and wondered what he was thinking. His expression was no longer hostile; it was more like confused and reserved. While Nicholas was changing Xavier, Jamal walked into the nursery.

"You really care for this baby, don't you?" he said with grudging respect.

"He's my son and I love him."

"Even though - "

"He might not be mine? Love has no color, Jamal."

"I'm beginning to see that. I don't know if I could be as cool and calm as you if the paternity of my child was a question mark."

"It's not a question mark to me, Jamal. Xavier is my son."

"I owe you an apology, man. I can see that you really love my sister and both of her children. I told Camille that once you found out you weren't the father, you'd leave her and go back to the mansion. Instead of leaving you've surrounded her and her children with deep unconditional love. I was wrong about you. I respect the person that you are. I never thought I'd say something like that to a white man."

Nicholas knew what it took for his brother-in-law to say what he did. If only his mother would come to the same realization that Jamal had: that color didn't matter. He was probably asking for the impossible. Phillip had told him that he'd hardly seen their mother over the last few months. When he had seen her, she seemed distracted, making him wonder if she was all right.

* * *

A few nights later Camille and Nicholas were relaxing in the living room, listening to music after having put the babies to sleep.

"Nicholas, I know you don't want a DNA test done, but - "

"Do you think it will make me feel any differently

toward Xavier to know for sure I am his father?"

"No, I don't. Not any more. It's not about that. I want to know for my own peace of mind."

Nicholas knew that his wife had been on edge lately. If it would ease her mind he had no choice but to concede to her wishes.

"All right, Camille."

"Thank you, Nicholas. I know how much you love our son. That isn't in question. This is for me."

Nicholas held her close. He would now have to do something that he had hoped he would never have to do. Why couldn't it have been obvious who had fathered his son. For Camille's sake, he knew he would have to steel himself against any negative feelings or resentment if Elroy King turned out to be Xavier's father.

* * *

Dr. Broussard did the test and told them she'd have the results the following Monday since it was the weekend. During that time the tension threatened to unravel Camille's composure. A sense of relief filled her when the doctor's nurse called to tell them what time to come in for the results.

Nicholas was anxious, but tried to hide it from Camille. The past few days had been pure torture. Now they would know for sure if Xavier was his natural son.

* * *

"Camille and Nicholas." Dr. Broussard smiled. "We are ninety-nine point nine per cent sure that Nicholas is Xavier's father."

"What!" Camille exclaimed. "You're absolutely sure!"

"Yes. Nicholas is Xavier's father."

Camille threw herself into her husband's arms. Nicholas arms automatically opened to embrace her, but he was too stunned to speak.

Xavier must have taken after Camille's side of the family, Nicholas thought. But still he would have expected to see something of himself in the boy. Knowing he was his natural father was a relief, though. Happiness at that fact made him want to shout.

* * *

When Nicholas and Camille got home they found his mother waiting in her car. What now? Camille thought as she watched her mother-in-law get out of her car.

Nicholas noticed how pale and strained his mother looked. He wondered what had brought her there.

Once inside the living room, Suzette spoke to Nicholas. "Phillip told me that you had a DNA test done and that today you had gone to find out the results."

"That's right, we did, Mother."

"And?"

"Both children are mine."

The part-time nanny they'd hired brought the babies into the living room. Nicholas took Xavier and Camille, Solange.

"I'll see you tomorrow," the nanny said with a smile and reached for her purse lying on the coffee table and left.

"Would you like to hold him?" Nicholas asked his mother.

She stood as if nailed to floor.

"No."

"Nothing has changed, has it, Mother. Because my children aren't all white you don't want to have anything to do with them. Right? No matter what color they are, they are still your grandchildren."

"I - I know." She cleared her throat. "I have a confession to make. And after I've told you everything I hope you can forgive me."

"Forgive you for what?" Nicholas asked.

"I'll get to that in a minute."

Suzette focused her attention on Camille. "I ran into your mother outside the nursery when you were in the hospital. Did she tell you what we talked about?"

"No. She never even mentioned seeing you. What does she have to do with this?"

"I'll explain it later, but first..." Her voice faltered. She swallowed hard and looked from Camille to Nicholas. "My whole life has been a lie."

Nicholas frowned. "A lie? I don't understand, Mother."

"You will." She paused as if gathering her composure. "My mother died when I was eight years old and I left New Orleans and went to stay with my grandmother in Texas. By the time I turned fifteen she was too old to take care of a teenager so she contacted my father's sister and arranged to have me sent back to New Orleans to live with her and her husband."

"Why are you telling me this now? I've tried for years to get you to talk about your past, but you refused. Now all of a sudden you're a fountain spilling over with information."

"When I saw Xavier in the nursery, I knew I had to tell you the truth."

Nicholas frowned. "The truth? What truth?"

"That I'm not who or what I seem be. And neither are you."

"What are you talking about? I don't understand."

"You will in a minute." She let out a heavy sigh.

"What does my mother have to do with this?" Camille again asked.

"It'll all become clear to you when I've finished." Suzette walked over to the lounge on the far end of the room, sat down and braided her fingers in her lap.

"My real first name isn't Suzette; it's Sally, and my middle name is Mae, not Lynn. My maiden name was Cotton. When I went to stay with my aunt and uncle, they agreed to legally adopt me if I changed my first name to Suzette. Aunt Laura was my father's younger sister and she had insisted that I do so."

"Why would she do that?" Nicholas asked.

"You see, although my father was white, my mother was only a quarter white the rest black. He never married her. She was his mistress. He was killed in a plane crash when I was five. My mother never got over it and she became so despondent that she literally wasted away after his death.

"Because my skin was so pale, my aunt urged me to pass for white and never acknowledge my black heritage. She insisted that I cut all ties with my mother's people. When I finished at Vassar, I met your father. We fell in love and got married."

"Did he know?" Nicholas asked through stiff

shocked lips.

Suzette lowered her head and looked at her hands. "No. I never told him."

"When Phillip and I were growing up you thought your secret might be somehow discovered if we associated with black children and played with them in the black neighborhood. Do we still have relatives in New Orleans?"

"Yes. You have cousins that my mother was never really close to."

"It must have been your worst nightmare threatening to come true when you found out that the mother of my child was black."

"You have to understand, Nicholas, that I—"

"That you were ashamed of being part black to the extent of keeping me and Phillip in the dark about our heritage."

"How does my mother fit into this?" Camille asked, equally stunned by her revelation.

"She remembered me from when we were little. Her mother and mine had attended the same church. Hazel and I had played together. The reason she recognized me is that I couldn't completely abandon who and what I am. I kept my mother's gold locket and have never been without it. My father had given it to her. It was unique he'd had it specially made for her. Hazel recognized it when she saw me and put things together. I told her not to say anything. She promised she wouldn't, on one condition, that I tell you the truth."

"So much makes sense now," Nicholas said absently.

"I always loved you and your brother and only wanted to protect you."

"Dad wanted to have more children, but you refused. You had lucked out when Phillip and I came out looking white. You were afraid that if you had any more children they might look black. Oh, my God, Mother."

"I know I shouldn't have kept this from you."

"You're damned right, you shouldn't have. You tried to separate me from the woman I love and my children in your desperate attempt to keep your secret hidden. If Hazel hadn't found out who you were and we hadn't had the DNA test done you would never have said anything. Would you?"

"I don't know."

"Don't be such a hypocrite, Mother. You know you wouldn't," he spat, his blood hot with anger and pain. "I begged you to tell me about your background and your family, but you wouldn't. Right now I can't stand to even look at you. I'm ashamed to call you mother. I don't want you here. Please leave."

"Nicholas, maybe - " Camille began.

"No, Camille. After all she's done how can you feel sorry for her." He glared at his mother. "I don't want you anywhere near me or my family."

"But, Nicholas - "

"Just get the hell out, Sally Mae. If that's even your real name."

"Please, Nicholas." Tears ran in rivulets down Suzette's face. "You have to forgive me. I'm so sorry."

"Sure you are. Now that your secret has been exposed."

Xavier began to squirm and whimper.

"Leave my house now, Mother. I can't stand being in the same room with you. Get out and don't come back."

Solange screamed, flailing her tiny arms and legs at the sound of Nicholas's raised angry voice.

"You'd better go, Mrs. Cardoneaux," Camille said.

With a dejected look on her face Suzette rose to her feet and quietly left the house.

Chapter Twenty-eight

"You were a little hard on her, don't you think?"

"No, I don't."

"You don't know what it was like for her, Nicholas."

"She turned her back on her own people, Camille. How can you defend her?"

"Back then people were really into color coding. White was considered right and Black get back. It's a harsh but true reality."

"My mother opted for the easy way out. All these years she denied Phillip and me any knowledge of our black heritage. Her marriage, her whole life was built on a lie. My life was built on that same lie."

Xavier started crying. "I'm going to calm my son and put him to bed. Then I'm going for a drive."

"Will you be all right?" Camille asked.

"Eventually." He kissed her forehead. "Why don't you call Jolie or Deja to come over and help you? I don't know how long I'll be."

"I love you, Nicholas."

He smiled. "I know. And I love you too."

Camille hated seeing the pained look in her husband's eyes, but knew there was nothing she could do to ease it away. This was a difficult time for him. The whole core of his life had been rocked down to its foundation.

Camille now understood the look of fear she'd seen in Suzette's eyes. How had she lived with this secret her entire marriage? What did it feel like to deny one's own heritage? And to deny it to her children?

Nicholas was hurting and had lashed out at his mother. When he finally came to grips with this startling revelation and was ready to accept it, Camille hoped he'd let her help him. Then maybe later there would come a time when he and his mother could talk rationally about everything. At least she hoped so for all their sakes.

* * *

Nicholas called Phillip and arranged to meet him in the park across the street from the hospital.

"What is it, Nick?"

"I don't know how to get into this."

"Is it something to do with the DNA results?"

"Indirectly. I've learned that Xavier is my son."

"That should make you happy, but I don't see any

evidence that it has. Why?" he probed.

Nicholas let out a soul-weary breath. "I'm happy about that, but what I found out later blindsided me. Mother came to our house and..."

"And what? Tell me, Nick," Phillip said anxiously.

"The reason Xavier didn't show any signs of his white heritage is because our mother neglected to tell us that she is only part white. Her father was white, but our grandmother was three-quarters black."

"What?"

"Our mother figured that she had hit the lottery when you and I came out looking white."

"Did Dad know?"

"No, she never told him the truth. She's lived a lie since day one of their marriage. And way before that. She's been passing since she was fifteen."

"Well, what else did she say? Did she give you any explanations?"

"She didn't have to. You know how important money and social acceptance are to her."

"But there has to be more to it than that."

"You're as bad as Camille. She feels sorry for her too."

"You don't, I gather. She must have felt that she had to do what she did. She has no other close family."

"No, her mother and father are dead. Our great-grandmother probably is too. Aunt Laura and Uncle Paul live in Europe. There had been no one around to trip her up."

"Nick, I'm sure that Mother is - "

"I don't want to hear her name. Oh, by the way it's not Suzette, but Sally Mae."

"You sound so bitter. I feel as shocked and confused as you do, I must admit, but she's still our mother."

"So you think I should just forgive and forget. Right?"

"You might try being more compassionate. You have no idea what she's gone through emotionally keeping this secret for so many years. Her feelings of guilt must be monumental."

"They should be. She tried to convince me to abandon Camille and our children, Phillip."

"I know that. She is going to need therapy to come to grips with everything, Nick."

"I thought that you of all people would understand how betrayed and lost I feel because of what she's done."

"I do, believe me."

"You don't act like it."

"That doesn't mean that I don't feel it." He

thrust his hands in his pockets and turned away. Then a few seconds later he turned to face Niçholas and said. "The way we perceived ourselves has been turned inside out. I'm not happy about it, but we can't change any of it."

"You might be able to forgive her, but I don't know if I ever will."

"Give it time."

"I don't know if time will make any difference. I've got to get away and think."

"Where is mother now?"

"I don't know. She's probably at Magnolia Grove."

"I'd better go and check on her. Are you going to be all right?"

"I can't answer that. I'm so - I don't know how I am."

"You need to go home to your family. You have Camille. Let her help you through this."

"I want to. But I feel so lost and confused, Phillip."

"It might take time, but we'll get through this."

* * *

Camille was worried about her husband. She had just come back into her bedroom after checking on the twins and was sitting in the window seat waiting for

Nicholas to come home when he'd called to say he wouldn't be coming home. That he was taking the Creole Lady out and didn't know when he'd back. She had called Jolie and asked her to come over. The doorbell rang and she rushed to answer its summons.

"You sounded upset," Jolie said as she followed Camille into the living room.

Camille explained all that had happened. "Nicholas was so distraught when he left."

"I can imagine. I know a little of how his mother must be feeling. My brother and sister went through a similar experience. You remember my telling you about them passing for white?"

"Yes, it's why I called you. I thought that maybe you could help, but Nicholas isn't coming home tonight."

"Maybe I can when he comes back, that is if he wants me to. He's got to be feeling confused and uprooted. To find out you are a part of two worlds when you always believed you were part of only one is pretty mind blowing, Camille."

The phone rang.

"How are you, sugar?"

"Mama."

"She told you the truth, didn't she?"

"Yes, my mother-in-law was here. She certainly

dropped a bomb on us."

"How is Nicholas?"

"Not good, Mama."

"Do you want me to come over?"

"Would you? Nicholas has gone away on the Creole Lady. I'm worried about him. He was so hurt and angry."

"That's to be expected. He'll get over it in time."

"I hope you're right, Mama."

Jolie patted Camille's shoulder. "I'll be going. If when Nicholas gets back he wants to talk, have him call me."

"I will, Jolie. And thanks for coming."

"You don't have to thank me. We're friends, aren't we?"

* * *

"What are you doing here, Jamal?" Nicholas demanded when he saw his brother-in-law waiting at the marina when he eased the Creole Lady into her berth.

"Camille told me that you took the boat out. Your skipper said you called to let him know when you were coming back. So I decided to wait for you."

"Why? I was never one of your favorite people. Am I that now since you know I'm black too?"

"I guess I deserved that. The last few months

I've grown to respect you as a person despite your skin color."

"I suppose Camille told you - everything?"

"Yes, she did."

"So why are you here."

"Let's go some place where we can talk."

"What is there to talk about? It seems that we are brothers under the skin."

"I'm not going to say I know how you feel because I don't and never will. What I do know is that you have to accept things."

"It's not as though I have a choice, is it?"

"Your mother needs you, man. I'm sure that underneath she's felt just as lost and displaced as you feel right now. She's lived with it a lot longer. Living a lie couldn't have been easy for her"

"I don't believe I'm having this conversation with you of all people."

Jamal laughed. "Me either."

"Let's go to Jaeger's beer garden."

"Sound's good to me."

A few minutes later they were sitting at the bar having a beer.

"There's something I need to tell you. A month before you drove Camille home from the clinic, I had applied for the master carpenter job at Cardoneaux Construction."

"You did?" Nicholas said, shocked.

"Needless to say I didn't get the job and I resented it. Seeing you was like waving a red flag in front of a bull. To my way of thinking it was just another insult."

"Another insult?"

"I'd been turned down by other companies like yours that were headed by white men. Back when I was in college and struggling to keep up, a guidance counselor suggested I leave and enroll in a trade school to become a carpenter since I was so good at making things. You see, I'd built several trophy cases for the college and he was impressed with my workmanship. I didn't take his advice as it was intended. Instead I considered it a put down."

"This counselor happened to be white? I take it."

"Yes, he was."

"I see where some of your resentment and attitude comes from. I had guessed that something had happened to make you so hostile toward me and white people in general. If you want me to, I'll talk to the head of personnel and - "

"No, I don't want you to do that. I'm happy working at Allenbys. Now that I've had time to think about it I wouldn't have been happy working at an industrial company like yours. If I had only seen that earlier."

"Hindsight is 20/20, Jamal. And I don't mean it as a put down."

"Jamal laughed. "I know you don't."

"I'm glad to hear it."

* * *

Camille had dosed off when she heard the jacuzzi jets come on in the bathroom. Nicholas was back. She threw off the covers and hurried in there.

"Are you all right?" she asked.

"I suppose so. How about joining me."

"All right," she said and slipped out of her night-gown and stepped into the bathing pool.

Nicholas pulled her into his arms, straddling her legs on either side of his hips; he embedded his aroused column of flesh in hers to the hilt.

"Oh, Nicholas," she cried out.

For a few minutes he said nothing just reveled in the feel of her tight sheath surrounding him. He moved her up and down on his shaft again and again.

He groaned. "Oh, Camille, you feel so damn good. I needed this and you to make sense of this con-fused jangled mess my life has become."

"I'm here for you, baby, in any capacity you need me."

He lifted her off of him, rose to his feet and picking her up laid her on the terry-covered mat beside the pool. Then climbed out and over onto her body. She parted her thighs and closed her eyes as he eased his manhood deep inside her. He kissed her mouth and trailed kisses down her throat to the valley between her breasts. He worshipped one nipple then paid equal
homage to the other.

Camille moaned her pleasure at this double assault on her senses. He returned his mouth to hers and as he did so, moved his lower body in rolling motions against hers.

"I love you so much, Camille Cardoneaux."

"As I love you Nicholas Cardoneaux."

And he brought them to a slow satisfying climax.

Later they lay entwined on the bed.

"You've been gone for a week, Nicholas. Did you resolve anything?"

"Not while I was on the boat, but when I got back your brother was waiting for me and we had a good talk. He explained a lot of things about himself and why he felt the way he did. It was much of what you'd told me about him and the past."

"What else did he say?"

"That I had to accept things, and I should find it

in my heart to forgive my mother. He said that if he could change his mind about me, I could change mine about my mother and show her a little compassion."

"He certainly has grown up."

"Yes, he has. He's really deep and he can be a likeable character when he wants to be."

"Well, are you going to talk to your mother? I'll go there with you if you want me to."

"I'm not ready to see her just yet, but when I am I'll do it alone. Knowing I have you lending me your support and love means more to me than you'll ever know, Camille."

Epilogue

"Your mother is going to spoil the twins," Camille said to Nicholas as they watched her playing with the children in the garden.

"They are her only grandchildren. It doesn't look like Phillip will be providing any anytime soon."

"You never know. He might surprise you one day. Your mother is a different person. I'm so glad you finally went to see her and talked about your feelings."

"After talking to Jolie and her brother, I came away with a whole new perspective. He told me how being accepted was important to him and that he had to find out for himself where he truly belonged. With my mother she got into a situation and wasn't strong enough to take a stand. She thought she would lose everything if people knew about her dual heritage. She really had no one to talk to or confide in who would understand. She wasn't willing to risk my father not understanding and was afraid of losing his love and being tossed out of the only world she knew."

"The group counseling sessions seemed to have helped her, don't you think?"

"Yes, I believe they have. She got to meet people she would never have suspected of living the same kind of lie as she."

"How about you?"

"I understand why she did it, but - "

"But you're finding it hard to completely forgive her. You've made a start by allowing her into our lives. She has turned into a doting grandmother. Her spirits seem lighter now that everything is out in the open and she doesn't have the burden of the secret hovering over her any longer."

"Have I told you lately how much I love you?"

"Not in the last six hours."

"Well I do and I'm going to prove to you how much - later."

"You prove it to me every day and every night, and in every way, Nicholas. I feel so lucky to have you in my life."

"Because of a twist of fate we not only have two beautiful babies, we share a deep all-consuming love. Don't we?"

"Yes we do." Camille kissed him.

"What's that for?"

"General principles. And to tide you over until later."

"I can hardly wait till then."